"It's still there, Annette."

"It's chemistry." She didn't try to deny it. "Chemistry without emotion is…" She shrugged, signifying nothing.

Steve had a different view to propose. "Chemistry *with* emotion is love, right?"

"Impossible." She looked up at him, letting him see the certainty now in her eyes. "Love without trust is impossible. At least for me."

Would telling her the truth make her trust him more? Or less?

But telling her, telling anyone… He was the one who took care of problems. He was the one who looked out for people. He was the one who accepted responsibility. He didn't burden other people with it. Especially not her.

Dear Reader,

Love is in the air, but the days will certainly be sweeter if you snuggle up with this month's Special Edition offerings—and a box of decadent chocolates. First up, award-winning author and this year's President of Romance Writers of America®, Shirley Hailstock is a fresh new voice for Special Edition, but fans already know what a gifted storyteller she is. With numerous novels and novellas under her belt, Shirley debuts in Special Edition with *A Father's Fortune*, which tells the story of a day-care-center owner and her foster child who teach a grumpy carpenter how to face his past and open his heart to love.

Lindsay McKenna packs a punch in *Her Healing Touch,* a fast-paced read from beginning to end. The next in her widely acclaimed MORGAN'S MERCENARIES: DESTINY'S WOMEN series, this romance details the trials of a beautiful paramedic who teaches a handsome Special Forces officer the ways of her legendary healing. *USA TODAY* bestselling author Susan Mallery *completely* wins us over in *Completely Smitten*, next up in her beloved series HOMETOWN HEARTBREAKERS. Here, an adventurous preacher's daughter seeks out a new life, but never expects to find a new *love* with a sexy U.S. marshal.

The fourth installment in Crystal Green's KANE'S CROSSING miniseries, *There Goes the Bride* oozes excitement when a runaway bride is spirited out of town by a reclusive pilot she once loved in high school. Patricia McLinn delights her readers with *Wedding of the Century*. Here, a heroine returns to her hometown seven years after running out of her wedding. When she faces her jilted groom, she realizes their feelings are stronger than ever! Finally, in Leigh Greenwood's *Family Merger*, sparks fly when a workaholic businessman meets a good-hearted social worker, who teaches him the meaning of love.

Don't miss this array of novels that deliver an emotional charge and satisfying finish you're sure to savor, no matter what the season!

Happy Valentine's Day!

Karen Taylor Richman
Senior Editor

Please address questions and book requests to:
Silhouette Reader Service
U.S.: 3010 Walden Ave., P.O. Box 1325, Buffalo, NY 14269
Canadian: P.O. Box 609, Fort Erie, Ont. L2A 5X3

Wedding of the Century

PATRICIA McLINN

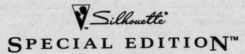

Silhouette®

SPECIAL EDITION™

Published by Silhouette Books

America's Publisher of Contemporary Romance

With many thanks to Pamela Dalton,
who has demonstrated Wisconsin's warmth
and graciousness all along. Cathy McDavid, who was
so generous in trying to steer me clear of construction
accidents. Lynda Sandoval Cooper—retroactively—
who not only knows about broken hips,
but really did e-mail the right person!

 SILHOUETTE BOOKS

ISBN 0-373-24523-8

WEDDING OF THE CENTURY

Visit Silhouette at www.eHarlequin.com

Printed in U.S.A.

Books by Patricia McLinn

PATRICIA McLINN

finds great satisfaction in transferring the characters crowded in her head onto paper to be enjoyed by readers. "Writing," she says, "is the hardest work I'd never give up." Writing has brought her new experiences, places and friends—especially friends. After degrees from Northwestern University and newspaper jobs that have taken her from Illinois to North Carolina to Washington, D.C., Patricia now lives in Virginia, in a house that grows piles of paper, books and dog hair at an alarming rate. The paper and books are her own fault, but the dog hair comes from a charismatic collie who helps put things in perspective when neighborhood kids refer to Patricia as "the lady who lives in Riley's house." She would love to hear from readers at P.O. Box 7052, Arlington, VA 22207 or you can check out her Web site at www.PatriciaMcLinn.com.

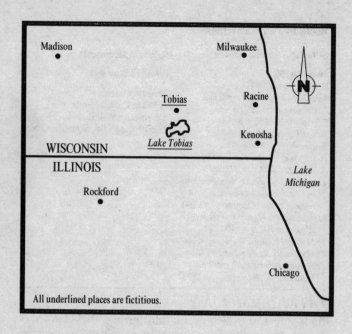

Madison

Milwaukee

N

Tobias

Racine

Lake Tobias

Kenosha

WISCONSIN

ILLINOIS

*Lake
Michigan*

Rockford

Chicago

All underlined places are fictitious.

Prologue

Seven-and-a-half years ago

"If anyone knows just cause why these two people..."

Annette heard the side door of the First Church of Tobias, Wisconsin, emit a high-pitched protest at being opened, but didn't turn.

It was the day of her wedding to Steve Corbett, the man she loved. The man who had pledged to love and protect her.

The man who'd withdrawn into abstraction and politeness in recent weeks.

The man, so went the dark whispers that had filtered to her, who had been seen recently in intense conversation with his old girlfriend.

Gossip. That's all. From people who'd never believed the elder Corbett son would marry Annette Trevetti. She'd been among those nonbelievers at first. She'd insisted they were dating casually for a full year. He would give her that half smile and say, "Maybe *you're* not serious...."

But this was their wedding day. A day full of promise, hope and joy. The happiest day of her life. It had to be. It was, as she'd been told times past counting, the wedding of the century in Tobias. The music, flowers, dress and ceremony were all exquisitely tasteful. Even the bridal party had been chosen with an eye to balance and proportion, which was the reason, she had been told, that her brother couldn't be in it—he didn't fit.

"That's crazy!" she'd blurted in front of the wedding consultant. Lana Corbett had gone stiff at that violation of the Corbett code of never acknowledging the existence of anything as ordinary as laundry, much less washing the dirty stuff in public. And Steve had uttered that Corbett standard, "We'll talk about it later." How could she both admire how self-contained he was and hate it?

When they *had* talked about it, Steve had said he would make sure Max was in the wedding—over his mother's objections and Max's refusal to wear a tux—if it was important to Annette. Annette had wanted to say there'd be no tuxes to worry about if the wedding had remained the simple, personal and small ceremony they had planned. She'd hoped Steve would stand up for that version without her demanding it. But he seemed so distracted that she wondered if he even noticed what the wedding had become.

Then he'd held her and said that what mattered was the two of them spending the rest of their lives together. How could she argue with that? And how could she push him into another family fight when she knew—thanks to the Tobias rumor mill—he was already defying his mother by marrying her?

So Lana Corbett decided every detail of their wedding,

since everyone in Tobias knew that Annette, poor all her life and motherless the past seven years, didn't have the faintest idea how to go about having a wedding worthy of a Corbett.

But these past weeks she'd begun to wonder. What if the wedding said something about the rest of their lives together?

"Why these two people should not be joined in holy matrimony—"

"I do!"

Despite the packed church gasping and the minister gaping, Annette didn't turn toward the side door—pleased that Lana Corbett couldn't blame this wrinkle in the master plan on her. The first real concern trickled up her spine when Max half rose from his seat behind her, his face set in his protective-brother mode.

Then she felt Steve stiffen beside her.

In that instant, the meaning of that all-wrong "I do" sank in like a blade into flesh.

She turned and saw Lily Wilbanks with her hands spread across her notably rounded abdomen.

"I'm the one who should be up there marrying him. Because this is Steve Corbett's baby."

The gasps turned to outcries. Distantly, Annette was aware of Lana demanding that someone remove that woman.

Lily had to be wrong. Mistaken. It couldn't be Steve's baby.

The rumors. Steve and Lily, sitting in his car at Lake Tobias Park, with their heads close together and their faces intent.

No. He hadn't asked Lily from the oh-so-perfect family to marry him, he'd asked her. He wouldn't betray her this way.

"Annette…"

It was Steve's voice. The same soothing tone he'd used over losing control of the wedding—their wedding, the start of their marriage. It held calming sympathy, but it held even more of the stiff Corbett proceed-with-dignity credo. Not to make a scene. Not to get emotional.

Not to be herself.

Through the gloves his mother had insisted she wear, Annette felt Steve's fingertips. They felt cold. Or maybe her skin was cold.

She stepped away from his touch but couldn't take her eyes off his hand, still extended in the gap between them, as she demanded, "Did you get Lily pregnant?"

The gasp from the wedding guests was louder, more shocked. Focused on Steve's face, she saw the stiffness come over him. Watched the life of the man she loved disappear behind the Corbett code.

"Annette," he said with a reasonableness that made her want to scream, "we'll talk about that later. For now—"

"No. We won't talk about it later. Tell me now."

If she let this go until later, she would let him—and her love for him—explain it away. And now she knew why she'd never asked him about being seen with Lily, why she hadn't pushed him about his mood these past weeks. She'd been afraid of the answers.

"Annette—"

"Now, Steve. Or never."

Something in his eyes flickered. "This isn't—"

"The time? The place? Well, I'm tired of having my feelings scheduled so they're more convenient for the Corbetts to ignore. And a church is the perfect place to face the truth—that this isn't going to work."

She turned, half kicking the full skirt out of her way, and escaped through a door to the minister's office. She tried

to pull her engagement ring off, forgetting the hated gloves
for an instant. Yanking at the material, she heard a rip, and
it released, pulling inside out as it came off her hand. She
dropped the glove on the desk, pulled the ring off and
dropped that atop the huddled glove.

She had the outside door open when she turned at the
sound of someone behind her.

Steve stood at the far door as if frozen in midstride, his
lips parted but no sound coming out. His gaze locked on
the glove and ring on a corner of the desk.

She kept going, hearing the door close behind her with
a solid thud.

Chapter One

"I still don't know why Juney called you, but as long as you're here let's get a move on."

"Because," Annette explained to her older brother for the third time in twenty minutes, while ignoring his equally persistent effort to hurry their exit from the hospital, "she knew I'd track her down on her honeymoon on Maui and pulverize her if she hadn't let me know that you'd been injured."

Annette had already talked to the doctor who had set Max's wrist, which had eased her worst fears, although it was too soon to rule out nerve damage. The cut on his head was closed and expected to heal well. The next big hurdle was getting Max home. After that she would figure out how to hog-tie him so he'd obey the doctor's instructions.

And how to keep the small construction business he'd built over years of achingly hard work running, with him on the injured list and his office manager and aide-de-camp,

Juney, just starting a month-long honeymoon, thanks to a contest her fiancé had won.

"Somebody has a big mouth—calling Juney on her honeymoon in Hawaii, for Pete's sake. And how'd you get here so fast? You shouldn't drive so fast. If—"

"I maintained a safe and reasonable speed." Her wry imitation of a public service announcement's tone drew a slight grimace from Max. Or maybe that was pain as he shifted to the edge of the examining table in the emergency room cubicle.

She truly hadn't broken the speed limit—at least not by much. But she might have set a land-speed record for throwing items into a suitcase. As Annette had headed out of the suburban Chicago town house that housed her, her business partner, Suz, and the headquarters of their company, Every Detail, Suz had grabbed her arm and reminded her that she would do Max no good by getting in a car accident. She'd repeated Suz's warning to herself every time the urgency to get to Max had pushed her foot down on the pedal. Thank heavens the recent patch of balmy weather had cleared even the side roads of signs of the big snowstorm from three weeks ago. She didn't care if March did go out as a lion, as long as it continued coming in like a lamb long enough for her to get Max safely situated.

"So, I broke my wrist. Big deal. It's not like I broke something serious. I can take care of myself."

"Right. You had surgery and now—"

"Not surgery. Pins and plaster is what they called it—a procedure."

"Okay. A procedure. And after this procedure, you're telling me you'll be able to cook and clean and drive and do the company books with Juney gone and make the business calls, and generally run your life and business—all with your left hand and *that* covering your right arm?"

She pointed to the brand-new cast that extended from the top of his fingers to halfway between his elbow and his shoulder. When she'd entered the cubicle and seen that irrefutable proof of his injury stark against his skin, plus the unfamiliar pallor of his face against the dark hair so like her own, she'd felt as if the floor under her feet had tilted.

Max hurt. How could that be? He was invulnerable. For as long as she could remember, he'd been her rock, her stability, her champion. *You and me against the world, kid. That's even odds.* How many times had he said that to her? From her earliest memories of him cleaning her skinned knees and drying her eyes when hurt feelings made her cry.

The feelings had been so much deeper and the hurt so much bigger after the wedding when—no, she'd closed off that path years ago. No sense in opening it now, of all times. Leave Steve and their wedding-that-wasn't in the past where it belonged.

Taking care of Max had brought her to Tobias, and that's what she would concentrate on.

"You heard the doctor," she added. "You can't drive and you shouldn't put any undue stress on the joint."

He ignored her points and continued with his own—some things never changed.

"You've got enough on your plate right now." He reached for his shirt on the back of the blue molded plastic chair she'd been too restless to sit on. "What with wrapping up selling your business and—"

"Suz is thoroughly capable of taking care of that," she said.

She and Suz had found a niche by matching busy professionals with the perfect service provider, everything from car repairs to lawn work to putting on an addition. Clients could hire them for one project or pay a retainer for ongoing help, and she and Suz did all the researching, finding, assessing, reviewing and overseeing. Terrific word of mouth about their service had grown the company even faster than they had hoped. An article in their alumni magazine had spawned local media and then national interviews.

That drew the attention of a corporation preparing to open franchises offering a similar service. To obtain the company name of Every Detail and clear out the competition, the corporation had made them an offer that would set them each up for life. How could they say no? They couldn't.

It would be strange to no longer have the business to occupy most of her waking—and some of her sleeping—hours.

She gestured for him to stay put and snagged his blood-stained green work shirt. But when she tried to hold it out to let him slip his left arm into the sleeve he scowled so fiercely that she handed it to him. The only way to make her point that he needed help was to let Maximilian Augusto Trevetti prove it himself.

"Yeah, but you need to be deciding what you're going to do next." He continued his agenda in his big-brother voice, which ranked half a notch below Moses handing down the Ten Commandments. "Besides, I know you don't want to be here."

As she watched him position the shirt with his left hand so he could put that arm in the sleeve, she had to admit that he had her there.

Only one thing had gotten her back to Tobias in the past seven years—to see Max on those few holidays when she hadn't finagled it so he came to see her.

Only one thing had gotten her back to Tobias now—Max needed her.

Nothing, not even her overprotective brother, would push

her out of town until she knew he was all right. That didn't mean she would enjoy this stay in her old hometown.

"So let's get out of here before…"

His words faded as he jiggled his arm to move the sleeve up. The muscles in his face tightened, but he didn't grimace at the jostling to his battered body. It had been a hell of a fall. Every move had to bring a new ache.

After all he'd done for her—even before their mother's death when she was twelve—keeping his company and his home running would constitute about a dime's worth of payback on a gift of millions. Whether he liked it or not.

Not was the smart bet. He had the shirt on his left shoulder and partway across his back. Putting his left hand over his right shoulder, he tried to grasp the collar to pull it up, but his fingers didn't quite reach.

"Let me—"

"I can do it," he insisted.

Definitely *not.*

Too bad. She was sticking around.

But she was no fool. She'd created a successful business with her partner, then helped drive a deal for an eye-widening package with the conglomerate looking to eliminate pesky competition. You didn't do that without facing facts.

Like the fact that this return to Tobias would be a whole lot different from the scattered holidays she'd spent here. She'd kept those few visits brief, and she'd gone nowhere but to their childhood home.

Taking care of Max and Trevetti Building meant full immersion into Tobias, Wisconsin, where everyone knew all the facts of her life. Including the luscious tidbit that she'd left Steven Worthington Corbett, elder son of Tobias's founding family, at the altar seven years ago after he'd gotten another woman pregnant. Good cause for walking out of a wedding, but still, to Tobias, the Corbetts were the top of the heap, and one didn't go against them. Especially one who'd come from near the bottom of the heap.

Well, the citizens of Tobias could cluck over the past all they wanted. She'd found success by leaving her past in the past in order to face the present and shape the future. She wouldn't abandon that strategy now.

Max grimaced as he stretched to reach the shirt collar.

"For Pete's sake," she muttered, dropping her purse onto the chair. "Quit tying yourself in macho knots, you idiot."

"I don't need help getting dressed like some baby."

But he didn't prevent her from pulling the shirt into place over his right shoulder.

"I seem to remember somebody buttoning my coat for me one cold day so I didn't have to take my mittens off."

His face darkened, but he said nothing as she slipped the top part of the shirt under his cast-covered elbow, then closed the bottom four buttons. She put his light jacket over his shoulders.

"There. That should keep any of the fine upstanding citizens of Tobias from turning you in for indecent exposure. Or any of the less upstanding females from drooling over you."

He dismissed that with a grunt.

She placed her hand on his arm as if to pat him, but really to be prepared if he needed support as he eased off the examining table.

"Thanks." From the wryness, she knew he hadn't missed her precaution.

"Get used to it, big brother. Annette's back in town." She jerked a thumb toward her chest like a gang member from an amateur production of *West Side Story*, then picked up her purse and raincoat and pulled aside the curtain that cut off his cubicle from the hallway. Looking toward her brother, she added, "For once, I'm in charge."

"There's no reason for you to stay. You can head back to Glen Ellyn. I'm perfectly capable of driving home and taking care of myself."

For the first time she chuckled. "Oh, yeah?" she challenged as he moved past her. "How're you going to drive yourself home when I have your keys and your truck's not here?"

"You're getting bossy, you know that, Annette? Pushy. And—"

A calm voice stopped both her chuckle and Max's grumbling like a door slamming shut.

"Hello, Annette."

The voice had deepened slightly, but she knew it immediately.

Steve Corbett stood directly in front of her.

The curtain dropped behind her, released by a hand robbed of any strength. The linoleum floor and the walls painted with primary-colored stripes wavered and closed in on her. Was this what Alice had felt like when she'd tumbled down that rabbit hole to Wonderland?

Only this wasn't Wonderland. This was Tobias. And Annette should have been prepared to run into the Corbett heir apparent. Had she imagined he'd disappeared, because she'd managed to avoid him on her few trips back? That was like a baby thinking the world disappeared because he covered his eyes with his hands while playing peekaboo.

God, please just let him keep going. She'd be prepared later. She wouldn't feel as if seven years had slid away and she had gained nothing in that time. She would have something planned to say. If only he would keep walking....

Giving a fine performance as the original immovable object, he didn't budge. The past stood face-to-face with her, blocking her path. Almost as if he were throwing down a dare—if such a thing weren't too undignified for a Corbett.

His face had changed. The bedrock of distinguished facial structure had asserted itself strongly. He would be a handsome man long after the thick, mahogany waves turned to silver. She'd daydreamed of watching that change happen, with their children and grandchildren around them, and—

Annette blinked hard, yanking her mind back to the problem at hand.

Okay, if he wouldn't move, then she should. Answer coolly and move on. This first meeting would be over, and if the fates were truly on her side, there would not be another.

She couldn't get a word out. Maybe her vocal cords could have produced the sounds of a word, but her mind didn't supply any raw material.

Steve smoothly covered her lack of response.

''How're you doing, Max? I wondered if you'd need a ride home.''

That snapped her head around to her brother.

Since when had he become familiar enough with Steve that he'd be accepting rides from the man she hadn't married? Max had tolerated Steve for her sake, but that was all. He definitely hadn't approved of her decision to marry before she'd finished college. He'd never once pointed out how much he'd sacrificed to give her the chance to go to college, but there had been dark predictions she wouldn't complete her degree once she was Mrs. Corbett. But Max, being Max, had supported her decision once she'd made it.

Through Max she'd learned the major turning points of Steve's past seven years—his marriage to Lily, the birth of their daughter, Steve's going to grad school instead of law school as had been expected, the divorce, then Lily's death in an accident and his becoming manager of both the town and county of Tobias.

If she'd thought of it at all, she'd figured Max knew these things because everyone in Tobias knew about the Corbetts. There certainly had never been anything buddylike between him and Steve.

Not until now.

"I'm fine," Max said, not looking at her.

Now she understood his hurry to get out of the hospital. He'd known Steve would come to offer Max a ride home.

Steve's brows lifted, along with one corner of his mouth. "They put full-arm casts on folks who're fine? And I thought we had a fiscally responsible hospital here in Tobias."

"They're being cautious."

"I heard different—I heard you broke your wrist. And you'll be out of commission for weeks, maybe months."

Steve flicked a look toward her, underscoring his final words.

She wouldn't be here as long as months, but weeks, yes. Weeks of being in the same town with him.

Max grunted. "Checking up on me? Now you sound like Annette. And if the doctors think I'm going to…"

The reality of seeing Steve had rocked her, no denying that, but that didn't mean she would curl up and whimper. She had to set the tone. Just the way she would in a business meeting. Start the way you mean to go on—that's what she'd learned. She couldn't keep standing here gaping wordlessly.

She hooked the leather strap of her purse higher onto her shoulder, produced a smile and cut short her brother's dismissal of the doctors' recovery timeline.

"So, how are you, Steve? Or are you going by Steven now?"

She'd learned to put a bit of a sting into her smile. It came in handy when dealing with repairmen, mechanics and contractors accustomed to running over women, especially young women. She and Suz referred to it as their don't-tread-on-me approach.

That was the tone she wanted with Steve Corbett. So that after this he not only would not block her path but would steer clear of her altogether.

An expression flickered across Steve's face. A charge of light in his blue-gray eyes, an infinitesimal lift of one brow, a pull at the corner of his mouth. It could have been admiration. Or irritation.

"Still Steve."

She nodded as if in approval. "Keeping the casual touch for now. You can always go more formal when you move beyond little Tobias."

"No plans here to leave Tobias."

Was there an edge of accusation behind those words? He couldn't possibly be faulting her for leaving Tobias, not when he'd left her no choice. She studied him for more evidence.

Under a battered leather jacket, he wore jeans and a faded Chicago Cubs T-shirt that showed that he had not lost his swimmer's build in the past seven years. The casual clothes also didn't detract from the clean line of his features. His straight nose, strong jaw and totally masculine mouth were what people thought of as aristocratic and what so few aristocrats truly looked like. His thick brown hair with the glints of gold and red was cut with casual precision.

A memory burst full and fresh into her head. The two of them, sitting on the pier in early October. She was a junior in high school, he was a senior. It was more than two years before they'd started dating. He'd still been with

Lily then—it wasn't until the school year ended that he shocked everyone by breaking up the town's golden couple—and Annette would have said she and he were more acquaintances than friends. But that one golden day they'd run into each other as she'd left the library.

Somehow they'd ended up on the pier eating strawberry licorice and talking. She'd been teasing him about cheering for the Cubs when they'd finished yet another season without a whiff of the playoffs. Most of the folks in town pulled for the Brewers. They weren't powerhouses, either, but it made sense to pull for the loser from nearby instead of going out of state for one.

He'd said Miss Trudi Bliss, a former teacher and distant relative, had taught him to appreciate the Cubs, telling him that pulling for an underdog was a test of character. To not give in to cynicism, to not give up hope, to not switch allegiance to this year's winner, to find value and pleasure in moral victories. And then he'd given her that half-grin. "And this way Zach doesn't steal all my stuff. That's a major benefit with a younger brother."

He never touched her that day. Their talk hadn't even qualified as flirting. But she might have started to fall in love with Steve Corbett in those Indian summer moments, sitting beside him while they looked out to where the trees wept golden and russet leaves into the lake.

Her first step into the rabbit hole. Falling had been so much easier than clawing her way out.

"We better get going," Max muttered.

She kept her social smile aimed at Steve. She would not only get through this, she would show that she'd picked up poise and aplomb to rival a Corbett's.

"And your family? I hope they're all well?"

"I have no idea about Zach." A tougher note came into his voice at the mention of his younger brother—a note she didn't remember. But, then, she'd been so besotted she probably wouldn't have noticed if he'd sounded like Bobcat Goldthwaite. "We haven't heard from or seen Zach since he took off out of town that spring."

Zach had taken off, all right. In a spate of loud, harsh words aimed at his mother and the lusty roar of a motorcycle revved to the maximum. Like so many things during that time, Annette hadn't asked and Steve hadn't volunteered an explanation, even when Zach had not returned to be his brother's best man months later. She was startled to hear that he hadn't returned at all.

"My mother," Steve added after a pause that made Annette wonder if his thoughts also had traveled to the past, "is in perfect health, as always. And Nell—" A smile started in his eyes, where it was personal and private, then spread to his mouth, like he couldn't hold it back. "Nell is amazing."

"Nell?" Of course, Nell had to be his little girl. His and Lily's. "Your daughter. How is she?"

He'd wanted children. They'd talked about that. So often. *Our babies,* he would say. And his voice would drop into a rumbling timbre she seemed to remember in her bones—because she'd not only heard it but had felt it communicated from her hand resting on his bare chest to where her body would cradle his child growing inside her—

Max's left hand touched her arm, and she jolted back to awareness of the present. And that Steve was telling her about his daughter, answering her automatic *How is she?* as if she were a doting aunt.

"She's an amazing kid and she sure makes life interesting. She doesn't settle on anything for long." The warmth in his eyes and voice contradicted the rueful shake of his head. "With her like this at seven, I can only image what she'll be like as a teenager."

Lily had been blond, slender and sure as a teenager, so unlike Annette, whose dark coloring and curvy build had not helped her youthful insecurities.

Max shifted his weight to his other foot. "Annette—"

Neither she nor Steve looked in her brother's direction.

"I was sorry to hear about Lily. About the accident, and her death." They were the first words she'd spoken to Steve during this encounter that sounded natural to her ears, maybe because they were sincere.

She was still surprised at the sorrow she'd felt for the loss of a woman who had never been a friend. Or had the sorrow been for a child she hadn't known? Losing her mother as a girl was something she understood.

"Lily made a lot of mistakes in her life, but in the end she made it so I had Nell, and I'm grateful for that."

It was an oddly distant way to describe how he had come to be raising his daughter alone. Yet there was nothing distant in his eyes or voice when he spoke of Nell. He loved the child.

The child he'd created with Lily while he'd been pledged to her.

Like a ghost materializing, the wraith of that long-ago pain wrapped cold around her.

She pushed through it, focusing on the now, which meant Steve talking about his young daughter.

At least that solitary good had come out of the situation. A little girl had a father who loved her. Annette knew first-hand how important that was, because she hadn't had it. She'd hated many tenets of the Corbett creed, but living up to responsibility was one part she admired. A lot of men would have found another way—an easier way. Not Steve Corbett.

"When you meet Nell, you'll see—"

A spurt of panic pushed out her next words. "I won't

meet her. I mean, I'm only here to help Max. And with all the things to do for his company, and, uh, doctors and things, I doubt there will be time to…'' She gathered her thoughts and her calm. ''It's good to know you're doing well, Steve, but I doubt we'll see each other again. So I'll say goodbye and good luck to you now.''

She gave it a nice edge of finality.

But the glint of challenge in his eyes warned her that not only did he not accept that, but that she wasn't going to like whatever he had to say next.

''Tobias is still an awfully small town. I'm sure we'll be running into each other. A lot.''

''So when did you start being friends with a Corbett, Max?''

Annette didn't ask the question until she had watched her brother maneuver into the passenger seat of her car, helped him with the seat belt, closed the door and settled herself into the driver's seat.

''I wouldn't say friends.''

''He came to check up on you and give you a ride home from the hospital—doesn't sound like strangers to me.''

''He was there after I fell, showing a new inspector around. He helped get me to the hospital.''

''Oh.'' Why was she grilling him about this, anyway? She could never doubt Max's loyalty. He was one man she could count on no matter what.

''But I do respect the guy,'' he said in a rough voice.

She turned to him, but he stared straight ahead.

''I mean, I don't like what happened—what he did to you—and it's not like I forgive him or anything. But he did stand up and do the right thing.''

''For Lily and the baby.''

''Yeah.'' But she knew there was more. He let out a huff

of air. "Remember when I drove into Evanston and told you he and Lily were getting married?"

"Yeah." Oh, yes, she remembered. Less than two months after Max had taken her to Northwestern after her hasty transfer to the school north of Chicago, he'd shown up at the campus apartment she shared with Suzanna Grant, her randomly assigned roommate. He'd said Steve was marrying Lily—and then he'd held on to her when she'd cried. After he'd slept on the couch that Saturday—Steve and Lily's wedding night—and returned to Tobias on Sunday, she and Suz had talked for hours, taking a long step toward becoming the friends they were now. And she'd cried her last tears for Steve Corbett. "I remember."

"Well, what I didn't tell you was nobody else in town knew about their getting married. Not ahead of time like that. They got married real quiet by a judge and nobody knew until after."

"But…then how did you know beforehand?"

"Steve told me."

"What?"

"Came out to the house and knocked on the door. I decked him."

"What!"

"Well, what did you expect? After the way he'd hurt you. I punched him in the mouth."

"Max, what were you thinking? You know how the Tobias cops treat the Corbetts. If he'd called the police—"

"He didn't call the police, because he understood. Didn't try to duck or anything—and he saw it coming. Stood there and took it." Respect edged his words.

She pressed her palms to her head, as if that would make the whirling ache go away. "I don't believe this."

"He said he'd've done the same if the situation had been reversed. So I gave him ice and towels—cut lips bleed like a son of a bitch—and he told me he was going to marry Lily. He didn't want you to hear it through the grapevine.''

Why? The Corbett version of courtesy? Sleep with someone else while you're engaged, get her pregnant, have it all come out at your wedding, but don't let your ex-fiancée be blindsided by the news that you've married?

Supporting his right arm with his left hand, he shifted in the seat.

''What else, Max?''

''There was a time—later on—when he wanted to see you. I told him no. It was a couple days after they buried Lily. And right before that first time you and Suz came for Thanksgiving. Must've been a year and a half after…you left. I never did know how he found out you were coming, but he did, and he said he wouldn't take no from me. Made me promise to ask you if you would talk to him.''

''But…you never did.''

He shook his head—at himself or refuting her words? ''I said there was something you should know. You said if it had to do with the Corbetts, I better keep it to myself. When you were leaving, I tried again. Remember?''

Standing at the front door, with the wind shaking leafless branches at the murky sky. Bracing herself to leave the warmth of Max. She remembered.

''And you said if I didn't honor your wishes on this, you'd stay away for good. Not just from town, but from me. I believed you. I wasn't going to risk it.''

Nothing on earth could keep her away from her brother for good. But the fog of grief and heartbreak had finally been starting to lift when she'd heard the news of Lily's death. The emotions of that—and, yes, the recognition that Steve was no longer married—had pushed her emotions close to an edge she never wanted to be near again. Being in Tobias was bad enough. She had been afraid if Max said one more thing about a Corbett, and especially Steve...

She couldn't blame Max for believing her threat—she'd believed herself.

"I'm sorry, Max. I never should have said that."

He went to hitch his shoulders in a forget-it gesture and winced instead.

She started the car, looking over her shoulder to back out.

"'Net?" Max's voice roughened on her childhood nickname. "Were you still in love with the guy then? Would it have made a difference if you'd talked to him that Thanksgiving?"

Not knowing the answer to the first question, she shook her head at the second. "No."

She didn't know if that was the entire truth. She *couldn't* know. Because that was in the past, and she was in the present.

As for the future, she'd help Max for this month, then she'd leave and find whatever waited in the next phase of her life beyond Tobias.

Steve was standing in the hospital hallway staring out the automatic doors that had closed some time ago behind Annette and Max when his cell phone rang.

A minor emergency would be good. A transformer out or a small flood, maybe. Something to get his mind off Annette Trevetti. At least for a while.

A call from his mother didn't qualify.

He started for the door to the parking lot, absently letting Lana have her say. He'd learned at an early age that it caused fewer fireworks to listen before simply doing what he wanted. Zach had never learned that trick.

"No, I'm not going to forbid her from going there...."

Miss Trudi is family.... Great-aunt by marriage might be distant, but Miss Trudi *is* family.... Eccentric's not a crime.'' He turned from the parking lot and headed toward downtown.

''Mother.'' She stopped talking. ''I'm picking Nell up because it's her time to come home, but Nell will go on seeing Miss Trudi as long as they both enjoy it.''

Not for the first time, he thanked heaven as he hung up that he'd insisted all legal *I*s be dotted and *T*s crossed before he'd married Lily. They'd shared a house but never a bed. Six months after Nell's birth Lily had moved out, leaving Nell. So there was no doubt after Lily died that he was solely responsible for Nell.

He supposed it was to his mother's credit that she wanted to be involved in raising her granddaughter, and he would never cut her off from Nell. But he was damned if Nell would be raised the way he and Zach had been.

Steve used to envy the bond between Annette and Max. Just the two of them, yet they had a stronger sense of family than he'd experienced in all his life.

Until Nell.

When he'd brought up Annette meeting Nell and she had backpedaled so fast she should have fallen off the edge of the earth, he'd wanted to goad her, to push her, to get a rise out of her.

And he'd succeeded. Her wide brown eyes had come to his face, looking almost hunted—and their expression had put him in the role of the one toting the weapon. The expression frosted over in an instant. But he'd known. The prospect of seeing him again had not pleased her.

He thought he would have accepted that—he didn't particularly relish reliving being left at the altar—if it hadn't been that she'd been so all-fired eager to get the hell out of Dodge. A little too eager.

It wasn't as if he thought he could recapture her belief in him, but why shouldn't he find out exactly what was behind that edginess? Maybe some hunting was in order.

Chapter Two

From the hospital, Steve headed his SUV toward one of the two best vantage points overlooking the lake and what qualified as downtown Tobias.

Tobias Corbett, founder of the town, the county and the family's fortunes, had bought both vantage points, as well as most of the valuable property around them. He'd given each of his two sons one of the plots, and the plots had been passed down through the two very different branches of the Corbett family.

Now Trudi Bliss, a seventy-eight-year-old independent thinker and the last descendant of Tobias's elder son through his only daughter, who had married one Jebediah Bliss, owned an eyesore of a house set in a square block of prime Tobias property. Compared with the improvements Steve had worked hard to bring to Tobias, the throbbing of that sore thumb kept getting worse, and the squeeze on Miss Trudi, as she was known to everyone, got tighter.

There were plenty of people who lectured him, telling him that as manager of the town and county and Miss Trudi's closest relative, Steve had a major problem brewing.

That was his job—to handle problems.

Like the one this morning. Steve, introducing the new electrical inspector around, arrived at the work site where Max Trevetti's company was turning a one-story house into two stories and found it in an uproar.

Somehow Max had fallen, obviously breaking his wrist. Homeowner Muriel Henderson had fainted at the sight of either the bones sticking out of Max's wrist or the blood from the cut on his head. Max's workers were divided between reviving her and trying to stop Max from driving himself—one-handed—to the hospital because he didn't want to waste man-hours. Steve instructed the new inspector to call for paramedics to attend to Muriel, then drove Max to the hospital to make sure the guy didn't try to keep working. He knew Max Trevetti.

That had surprised Annette.

It used to be that every one of her emotions registered immediately on her face. God, it had been like an oasis of clear water and lush plants after a lifetime in the arid landscape of Corbett House. At movies, he used to watch her more than the screen. It had been a revelation seeing someone respond that way.

Not anymore. In the hospital hallway she'd guarded her emotions like a judge. Even when she'd first seen him. Nothing.

But he had seen her moment of surprise later.

Yeah, she'd definitely been surprised that he and Max had become…well, not friends, exactly. Perhaps colleagues.

After Max had punched him that night, then sopped up his blood, the next time they'd passed in the street there'd been a nod. Then a civil conversation about a permit application. They didn't seek each other out, but when circumstances put them together they got along. In a town this size and with their respective positions, circumstance put them together fairly often. Like today.

Steve had gotten the doctor's initial diagnosis before he called Gert, who usually looked after Nell after school and whose daughter Juney was Max's assistant. That was another thing about a town this size, everybody was connected to everybody else. Steve had been sure that Gert, home with the flu, would know how to get in touch with Juney, who would know how to get in touch with Annette. A roundabout way to notify Max's sister, but Steve had figured that getting the call from him would have made the situation worse for Annette.

Or maybe he hadn't known how in hell he would start that conversation.

Max had insisted Steve get to Town Hall to keep appointments and to change out of his blood-smeared clothes. When he could shake loose, he'd returned to check on Max. Well…maybe he'd wondered, with Juney on her honeymoon, if Annette would come to town.

Curiosity. It was natural.

Physically, she'd hardly changed at all.

The impact of that realization had stopped him in his tracks in the instant she'd faced him.

Her hair turned neatly under at her shoulders instead of falling well beyond, and was more controlled than before. But it was still that rich, thick chocolate, the same color as her eyes. And her figure—

His tire bounced from the curb he'd kissed while parking, jerking his mind to the here and now.

He had another female to think about.

He had his hand on the iron gate flanked by brick walls

when he saw two figures approaching. He started down the hill that sloped toward the lake to meet them. Last summer's crop of weeds had dried in the cracks of the brick wall and through the ironwork atop it. If weeds were a cash crop, his relative would be sitting pretty.

Beneath an open red raincoat, Miss Trudi wore her usual smock and loose pants, which his mother unstintingly called *disreputable*. The older woman's alternative was chiffon of various hues and lengths that frequently became tangled in furniture, plants and people. From a safety standpoint, he preferred this get-up.

The other figure flipped his heart and brought a smile. She'd had that ability from the first time he'd held her and looked into her eyes. He'd seen neither of her parents there, but another person entirely. All her own.

He waved and called hello. "Thanks for looking after Nell, Miss Trudi."

"It's my pleasure. How is Gert?"

As he gave the unpromising update on Gert, he reached for the books Nell carried. She shifted them away. "I can do it." One of her favorite phrases. She scowled and added, "Girls can do anything boys can do *and* have babies."

If Miss Trudi had accurately conveyed the facts of life to the seven-year-old, he'd both mourn that step toward maturity and be eternally grateful that he didn't have "The Talk" looming somewhere in his future.

"Sketched in the broadest strokes," Miss Trudi murmured with an amused glint. "We have been exploring the realm of potential role models for our Nell." Then she added to the girl, "Being a strong woman does not suspend the rules of courtesy. And a smart woman does not dismiss realities. Are the books heavy?"

Nell considered. "Yeah." She extended the stack to Steve. "I can be anything I want to be."

"Absolutely," he agreed.

"Like the president of India."

"Indira Gandhi," Miss Trudi filled in, nodding to the books, which Steve noted were biographies for children. "However, Indira Gandhi was prime minister, dear."

"You might start closer to home," he told Nell.

"Tobias doesn't have a president."

"No, but the United States does."

Her furrowed brow and intense look informed him she was weighing that. "Maybe after India," she said.

"No need to decide just yet, dear," Miss Trudi said in absolute seriousness. "Now, Steve, won't you come in and have a cup of tea? You look tired."

Absently, he thanked her and followed them in.

Annette hadn't looked tired. A little worried about Max, sure. But in that moment before she became aware of his presence, what else he'd seen in her had been laughter and confidence. Bone-deep confidence. That was new. Her looks might not have changed much, but a lot had happened in seven-and-a-half years. He knew each step of her success—a proud brother and Tobias's grapevine saw to that— but they were strangers to each other now. Maybe they always had been.

"Dad!" Nell rolled her eyes. "Told you he wasn't listening."

"Sorry. Got some, uh, business on my mind."

"That's okay, dear." Miss Trudi patted his hand. "We're talking about women."

Nell giggled, and he gave her a fake glower. "Hey, I know about women."

"Of course you do, dear," Miss Trudi said soothingly. "That's why you're having tea with me instead of preparing for a date."

A flash of the first time he'd picked up Annette for a

date crossed his mind. His heart going like a trip-hammer at the idea of spending time with her...

But Miss Trudi and Nell didn't mean ancient history. He'd dated since the divorce. Been serious a few times, too. Serious enough to almost make some damned fool mistakes.

The first serious one had wanted kids—just not some other woman's. He'd made sure the next woman hadn't objected to raising a child not her own. She hadn't; Nell had. Seeing them together, he knew Nell's instincts were on target.

Then he'd almost made the biggest mistake. A few years ago, Fran had moved back in next door to care for her terminally ill father. She was funny, endearing and wise. Nell adored her, and vice versa. He'd brought up marriage.

Fran had smiled, touched his cheek and said simply, "You don't love me."

When he'd tried to fumble out a response she'd added, still with that wise smile, "And I don't love you. If I had any sense, I would—but I don't. And neither one of us wants Nell to have an example of a marriage not built on love."

It had hit him then that although he hadn't made the same mistake twice, the potential for new and different mistakes might be infinite.

He hadn't dated much the past year.

"Time to go, Nell." He stood. "Say thanks to Miss Trudi."

He buckled Nell into the back seat and circled to the driver's side. A blurry figure in an unfamiliar car tooted in greeting. He smiled and waved automatically.

Talking about the Corbetts was considered a right of residency in Tobias. The whispering that Annette would come crawling back had evaporated after he'd married Lily. It regained life when it became clear he and Lily weren't living together even before the divorce. And it flourished after Lily died. But he'd known Annette never would. He'd known that the instant he'd seen his ring discarded on the minister's desk.

He could have caught her before she left the building, much less town. He'd remained rooted to the spot.

"Why're you just standing there?"

Nell's call from inside the car jerked him out of his reverie. Producing a smile, he tossed the keys in his hand and found the right one. Inside, he checked the rearview mirror, catching Nell's face in its frame.

"What's the matter?"

He smiled. "Nothing's the matter. Looking at my favorite girl."

She tipped her head. "You had a different favorite girl before. The lady at the library told the other lady that the girl Steve Corbett loved a long, long, long time ago is back."

That was fast, even for Tobias. He put the car in Neutral and slung around against the pull of the seat belt to look at her directly. "A woman I used to date—"

"Like Fran?" she asked.

"Yes, dates like I had with Fran. But more dates. We…we liked each other a lot—but it didn't work out, and she went away. Now she's back because she's helping her brother, who got hurt. Remember Max, who builds rooms onto houses and has that big toolbox? That's Annette's brother."

Maybe he'd hoped to distract her by throwing in Max and his tools, which had fascinated Nell. No such luck.

"Are you going to date her now?"

Date Annette. Looking over to see her eyes, bright and interested. Laughing as a rubbery string of cheese stretched into a slapstick routine as they shared a pizza. Holding her hand as they walked across campus. Holding her. Her mouth on his. Her taste. The hot, tight feel—

"Are you?" Nell demanded.

He pushed down the college kid in love he'd once been and grabbed for the father he'd become. "I can't tell you that, Nell. But I can tell you that no woman I date could ever change how much I love you. Do you understand? What I might feel for a grown-up woman won't change that you're my favorite girl. Okay?"

She met his eyes and nodded. "Okay."

He turned and put the SUV in gear.

"But maybe you're not gonna date this one because she's going to hightail it out of town first chance she gets?"

He raised his eyebrows at Nell through the medium of the rearview mirror.

"That's what the lady at the library said to the other lady at the library."

"Ah. Well, ladies at the library don't always know everything."

She frowned. "So she's gonna stay?"

"We'll have to wait and see." He pulled away from the curb, knowing that answer was unsatisfying all the way around.

Nell didn't like waiting.

Annette would surely prefer the library lady's prediction—if not her phrasing—that she'd be gone as soon as possible.

As for him... He shouldn't want to be reminded. He didn't need distractions from Nell and his job. But... Hell, he didn't know what he wanted.

"Daddy, remember I'm going to Laura Ellen's to practice for the parade."

He would have remembered Nell and her friend were

preparing for the St. Patrick's Day parade as soon as he'd spotted the calendar on their kitchen wall. "We'll get you some dinner and get you to Laura Ellen's in plenty of time."

Another exciting night in his social life.

Maybe Miss Trudi was right. Maybe he should start dating again.

Annette dropped her purse and duffel on the sofa that pulled out into a bed and looked around at the room Max had built on for her after he'd dropped out of college and came home to raise her.

Until then she could remember only sharing the one bedroom with her mother while Max slept on an old couch in the main room. That was after their father had deserted his family.

The house had been a one-room fishing cabin when Anthony Trevetti brought his wife and baby son to Tobias, Wisconsin, from a slum in Boston.

Annette couldn't even imagine what it must have been like in the unheated single room with no kitchen or bathroom. By the time she could remember, Max and their father had put together a serviceable bathroom and a kitchen area and added the bedroom. After their father left, Max used his earliest construction skills to add insulation and drywall to what had been open-stud walls.

Then, after Mama... Max had said neither of them should have to sleep in the living room. So in addition to working overtime, he'd built this room.

You and me against the world, kid...

Her own room. A bed and a closet all her own. She had painted the walls sky blue and the trim a barely-there yellow and turned sheets from a yard sale into curtains and matching pillowcases sewn—badly—by hand. The room had made her think of summer all year round. A refuge for a lonely and uncertain girl.

And then a place to marvel that she was falling in love and Steve said he loved her back. A place to build dreams…then to survive the first hours after they shattered. She blinked hard against hot moisture in her eyes, focusing on the present.

The walls were painted parchment now with precise white trim. Businesslike shelves and cabinets tidily lined three walls with the fourth wall taken up by the sofa, in a muted plaid of earth tones. Juney's desk, swept unnaturally clean in her absence, protruded into the room, facing the door.

Max was asleep, knocked out by the pain pills and perhaps by the pain.

She should use this time to settle in. To unpack and arrange her belongings so she could hit the floor running in the morning, so she could do what Max needed done and keep him from doing what he shouldn't.

She would make the sofa bed, put on the silk pajamas that made her feel pampered, pile pillows and curl up with a book like she used to…when she had been that lonely and uncertain girl. *Poor little Annette Trevetti.*

From the second-grade classmate who'd asked in all innocence why she wore the same clothes so often to the teachers who had scurried past the fact that her father was gone and her mother worked too hard to attend events to a smattering of adults who had complimented her for doing so well, *considering,* she'd learned that even comments meant to be supportive could hurt.

And the mean-spirited ones could crush…if you let them.

She hadn't let them. But she had promised herself she would get away for good as soon as she could.

Instead, she had lost her head and her heart to a pair of

mysterious blue-gray eyes. Eyes like a day with the potential to shift from sun to rain in a heartbeat. She'd dreamed of spending the rest of her life keeping them sunny, even if it meant staying right here in Tobias.

She picked up her purse and walked out.

Waiting at the stoplight on his way back from dropping off Nell, Steve idly looked to the left. A figure walking through the shadows in the Video Barn parking lot caught his eye and his heartbeat.

Annette.

Didn't matter that she was swathed in a long black coat turned even inkier by the shadows. He knew. Something about the way she moved.

A hunter's instinct for his prey?

His mouth twisted at that thought. More like a conditioned response he hadn't quite shaken. Drooling, like one of Pavlov's dogs.

She was inside before he pulled into the parking lot. He scanned the aisles between the rows of videos and spotted her on the right side, short of the new releases. The classics section—that figured.

Passing the new animated video Nell was badgering him to rent, he circled wide, hoping Annette wouldn't be alerted by the *Hi, Steve*s that trailed him.

So far so good. He came up behind her left shoulder. She had her head bent, reading the back of a tape. Her hair swung forward, obscuring her face. Didn't matter. He could have traced that curve from behind her ear, around the corner of her jaw and the point of her chin by memory.

Dammit.

He leaned in close to say in a low voice, ''Told you it's a small town.''

She jolted, audibly sucking in air. Trying to spin away

from him, she banged her right elbow against a stack of tapes, knocking down two.

She adjusted the tapes she held to prepare to corral the runaways, setting the bottom of her coat into swirling motion. But he'd already bent to pick up *Ball of Fire* and *Bad Day at Black Rock*. Was this the fates' idea of a joke?

With his eyes momentarily at knee level, her open coat revealed her legs encased in black leggings that hugged every curve. Definitely not *Bad Day at Black Rock*. She used to lament that she didn't have straight-as-sticks legs, and he'd thought she was nuts. He'd loved her legs. From the appreciative fizz stirring his blood around, that hadn't changed. *Ball of Fire*.

She freed a hand from the tapes and used it to overlap one side of the coat's bottom over the other. Which meant there was no reason not to stand, so he did.

"Did you want to look at these?"

"Thank you, no. You may put them away."

He used to be able to read every nuance of what she felt from hearing her say one word, one syllable. His inability to decipher that now was more than being out of practice. Just as at the hospital, her tone gave nothing away. Totally unlike the voice he remembered, covering the emotional scale like the run of keys on a piano, from the depths to the heights. Each one beautiful and distinct.

When he turned back, she had moved two steps away. Not enough to spell retreat, yet enough to establish distance and to let him simply walk away.

The way she had?

Hell no, *he* wasn't a runner.

"Nice to see you getting reacquainted with Tobias, Annette."

"It can't be considered reacquainted, since this place didn't exist when I last lived here." Her voice had that same cool dignity she'd used for their exchanges at the hospital, like she was talking from behind frozen glass.

"I guess not," he said easily. "Lots of things have changed since then. So what are you doing here?"

She cut him a look. Could that be humor lurking? He used to love to make her laugh, to lift the sorrows from her eyes. "Oddly enough, I'm here to pick up videos."

"You always did like movies."

Her mouth tightened. "I thought Max might like to watch some movies."

He tipped the top video down enough to read the title. *Pride and Prejudice.* "Either I don't know Max very well or he must be really bored."

She backed up, a definite retreat. Color flowed into her cheeks. Her facial muscles didn't change, but she couldn't control the color or hide it behind glass.

"You don't know Max at all." He'd bet Tobias's next fiscal year's budget that those words had sounded less certain than she would have liked. "But this one is for me. Max is asleep. The doctor gave him painkillers for the next few days."

"So, you're bored. Back in town less than a day, and you're bored." That came out as more of an accusation than he'd intended.

"Max is supposed to take it easy for the next week. I'm stocking up."

She looked and sounded assured. His unexpected arrival had knocked her off balance, but the edge of his accusation somehow gave her power. He'd have to remember that if he was going to... What? What was it he was after? Oh, yeah, figure out why the hell she was so set on getting out of town fast. Nothing else.

"So you're going to stick around for a while?"

"As I said at the hospital, as long as Max needs me."

"People change their minds…about sticking around, I mean."

A bolt of light and fire flashed across her eyes. It should have broken that damned frozen glass from the inside, but she reined it in immediately.

"When they're given a reason, they do. Max has never given me a reason not to trust him completely."

Giving him no time to respond, Annette walked away, returning a video to its rack on her way toward the checkout lines.

After a quick detour to pick up that animated video for Nell, he followed.

Annette's shoulders tightened under the black coat as he came up behind her. Using his elbow, he gently nudged her toward the checkout on the right, the one with the teenage clerk. Her momentum carried her two steps in that direction before she stopped in the open area between the lines.

"I'm going in the other line."

He shifted his weight to partially block her. "I wouldn't advise that."

"The other line is shorter, and I don't want your advice."

He ignored the second part. "Shorter, yes, but there's a catch." He waited until she met his eyes. The chili he'd had for dinner chose that moment to somehow lodge in the center of his chest. The stuff hadn't even been that hot. "Recognize the clerk on that shorter line?"

She looked at him another beat, then glanced toward the white-haired clerk. "Miriam something. She worked in the front office at the high school."

"Miriam Jenkins," he said, standing close just so they wouldn't be overheard. "She's retired from there now. She works here to help the pension, but it also supplements her store of knowledge of what's going on in Tobias. Forget the *Tobias Record,* Miriam's the real source of news around the county. How many questions do you feel like answering—or avoiding—tonight?''

She gave a soft tsk of irritation. "Fine. I'll stay in this line, but there's no reason for you to."

"You kidding? After being seen talking with you in public? I don't want to be here all night answering her questions, either."

"You could have avoided the whole problem by not talking to me tonight."

"Oh, I think the problem started long before tonight."

Before she turned away, he saw color push up her throat and that hunted look cross her face again.

Chapter Three

"Yes, but is the roofing at least R-eleven? What material is he going to use for the roof?" asked the man behind the permits office counter at Town Hall.

"Bubble gum and straw," Annette muttered. The morning was not going well.

Max had been beyond cranky when she'd left. She didn't know if it was the result of pain or concern about his injury's effect on his business or lack of sleep or all three. She'd awakened several times last night, and each time she'd heard him moving around the house, so he clearly had even less sleep than she did.

As for her wakefulness, being in an unfamiliar bed and in a once-familiar room that was no longer hers was bound to produce a restless night.

Max had said he had to get this permit application in this morning. He'd delayed a day because of his wrist and he didn't want the company's reputation sliding because he had a little pain.

A little pain, a cut on his head, a cast on his right arm, doctor's orders to take it easy and potential permanent nerve damage if he messed up his recovery. He hadn't taken her listing those reminders well, lecturing her about how running a company was all about word of mouth, and complaints spread three times faster than compliments. He'd already had client calls that had mixed sympathy for his injury with anxiety. He had to make sure the work stayed on schedule as much as he could, and that started with getting this permit application in. Today.

She'd had to be firm—and a little sneaky. Holding on to the keys to his truck yesterday had shown great foresight, since one of his workers had delivered the truck last night.

She'd assured him she could do whatever he needed doing. How was she supposed to know that would require a stint in purgatory, otherwise known as the permits office, with Trent Lipinsky as the gatekeeper?

She had already called Max once on her cell phone— and woken him from a nap. She wasn't going to call him again. Instead, she'd deflected Lipinsky's picayune demands by writing down the detailed requests to relay to Max. She rubbed the spot between her brows that announced an impending headache.

"I've given you the dimensions, along with the location, the contractor's license number, the sales tax, the bonding company and the scope of work. Does the specific roof material matter at this point? Since this is only the application, and we will, of course, be providing all the details with the completed paperwork. I'll write it down on my list, and Max will know all the answers. When I bring back all the documentation you've so kindly enumerated and explained—" in tedious detail "—I'll have his answers."

She smiled at him. He smiled broadly in return.

"You know, Ms. Trevetti, I really should have all the details, but for you—"

"Is there a problem here?" The voice came from behind her.

At one point during last night's wakefulness, she'd decided to put the time to good use by preparing herself for running into Steve again. She'd tried. Memories kept hijacking her thoughts—because she was tired and worried about Max. Questions about why Steve had told Max about his impending marriage or why he'd wanted to talk to her after Lily's death were moot. Totally hypothetical, because they couldn't change what happened, and that was that.

Besides, she'd told the few stars winking through a dark curtain of blue spruce trees beyond her bedroom window, what were the chances that she would see Steve a third time so soon?

So much for her ability as a psychic.

"No, no problem, Mr. Corbett. I was just explaining to this lady how to apply for a building permit."

"Really?" It was Steve at his most controlled. From Lipinsky's bland expression he didn't realize the ice under his feet had become mighty thin. "I can't imagine Max Trevetti sending his sister without all the customary information needed to get the permit application in. Does Max strike you as someone who would suddenly forget what was needed for a routine application?"

"I, uh—"

"I'm handling this, Steve." She faced him. His protectiveness was seven years out of date. "There is no problem."

Without moving his head, he shifted his eyes to her.

"Glad to hear there's no problem." His face gave nothing away. He turned to the clerk. "So this permit application is all ready to go?"

"There's still the fee."

"Yes, here's the check." She handed it over, not sorry to turn her back on Steve.

Trent looked at it. "Oh. Sorry, Ms. Trevetti, but there's the water and sewer fee. That's not included in this."

Max had said that was paid at a later stage. In other circumstances she would have argued. But that would prolong having Steve Corbett stand behind her like he thought he was some six-foot-tall guardian angel.

"How much?" She shifted her purse to reach for her checkbook.

"I'm sure we can—"

She spun to face Steve. By clenching her teeth she kept her words too low and even for the clerk to hear. "I do not need you charging in and slashing around with the great sword of your name."

Catching only the start of his eyebrows rising, and not waiting for his answer or letting herself consider that would-be guardian angels should not wear shirts with seaming across the shoulders like guidelines for the caressing hands of a lover, she turned to the clerk, opening her checkbook with a snap and grabbing the pen chained to the countertop.

"How much."

"One hundred and fifty dollars, but—"

"Do I make it out to the county or the town?"

"I'm sorry, we don't accept personal checks from out of state."

She thought she heard a sound from behind her, and the clerk's eyes flicked to where Steve still stood.

She closed her checkbook and pinned the clerk with her don't-tread-on-me look. "I'll be right back. And when I return, I expect you to have a receipt prepared, the rest of this paperwork in order and no additions, glitches or delays. Nothing lost. Nothing missing. Not *oh, one more thing.* The application done and in the system.''

She didn't wait for his answer. She turned, circling wide of Steve, and went out the door into the main hallway, heading for the exit.

He caught up with her on the outside steps leading to Hill Street.

At least his following her meant he wasn't back there throwing his weight around with Lipinsky, supposedly on her behalf.

''Annette—''

She had been away long enough that it took her a moment to locate the Bank of Tobias. She spotted the sign to her left and angled down the town hall steps. Her unwanted escort easily kept pace. ''Please go away.''

''Part of my job.''

''Harassing former residents?'' He reached to take her elbow as they crossed the street. She avoided the touch by speeding up slightly.

''Keeping tabs on whether people have satisfying interaction with Tobias bureaucracy. I had a report Lipinsky was stringing someone along. That's why I came down.''

''Well, check me off as a satisfied customer and close the file.''

''Ah, but it wasn't your satisfaction I was concerned about. It was mine.''

That wasn't true. He'd always been exquisitely, tormentingly, soul-shatteringly concerned with her satisfaction.

Let me, Annette. Touching her, his long fingers so gentle, so persistent...

She stutter-stepped, and the toe of her shoe caught the curb.

This time she didn't have enough balance to avoid his grip. His hand wrapped warm and solid around her elbow, his strength holding her upright from that single contact point.

Warmth also flowed through her from that single contact point. No. She was doing this to herself. With her wayward thoughts about a long-dead first love. Making him into some paragon of sexual consideration. Why, he'd been no better at making her feel wonderful in bed than—than... Comparisons were pointless.

"You okay?"

She shook her head to clear it, belatedly registering his question and that her gesture would be construed as an answer—and that his grip had slid up her arm and had drawn her close to his side. He wore only the shirt; in a warm spell, March was far from shirtsleeves weather in Wisconsin, yet she felt heat radiating from him.

"Did you twist your ankle? Hurt your—"

"No." She stepped away. "I'm fine. Thank you."

Crossing the sidewalk to the ATM kiosk, she drew in a breath, regaining another kind of balance.

She started to punch in her PIN, paused and pointedly looked over her shoulder to where Steve stood, once more just behind her. "Do you mind?"

He wanted to grin. How she knew that when his face was wiped clean, she couldn't say. It wasn't like she knew the guy anymore...or, as events had proven, had ever known him.

They came from the same town but different worlds. She'd once had some foolish notion that despite their differences they'd truly connected in a way that could last a lifetime. She'd been wrong. That had changed her life, but it hadn't ended it. She wasn't going to let memories of those events disrupt her life now.

He turned his side to her but didn't move back. From a privacy standpoint it was perfect. From her standpoint it was little improvement.

"You don't need to do this," Steve said as she started pressing the keys that would withdraw a cash advance against her credit card. Ordinarily, she hated paying the fees, considering them a waste of money. But on rare occasions, the expense was worthwhile. "He's jerking you around."

"Thank you, I'd figured that out myself. It's worth the money to have this completed today. I'm not *poor little Annette* anymore. Things have changed."

"You never were *poor little Annette*—not in the ways that count. And I know things have changed." There was nothing to hear in Steve's voice. Certainly not sadness. "I hear they've changed a lot for you lately. Selling your company, right?"

"Yes."

"For a lot of money."

"Yes."

"Tell me about it."

Giving the spiel was second nature. And comfortable. "We find the right service for busy homeowners—car repairs, lawn work, tree service, additions, repairs. They can hire us for one project or on a retainer. If they don't know what kind of workman they need, we can find that out, too. We can either bring the client three to five bids, with background material on each, and let them decide which to take, or we will select one for them. Our company's name is Every Detail and that's what we see to—we do all the vetting of workers, researching their quality and prices, assessing the job and following up."

"Sounds like a lot of work."

"It is. That's why people are willing to pay us to do it."

"Must be hard, though, to let go of a company you created. Something you started and loved and thought you'd be doing a long, long time." While the machine whirred, she glanced over her shoulder to see him shake his head. "Then to let all that go."

"Sometimes circumstances combine in such a way that you realize that what you'd loved and expected to last a long, long time was merely temporary. The corporation pursuing Every Detail made us an offer of serious money. Enough to free us from working if we don't want to, and to give our associates a bonus, plus the promise of more work for our lineup of service people. How could we say no to that? There was no other choice to make."

The money came out of the slot, followed by the receipt and her card.

"We all have choices. We all make choices."

He'd made his choice. He'd probably thought he could have both her and Lily—that he could have anything he wanted, that he was entitled to it.

She put the card into place in her organizer and the receipt and cash in the billfold area.

"We make choices. And some of us never look back," he added.

She turned and found him facing her. She squared off to him, her calm intact.

"Is that what this is about? Is that what's bothering you? That when I left here I never looked back to Tobias, or you? That I succeeded without you? That I've made something of my life?"

"No, it doesn't bother me. It makes me proud."

She should have scoffed, laughed, something. He was so darn convincing. He always had been. That aura of sincerity had drawn her from the start…and had been her undoing in the end.

"Steven!" A man emerging from the bank steamed toward them.

Steve looked toward the man as he muttered, "And I wish to hell I knew what this is about."

She'd meant this conversation. His *this* sounded broader. Maybe he was talking about the approaching man. Or maybe she had misunderstood.

"Steven, how nice to see you. Great weather we're having, isn't it? We should get eighteen holes in at the club while it lasts, eh?" His well-tailored suit couldn't mask that he was built like a top—wide through the bottom. She had a sudden vision of a top trying to swing a golf club. "Had dinner with your mother and some of the other board members last week and we were saying how we had to get you to join this year—"

"Sorry, Jason, I'm not much of a golfer. But I'd be happy to talk to you about increasing the bank's commitment to the Tobias Fund. And I'd like to introduce—"

"Oh, well, uh…the board…"

"—a former resident who's come back. Annette, this is Jason Remtree, president of the bank. Jason, this is Annette Trevetti. I think you know her brother, Max, the owner of Trevetti Building."

"How do you do, Jason?"

Annette hoped that if Jason ever played poker she could be at the table. Betting against him would be a snap. The way he goggled at her, then Steve, then her again, he might as well have shouted that he'd heard all the gossip about them and remembered every shred of it.

"Uh, fine. It's nice to… Uh, Max—" He latched on to that name like a life preserver. "Max is a good customer of ours. Sorry to hear he got hurt."

"Thank you, I'll tell him you said so. And, yes, he is a good customer—a very good customer, so you can imagine my disappointment when I called about arranging to be added to the signature card while I'm here *temporarily*—" she emphasized the qualifier to let Steve know she hadn't missed that *former resident who's come back* "—for the account and was told no one could accommodate us today, even though Max's injury makes it impossible for him to sign. But now that I've met you, I'm sure you can personally arrange for someone to come out to the house this afternoon to take care of that and other matters. Three o'clock would be convenient."

"I, uh—"

"And next week, I'll be coming into the bank to talk about what services you're offering online. Online banking is so essential to business in this economy, don't you think? Yet I couldn't find any reference to the services offered by the Bank of Tobias in the material Max has."

"No, well, um…"

She took his limp hand and shook it firmly, adding a small smile. "It's been a pleasure to meet you, Jason, and I look forward to doing business with your representative this afternoon. I hope we can continue to do business in the future. Goodbye, gentlemen."

She couldn't say she was surprised when Steve ignored the hint, said a quick goodbye to Remtree and caught up with her in two strides.

"That was impressive," he said from her right shoulder as they crossed the street. "Remtree might leave bloodstains on his designer shirt from a few of those nicks, but impressive."

"He needed to be put on notice that if the bank doesn't provide services, Max will go elsewhere."

"Does Max know that?"

She said nothing. Max would be hard to budge on this. He didn't like change and he had a sense of loyalty that sometimes got in the way of his business sense.

"That's what I thought. You know, my mother couldn't have done that any better. Although I'll give you points for being smoother."

It was a good thing they'd reached the sidewalk, because that stopped her in her tracks.

"You, of all the people in the world, saying *I'm* like your mother?"

"Me of all the people in the world? You can't be trying to say I'm like her—you're too smart to make the same mistake Remtree does."

"You're either just like your mother or you give in to her all the time."

He raised one eyebrow. "Have any examples of *all the time?*"

"Swimming."

Both eyebrows went up. "Swimming? I quit competitive swimming after high school."

Steve had told her that Ambrose Corbett had encouraged both his sons to play sports as boys, approving only victories but also citing the benefits of learning teamwork and leadership, not to mention the connections that could later help a political career. When Lana objected that they were mixing with children from families beneath them, Ambrose had said, "If a Corbett only won the votes of other Corbetts, they'd never be elected."

Zach had reveled in the rough-and-tumble physicality. But for Steve the primary pleasure had been the unfettered interaction with other kids—kids he never would have met if Lana had had her way.

And she did have her way after Ambrose died.

Having reached six feet early in high school, Steve had

wanted to play basketball, but his mother refused permission. She would accept only tennis, golf or swimming—sports pursued at Tobias Country Club. He had decided to focus on swimming. Zach quit sports entirely.

When Steve was a Tobias High swimming star who dated glamorous Lily Wilbanks and she'd been little nobody Annette Trevetti in the class behind, she'd noted that while most swimmers shaved their times bit by bit, Steve had a reputation for dropping his times from practices to races in chunks. She'd also noticed how much she'd enjoyed watching his broad-shouldered, lean-hipped body slice through the water ahead of everyone else.

At the time she'd fooled herself into believing that the pleasure was a form of school spirit. When they started dating she'd recognized it for what it was—attraction, if not downright lust.

"Exactly. You quit competitive swimming. Your mother never wanted you to compete in sports, and you gave in to her."

"I didn't need swimming in college."

"Need it?"

He waved that off. "The point is I was on the swim team when I wanted to be and wasn't when I decided I no longer wanted to be. You'll have to dig deeper than that for an example."

"You're still here in Tobias, aren't you?"

"You of all people should know that was my plan all along, because it used to be *our* plan."

He'd talked about getting a law degree, then returning to Tobias and opening a legal clinic to help people in town. She was going to finish her degree so she could run the business side of the clinic. She had never mentioned her dream of leaving Tobias for good.

"It was *your* plan, because returning to Tobias is what's expected of Corbetts."

"You say *Corbett* like it's a dirty word. You were once willing to be a Corbett—said you would be for the rest of your life."

"If I hadn't realized my mistake in time, I would have been a Corbett by law and a piece of paper. I never would have been a Corbett in all the other ways—peering down my nose at the rest of the world, ordering people around and thinking I'm bet—"

"Honey, you've spent the past half hour doing a fine imitation of what you're describing as Corbett. I'm not saying Trent and Jason didn't deserve it, but—"

"I am *nothing* like—" She sucked in a quick breath and adjusted her shoulders and her dignity. "I do not have time for this useless discussion."

He didn't follow her as she returned to the permits office and finished her business with Trent Lipinsky. Finally, Steve had left her in peace. Left her to deal with the situation. Left her to her own thoughts.

Had she been too severe toward Lipinsky and Remtree?

She was so used to operating as half of a team with Suz, and yes, she supposed she did take the bad cop role more often than Suz. Much more often. Had she unconsciously patterned that role after the Corbetts?

She had found no answers when Trent handed her the completed paperwork to take to Max. She gave him a big smile, then felt a jab of guilt when his eyes sharpened and his smile stretched as he said, "We could discuss the ins and outs of permit applications over dinner tonight so it will be a smooth trip for you next time."

A jab of distaste joined the guilt. To top off his anti-charm, he'd stretched out *smooth* like some campy lounge singer. But she *had* smiled at him that way, so it wouldn't be fair to zing him, no matter how tempting.

"I'm sure it will be a smooth trip regardless, Trent, since you and I are both professionals. And that's what makes dinner out of the question." She shook her head in would-be sorrow as she turned to leave. "Conflict of interest."

She could ordinarily handle a dozen Trent Lipinskys. Why on earth had she fumbled this? Okay, that was obvious. Steve had thrown her off. She had let Steve's comments get to her, leading her to overcompensate with a smile that opened a whole new can of worms.

Overcompensate.

There wouldn't be anything to compensate for if she hadn't been harsh. *Doing a fine imitation of what you're describing as Corbett.*

She passed through the open doorway and turned the corner—and there stood the speaker of those words.

More accurately, there lounged the speaker. Steve had his shoulders propped against the wall, one ankle atop the other, arms crossed over his chest.

The notion spurted through her that she would almost be glad to see him if it meant a distraction from her doubts. But *almost* fell far short of *was.*

"Eavesdropping, Steve?"

"Keeping tabs on what's going on, and there's nowhere better to do that than these halls. So I'm here a lot."

"You're not asking me to believe you work all the time, are you? Besides—"

"I know better than to ask you to believe."

"—I wouldn't think you'd have to work all that hard to keep this job."

He raised his eyebrows at her reference to the position in town his name gave him. "That reminds me, you accused me of using my—what was it? *Great sword?*"

Heat surged up her neck, preparing to fly like flags in both cheeks. "Your name."

He grunted, but the lift of his mouth gave him away. "Did it occur to you that I'm that clerk's boss's boss, and that position might have more weight than my last name? No, I can see it didn't."

He was right. It hadn't occurred to her. And his explanation was reasonable. Before she could formulate a response, though, he went on.

"And you're probably right. I don't think so, either. I think the answer's more basic."

"He's an idiot," she grumbled.

"I wouldn't say that. I'd say his motivation this morning was to extend the time he was looking at a beautiful woman to the maximum. That's not a sign of idiocy."

"You think you know everything, don't you?"

"Well, I know you're free for dinner tonight."

Was there an invitation hidden in that? Was he nuts? Or was she? Reading into an offhand comment all sorts of meanings that weren't there.

No wonder her nerves were jumping.

"Goodbye, Steve."

That goodbye at the town hall yesterday had been premature.

Annette pushed against the handle of the grocery cart as she looked over her shoulder. It made her feel a little paranoid. But looking over her shoulder had paid off, because she'd spotted Steve before he saw her. Finally.

Yesterday afternoon as she typed letters Max dictated, then met with the bank representative Jason Remtree sent out, she had decided the encounters Monday at the video store and yesterday at the town hall had been happenstance. The likelihood of that benign explanation had faded when Steve walked into the post office behind her first thing this morning. A young mother with two active toddlers got into line between them, and she'd avoided eye contact with Steve, so there'd been no conversation.

But as she'd left with an array of stamps, he'd turned from his spot at the counter and given her a slow, deliberate smile, along with a *good morning, Annette,* in a smoky voice that had every head in the place turning toward her and had her remembering mornings when he'd said those words just that way when there had been no one else to hear.

She returned the greeting coolly and walked out more slowly than she would have normally, so he wouldn't think he'd gotten to her.

And not ten minutes later he was there again.

At the gas station, she had swiped her credit card and inserted the nozzle into the gas tank. He pulled up behind her, then got out and stood, waiting for her to fill the tank. As if this were the only pump he could use. As if three of the seven other pumps weren't empty. As if the people at those four occupied pumps weren't gaping at them.

And he just stood there, arms once more crossed over his chest. As if he knew…knew that all he had to do was *be* to make her remember what it was like to have those arms hold her against that chest.

She turned her back to him and was telling herself that at least he wasn't trying to talk to her when the pump clicked off because the tank was full. Before she could pull the nozzle completely out of her car, his hand wrapped around hers.

"Let me help you."

That wretched smoky voice again. Making her think of… No.

"I don't need your help."

"It can make a mess if you pull it out too fast. We wouldn't want that."

Before she could stop herself, she looked up, and the heat and laughter in his eyes held her like a vise. She was unable to move, unable to dodge a memory of two young lovers who'd thought they were about to be walked in on by his roommate. A false alarm, as it turned out, but the consequences remained. As they had cleaned up, they had started to laugh. And as so often happened then, their laughter had led to—

Annette jerked her thoughts from the memories, turned on her heel and got in the car. If he didn't pull the nozzle free, she would drive off and yank the damned hose out of the pump.

He not only got the nozzle out, he refit the gas tank cap before she pulled out. That didn't improve her mood any.

She went home, and the first thing out of Max's mouth when she walked in was, "I'll bring in the groceries."

Groceries. She'd totally forgotten.

"No, you won't, because you're not supposed to do anything strenuous for at least a week. And—"

He'd snorted. "Carrying groceries is not strenuous."

"—there aren't any groceries to carry. Yet. I, uh, I thought you might need the stamps right away so I brought those home first."

"Why would I need stamps right away?"

"Well, I don't know, do I? It's your business."

Before Max could question that, she had headed back to town.

So here she was at the grocery store. But this time she wasn't going to be ambushed by Steve Corbett.

Her first over-the-shoulder check had shown Steve walking across the street toward the store, but he didn't appear to have noticed her. She jiggled the grocery cart to get all the wheels aligned enough so the thing would roll. A grocery store was perfect for staying out of sight. And she used to work in this one, so unless it had been renovated lately, she should have the advantage.

"Annette Trevetti, as I live and breathe! It is you! I thought I saw you yesterday crossing Hill Street, but then I saw the man was—well, then I decided I had to be wrong."

Annette turned toward the voice with a smile at the first words. Her smile dipped at the reference to being seen with Steve, but not much. Kim Jayne had shown her the ropes when she'd been hired here and had been one of the few seated on Annette's side of the aisle at the First Church of Tobias.

She moved near the checkout lines, even though that left her visible to anyone coming in—she could never hurt Kim Jayne's feelings by ignoring her.

"Kim, it's great to see you. How are you? How are Ray and the kids?"

"We're all still kicking, but those kids aren't such kids anymore. Dee goes to college next year, and Heather's in high school."

"Oh, my gosh. I can't wait to hear all about them. Do you have pictures?"

Kim snorted. "Do I have pictures? Are you kidding? But…"

She dipped one shoulder toward the register she'd been running all the time she talked, and to the line of customers. Kim wouldn't make customers wait while she held a personal conversation. Plus, the way she'd steered clear of naming Steve Corbett as the man she'd spotted Annette with was a reminder of how fast a personal conversation could become public property in Tobias.

"When's your break?"

"Fifteen minutes. Will you still be here?"

Annette looked over her shoulder again. Steve was outside the door. He stepped back to let a gray-haired couple enter before him. "I'll make sure I am."

"Great, see you then."

Annette zipped the cart along the aisle across the front of the store, using the people waiting in line as camouflage. She ducked down the paper goods aisle near the middle of the store, which would allow her maximum maneuverability.

"Annette! Oh, that is little Annette, isn't it?"

She jumped at the voice behind her, though not only did it come from the wrong direction, but clearly the light, clear tone did not come from Steve.

"Miss Trudi. It's so nice to see you. How are you?" She reached out a hand, but the older woman in the red coat instead engulfed her in warmth and color.

Miss Trudi had been her art teacher when Annette was in grade school. After retirement, she frequently invited former students for tea in her front parlor, when she poured out knowledge and culture as generously as the tea.

"I'd heard you'd come home. I'm delighted to see you again." Miss Trudi held her at arm's length. "You look tired, Annette. Oh, I don't mean to insult you, because you're lovely—even more lovely than as a girl, but it appears you have been working too hard. It's high time you came home. You'll be able to rest."

"I didn't come home to rest—I mean, I'm not coming home, it's—"

"I do hope you'll come to tea, my dear. We can catch up on everything."

"That's so nice of you, but—"

"Wonderful! Come at four tomorrow afternoon, and we can have a nice chat." Miss Trudi released her hand and backed up. "Must run now, but I look forward to seeing you at four."

"What? No—I mean, I'd love to. But—"

She followed Miss Trudi, but the older woman had disappeared into a knot of teenage girls using their lunch hour to buy candy bars and acne cream.

A raised arm trailing blue chiffon from the cuff of a red coat became visible beyond one girl's head. "I'll see you at four tomorrow, dear."

"Miss Trudi, tomorrow isn't…"

The first of the double exit doors closed behind the short figure in red. How did the woman move that fast?

"Talking to yourself, Annette? Pick that habit up in the big city?"

She closed her eyes but knew that wouldn't make Steve Corbett disappear. "What are you doing here?"

He raised his eyebrows as he hefted a bag of coffee in his right hand. "My turn to replenish the supply for the office. And you?"

"Getting food for Max, of course."

He looked at the contents of her cart—a solitary package of flower-strewn paper towels.

"I've seen Max eat down at the Toby, and I don't think this is going to cut it, Annette." Before she could do more than open her mouth, he continued. "Sorry I can't stick around and talk, but some of us have to work for a living, you know."

And he was gone nearly as quickly as Miss Trudi. Though that made more sense with his long, powerful legs, legs with the ropey muscles of a swimmer—

Dammit! She wasn't going to let the memories of hormones take over. He was gone, that was the important thing.

So, why had he left so easily? What was—

She put a hand to her throbbing forehead.

Steve was gone, but she feared her headache was just starting.

Chapter Four

Max met her as she pulled in, determined to carry groceries. "How'd it go?"

"Fine. This wasn't a trek to the North Pole, you know. I am accustomed to buying groceries on my own."

"You were gone long enough to see reindeer."

"I ran into, uh, some people." She handed him the package of paper towels.

He growled. He balanced the paper towels against the cast on his wrist and reached around her to grab the plastic handles of one bag knobby with soup cans and another with laundry detergent, both with his uninjured hand.

"Show-off," she muttered.

He ignored that, though his mouth twitched. "Who?"

She paired a medium-weight bag with a light one in each hand and followed him to the house.

Steve.

Everywhere she went. Even when he wasn't there, she

felt as if he were or might be any second, and that was just as bad. And now the memories…

For so many years she'd thought that the last memory of him, the one where she'd had to face that he didn't love her the way she'd loved him in the most public way imaginable, had obliterated all others. Now it turned out those other memories had been lying underneath the surface, waiting to pop up and torment her like…like locusts. Flying at her from out of nowhere and constantly whirring in her ears.

"You don't remember who you saw?"

She gave her head a shake to tumble her thoughts into order.

"Miss Trudi—I'm invited to tea tomorrow. Muriel Henderson was there, so after she asked about you, I heard all about Mandy and her family in Minneapolis, and she wanted to hear all about me." Annette didn't mention how much her high school friend's mother already knew about Annette's accomplishments. She wasn't surprised Max told them, but she was surprised the woman remembered them and congratulated her with such pleasure—and she was touched at both. "I had coffee with Kim Jayne, the clerk who trained me. Remember her?"

She frowned as she remembered that both Muriel and Kim had mentioned seeing her with Miss Trudi and seemed concerned about the older woman, though neither pursued it.

"Sounds like you're picking up your friendships again. That's nice."

She stared after Max as he disappeared toward the pantry in the hall that connected to his workshop. Friendship was not something she associated with Tobias.

The house was quiet, the floor lamp was angled perfectly on Steve's favorite chair, and he wasn't sleepy. Should have been the perfect combination to read the reports he'd brought home. He hadn't gotten to them because he'd spent too much of the past two days dogging Annette's steps and wondering about hunting, frosted ice and memories.

He hadn't spent the past seven years focused on what Annette Trevetti might be doing at any given moment. Even times when he'd known or had reason to expect she might be in town. A fleeting thought now and then, sure. An extra glance at a car with Illinois plates or a medium-height woman with dark hair, yeah, he'd admit to that.

This was different. This was as if talking to her had flipped on some strange mechanism inside him. Annette radar. His mouth twisted. She'd laugh at that.

No, maybe not. Not now.

Just after he'd dropped Nell off at school this morning, his cell phone rang. It was Jason Remtree, falling all over himself to apologize in case he'd said anything awkward during their encounter the day before. The guy had a tin ear for relationships—he kept buttering up Steve thinking that would safeguard him against a morbid fear that Lana would get him kicked off the country club board. Remtree was her lapdog, so why would she bother? Not that Steve would have any influence to stop her if she decided to do that.

Remtree probably thought he was returning a favor when he suggested Steve steer clear of the post office because from his office window he'd seen Annette pull in there. Steve had been a block away at the time. One quick turn, and there he was. In Tobias's compact business district, following her from the post office to the gas station had been even easier.

He'd suffered the consequences of recalling that incident

in his dorm room with an hour spent staring out his office window, punished by memories.

Maybe it was that ear warmer she wore that held her hair back. She'd had a habit of pushing her hair back with both hands. A simple gesture that got to him every time. He'd had no idea why until one night, after they had made love, lying there with his body covering hers, still joined, his possession of her complete, the certainty of their connection powering his hammering heart, he'd stroked her hair back. He'd realized he did that often when they made love. Just as her gesture did, his hands revealed her face, its beauty and its vulnerability. Only this revelation was for him alone. An intimacy even beyond their physical bond.

So maybe it was her hair being pulled back that had pushed him toward those memories and taken the guard off his mouth.

What had yanked him out of that was spotting her car go by. The grocery store had been a guess that paid off when he spotted those Illinois plates again. He was starting to feel a real affection for the Land of Lincoln.

He'd wanted to rattle her. Wanted to crack the glass and melt the frost. He wanted to see the Annette he remembered.

The fall of his senior year at Tobias High they'd stumbled into a long, rambling conversation. There'd been a zing of attraction, but he'd been dating Lily and he'd packed the zing away. Then came a Saturday near the end of swimming season.

He was hoisting himself out of the pool at the district meet. He'd qualified for state, as expected, and trimmed his record from the previous year, as expected. The night before, Lily had proclaimed that he would set a record for her.

Nothing like a command performance. In fact his entire

relationship with Lily had begun to feel like a command performance. She had opted for the University of Wisconsin at Madison after he chose it over objections from his mother, who'd wanted Ivy League. Now Lily was talking about their future together—college, law school, prosecutor and politics. The same future his mother had mapped out. Not even swimming had provided much escape.

So he'd come out of the pool, knowing he'd done what was expected, hearing what hit his ears as perfunctory applause, and there was Annette Trevetti in the stands in front of him.

She was part of a crowd of students. She wasn't yelling any louder than anyone else. The humidity was wildly wisping her thick hair around her face in a way that would have sent Lily screaming for lotions and sprays.

But Annette grinned so hard it made his cheeks ache. And her eyes were so bright with joy that he could almost believe his small achievement was the most important thing in the world to her for those few seconds.

And then he realized his cheeks hurt because he was grinning, too. The crowd, perhaps picking up on his reaction, cheered harder, three of his teammates gave him celebratory high fives while two punched his shoulders and Coach Boylan clapped him on the back.

He had never before celebrated a victory that enthusiastically. It was an odd sensation. A little raw from letting the world see his reaction. And more than a little tingling. At the time he'd written that off as the stinging contact of his teammates' and coach's approval. Two years later, when he encountered Annette on campus at Madison, he'd recognized the real source of the tingling.

A lifetime, that's what he'd thought he'd won when she'd said she would marry him.

He'd known his mother would be a problem. He would

have been happy to elope, but he hadn't suggested it. Max would have objected, thinking people would interpret that as Steve being less than proud to be marrying Annette. He might have fought Max, but he suspected Annette would have felt the same way.

So it had to be a public wedding in Tobias. Now, with the absolution of time, he could admit he'd hoped Lana might wash her hands of them. Instead, after he'd convinced her that nothing she said could stop him from marrying Annette, his mother took over the wedding like it was one of her precision-run fund-raisers.

He'd known Annette wasn't happy, but she'd closed up in a way he'd never expected her to. He had hoped she was simply stiffening her upper lip and looking toward their life after the wedding, the way he was. Even after Lily came to him, he'd thought he could hold it together and work it out.

And then it was all gone. In the opening of a side door of the First Church of Tobias, and the closing of a rear door.

Regret.

Was that the sharp taste in his mouth?

Maybe. But it didn't explain the sensation that jangled just under the surface of his skin like sheet lightning across a night sky. It was like the cells protesting that they'd been denied some basic nutrient for far too long.

Annette. His body craved her. To touch her...

His fingers curled around the arm of the chair, needing to direct the impulse somewhere other than his muscles' real desire.

To be touched by her.

The skin along his forearm prickled with awareness of a woman who was nearly two miles away. And had no more intention of touching him than—

"Daddy!"

He jolted, his heart hammering with entirely different cause than the second before, even as his mind recognized the tenor of Nell's call as run-of-the-mill waking up in the middle of the night. Not a nightmare, not illness. She was safe and healthy. If he left her on her own she'd fall back to sleep in moments.

Tell that to the protective adrenaline pumping through him.

He used the arrow of light from the hall to thread through the accoutrements of a girl whose ambitions ranged from grand actress to FBI agent to president of several countries, but who was still a little girl.

"It's okay, Nell. I'm here."

"Daddy!" Sitting up, she stretched both arms toward him.

He sat on the bed with his back against the headboard, drawing her to him so he held child, pillow, comforter and stuffed animals all in his lap. "Go to sleep now. I'm here."

She curled tighter against him, one elbow digging into his ribs. He didn't move. After a few minutes, he felt the shuddering sigh of relaxation go through her, and then her breathing smoothed and deepened.

This was what had come into his life that day at the First Church of Tobias. He hadn't known it then—he'd known only the searing pain. Obligation and responsibility had made him put one foot in front of the other. But from the first time he'd seen Nell, they had shriveled to a pair of solitary drops in an ocean. Everything that happened had come together to bring him to this moment. Even if he could have changed pieces of the past, how could he risk that those changes might have set in motion a sequence that would have stopped him from having Nell? He couldn't.

So he couldn't regret—not what had happened and not what hadn't.

He adjusted enough to let a different square inch of his rib cage be punished by Nell's elbow.

But did that mean he had to let the past predict the future?

An elderly man Annette didn't recognize was entering Lakeside Dry Cleaners as she prepared to leave. He held the door for her, and she smiled at him.

The smile melted as she recognized the lithe walk of the man approaching diagonally across the parking lot. Geometry had never been her strongest subject, but she didn't need to know how to work this equation to estimate that Steve's path would intersect with hers in a matter of seconds.

She pivoted and walked into the dry cleaners ahead of the elderly man. He gave her a bemused look and followed her in.

With her back to the door she looked around as if she'd misplaced her keys then shifted the clutch of hangers to her other hand and patted her pockets.

Another shift, swinging the hangers over her shoulder, and another round of pocket patting, and she came up with the keys in the hand that had always held them, said aha, bestowed a big, relieved smile on the elderly man and clerk who had watched her pantomime and went out the door.

Steve Corbett occupied a slice of real estate four feet away, leaning against the front grill of a parked pickup across the sidewalk from the Lakeside Dry Cleaners.

She stopped dead, but only for half a second. Railing against the inevitable was not only a waste of energy, it was undignified.

''Problem?'' he asked. Creases at the corners of his eyes belied the solicitous tuck between his brows.

''Not at all.'' She started to sweep past, but he grabbed the hangers she held over her shoulder. With her fingers still tucked under the curved metal, she had to stop or risk tipping over backward.

''Here, let me help you.''

''I don't need—''

But he'd gained control not only of the hangers and clothes, but of her hand. He lifted her fingers from the metal, removed the hangers with one hand then curled her hand within his other one, still over her shoulder. He exerted slight pressure to make her turn to face him, as if guiding her through a dance.

A dance that stirred too many memories. A dance that brought them too close, so that this moment and those from the past threatened to blur. That couldn't happen. The chasm between then and now would not be crossed.

''What are you doing?''

''Just trying to help.''

She yanked her hand away—forget dignity. ''You're not helping, Steve. You're not helping at all. And I think you know that.''

''The clothes looked heavy—''

She scooped her hair from her face with both hands. ''Not just now. Ever since I came back. I don't understand it. I would think you would be as eager as I am for us to stay far away from each other. To not stir the gossip or…anything else.''

''Anything else like memories? There were good ones, a lot of good ones. C'mon, Annette. Let's find someplace, get a cup of coffee and talk. You can tell me about your company. And I'll tell you what's happened in Tobias. All the things you would have seen if you hadn't felt you had to stay away—''

"I never wanted to come back. I told you yesterday, those plans were yours, not mine.''

He gave her his half grin. "That's crazy. We made those plans together, plans about coming back here and the good we could do. You can't tell me you didn't want to make this your home—''

"I didn't. I went along because coming back to Tobias was a given for you. I wanted to get out and stay out.'' She swallowed. Her first words had wiped his face clean of expression, especially the half grin that made him look so like the boy she'd known. Maybe it would come back if she— *No.* "I don't need to hear how the town's improved. My only reason for being here is to help Max. As soon as Juney's back, I will be leaving. I don't look to the past, Steve. It's over.''

"It's not over.'' He said the words so sure and flat. So Corbett. "It's not over and it's not finished. There have got to be questions—''

"No.'' Her attempt at a smile felt like a grimace. "I already know who and what and when. I don't care about where. And how and why—no, thank you. It's gone. What happened seven years ago is water under the bridge—no, it's more than that. The water wiped out that bridge. It's gone. It was demolished when you chose to fool around with Lily.''

If the water still eddied and rippled around the ruins in ways that stirred the remnants of long-ago desire, that was her problem to overcome.

"If it's been wiped out why are you so set on burning it down now?''

"You burned it down seven years ago, with you on one side and me on the other. That's how it's going to stay.''

"The foundation's not gone, Annette. It wouldn't be hard to rebuild. Not hard at all."

"Some foundations aren't worth salvaging, and some never should have been built in the first place."

He stepped back. She'd hurt him. She saw that in the split second before he closed down.

He handed her the clothes with a cool nod. "See you later, Annette."

We'll talk about that later.

Yes, she would see him later. In a town this size, as he'd said, it would be hard not to. But they wouldn't talk. Not about what had happened. Or how or why. Not about any of it.

Not now, not later.

Max was watching basketball on television. What was it with men and their TVs? Even Max—sane, feet-on-the-ground Max—had one with a screen larger than his dishwasher. And much better cared for than his dishwasher, which only worked on pots and pans and apparently ate the lasagna dish she'd found in the refrigerator Monday. She'd intended to use that dish for baked chicken last night but hadn't found it anywhere.

After returning from the dry cleaners, she'd devoted herself to learning Juney's system. A much better use of time than doing errands that could wait. After lunch with Max, she'd searched the Internet, printing out the most helpful articles to go over with him before leaving for Miss Trudi's for tea.

"Here's material about using the Internet for business efficiency."

He turned his head as if to look at the stack of printouts, but his eyes never left the television screen. "Uh-huh. Okay. I'll look at it."

"Max, you're usually so busy working that you don't have time to look at the big picture of what you want to do and how to do it. This could help you expand and get more business—around the state, the region or beyond."

"If I get much more business I'll need two of me to keep up."

She sat on the couch, watching the camera follow a knot of players from one end of the court to the other, then back again.

"What?" Max asked, still focused on the screen.

"I didn't say anything."

"You sighed. If it's about this Internet stuff, Annette, I'm sorry, but I'm not interested. I'm happy doing business the way I have been—face-to-face."

She heard herself sigh again. "I know."

"Then what's wrong? Ever since you came back fr—" He faced her and used his big-brother voice. "Did somebody say something to you in town?"

"It wasn't anything like that, and I could take care of it myself if it were. It was just…Steve said…"

"I heard you two were hanging around together. Lenny reported in from our work sites."

She'd spent too many years in Tobias to be surprised Max had heard things. *What* Max had heard, however… "Hanging around together? Hanging around? We were not! He kept showing up. Everywhere I went, every time I turned around. I had no say in it, and I most certainly wasn't hanging around with him."

"You want me to tell him to get lost?"

Tears welled up. She grabbed the TV listings from the coffee table and flipped through them. She'd teared up because of Max's offer, not for any other reason. Steve had been lost to her for seven years. Her words to him outside the cleaners had simply set the record straight. "No. I told him. It's all taken care of."

"I heard the new guy in permits gave you a hard time. I should've gone."

"No, you shouldn't have. Besides, I already had Steve hovering around pulling that protective routine. Having you there would have been overkill."

Her tone was perfect—light, but with a faint tartness of sarcasm. To Suz—probably to any woman—it would have been a clear signal that there was more to the words than met the ear. Max swatted away the subtleties like a hammer going through gauze and went straight to the literal meaning.

"Good. With Steve running interference, the guy wouldn't be too much of a jerk." And he returned his attention to the screen.

Great. Max thought that as long as Steve was looking out for her all was right with the world? *Hey, guys, what's wrong with this picture?*

Besides, she could look out for herself.

You've been doing a damned fine job of being like what you call Corbett in the past half hour.... Just because she'd learned to stick up for herself didn't mean she'd become like a Corbett. Did it?

"Max, have I changed?"

"Changed?" He blinked from the TV to her, scanning her outfit of jeans, sweatshirt and slippers.

"Not clothes. I mean, am I a lot different from before I left Tobias?"

He frowned slightly but didn't hesitate. "Sure. You've gotten an education. You've become a smart business-woman. You know all about stuff like the Internet and the right wines and all that fancy stuff."

She waved that off. "I mean...have I gotten hard?"

"Steve said that to you?" Sometimes her brother was startlingly perceptive. Never when she wanted him to be.

"Not exactly. He said I was acting like a Corbett."

"You sure he thinks that's an insult? You and Steve see the Corbetts from different angles. He's looking from inside out, but he's got plenty of people to tell him about the other way. You're looking from outside in, and the only one you ever had to tell you what it was like inside was Steve."

"He didn't talk about it."

"Did you ask?"

She stood. "It's all water—" Oh, no, she wasn't getting tangled in that metaphor again. "It's a long time ago. It doesn't matter. I just wondered—"

"No, you're not hard." He grinned slightly. "But you are loud when a guy's watching basketball."

"In the middle of a weekday?" What she'd been watching finally registered. "These aren't even games."

He cut her a look. "You've been away too long, Annette. It's previews for the weekend conference tournaments. Getting ready for the NCAA tournament."

Clasping her hand to her throat in mock horror, she gasped. "And you let me interrupt—we need to get you back to the doctor to check for brain damage!"

The TV listings he tossed at her and his chuckle followed her out.

One of the smartest things Steve had done when he'd accepted this job was hire Bonnie Hedley as his assistant. She had just moved into the area and had never heard of the Corbetts. So when Bonnie buzzed him at 3:45 p.m., she said, "Are you available to talk to your mother? You have a meeting at four." Any Tobias-raised secretary would have let Lana Corbett in and rescheduled the meeting.

On the other hand, he'd been so clear Lana wasn't going

to influence him that a visit to his office was rare enough to make him curious. "Send her in, Bonnie. Thanks."

He hadn't been getting work done anyhow. The confrontation with Annette this morning kept gnawing at him. At least that damned frozen glass had cracked.

I went along because coming back to Tobias was a given for you. I wanted to get out and stay out. Surprise gave that one sharp teeth. Or was it guilt because he'd never known she'd felt that way?

But why had he invited Annette to ask questions in front of the dry cleaners? What would he have said to her? The whole truth and nothing but the truth? Not likely, considering his lifetime of training and what was at stake. Even less likely considering she'd as good as told him to stay away. Which had been a hell of a time to own up to himself that he wasn't half as interested in why she wanted to leave town fast as he was in being around her.

As soon as his mother stepped into his compact office he knew she was upset. Oh, not that she displayed any of the usual signs people showed. Instead, she wore her lacquered look. One she assumed if her ironclad control on her emotions showed any inclination toward a rust spot.

"Coffee, Mother?"

"No. Thank you." She clipped her words and sat without smoothing the back of her cashmere coat.

Definitely upset, he decided, as he poured coffee from a thermos into the oversize mug that said Manage This—a present from his oh-so-respectful staff two Christmases ago.

As he sat, he noticed the new precision of her haircut, which meant Chicago. "Just back from the city, Mother?"

"Yes, I left yesterday morning, accompanied by Martha. I left the information with Mrs. Grier."

The second sentence was old news. She left contact information with her latest housekeeper because she refused to leave it with Bonnie, having maintained from the start that Bonnie didn't give her due deference.

But the first sentence was different. Martha Remtree, the young wife of the bank manager, was the latest to join his mother's pool of protégés. Steve wasn't surprised the younger woman accompanied Lana to Chicago. Despite being a widow for a decade and a half, Lana didn't take such trips in the company of men. But her cool voice chilled an extra couple of degrees when she said the woman's name, and that was news. What could Martha Remtree, a biddable woman if Steve had ever met one, have done to irk his mother?

"I hope you and Martha had a pleasant time."

"I would have had an entirely pleasant time," she said, ignoring his inquiry about the other woman as being of no importance, "if I had not been subjected to hearing news of my son's life from a near stranger."

Ah. Martha had been the unwitting messenger, and his mother had her lined up for a firing squad. He or Nell had done something, said something or been somewhere Lana didn't approve of. Although it had never before moved his mother to come to his office, it was a frequent enough occurrence that he had the timing perfected. He'd let her get this off her chest, then they could all go about their business. But don't make it too easy....

"A stranger? You and Martha have been thick as thieves since Christmas."

"That's a vulgar expression, Steven. Moreover, it is not the point."

"And what is the point, Mother?" The clock said eight minutes until he would leave for the meeting down the hall. He sat back, sipping lukewarm coffee.

"Why didn't you tell me she was back in town?"

He tensed without changing position. "Who, Mother?"

"That…that girl."

You can't be serious. You want to marry a nobody? A girl with no name?

She has a name—a good name—Annette Trevetti.

"What girl?" He looked at her over the coffee cup.

"Annette Trevetti." Her tone set his teeth on edge, but at least she'd said Annette's name.

"I didn't know you would be interested." She daggered him with a look. He didn't flinch. "Max Trevetti hurt his wrist on a building site, and Juney's on her honeymoon, so Annette came home to help him out."

She flicked her hand as if to say she didn't know these people and didn't care to. "You've been seen with her. You are not stupid, Steven. Why you insist on these self-destructive actions, selecting someone so unsuitable to marry, refusing law school, all that with Lily and this job. Over and over the same mist—" She drew in a breath. "You will not take up with her again. You can't be that foolish."

He leaned forward, putting the cup down.

"I never *took up* with Annette. I dated her, then I asked her to marry me. I seriously doubt that sequence will be followed again. But whether it is or not, whether I see her or not is my business. My business, and hers."

The lacquer hardened.

Lana stood, pulling on her gloves. "You had every advantage. I did everything I could for you—more than you'll ever know. I will never understand why you want to throw your life away."

"Whatever you did was for the Corbett name." She shifted her shoulders in a faint shrug. "What I'm doing is living my own life."

He should have known she wouldn't let him have the parting shot.

''You are doing a poor job of it when it means sending Nell to Trudi's hovel—''

He didn't know if a seventeen-room house, even one as run-down as Bliss House, qualified as a hovel, but that wasn't the fight his mother was picking.

''—and exposing her to your penchant for oddities. And now Miss Trudi has invited the Trevetti girl for tea at four o'clock this afternoon.'' He did his best to show her nothing. ''You forget. I have connections in this town.''

''Nell will have a great time with Miss Trudi, as she always does.'' Ah, that landed a blow, because Nell was not shy about saying she did not have a good time on the few occasions she'd been at her grandmother's house without him—not enough adventure and too many rules for her taste. ''If your gossip is right, and Miss Trudi has invited Annette, too, the three of them will get along fine. And now—'' he stood ''—if you'll excuse me, I have a meeting.''

She went to the door, a trim, elegant figure with not a hair—or an emotion—out of place. ''As long as you insist on exposing that child to low company, you—and she—will pay the consequences.''

Even before the door closed, Steve's thoughts were on Nell…and Annette. How fast could he wrap up the meeting and get to Bliss House to see what the hell Miss Trudi thought she was doing to those two—one who wouldn't understand the ramifications of their meeting and one who would understand all too well?

Chapter Five

"Miss Trudi?" Annette called, hoping she could be heard over the operatic music inside. She'd knocked, but her gloved knuckles on the solid wood had drawn no response.

Following instructions on a sign hanging crookedly from a nail in the front door—Bell Doesn't Work. Come To Back Door and an arrow—Annette had followed a narrow, muddy path around the shambling Victorian through dried vegetation knocked flat by snow. The back door showed signs of occupation, with the porch swept clean, a gnarled mat in front of the door and a bulb lit in a simple sconce against the cloudy day.

Miss Trudi's grounds had always tended toward wildness, and Annette never remembered the house being in what she would consider pristine condition. But the dismay she'd felt at pulling up in front of Bliss House had deepened with each step into the property. It could have used all the skilled workers on Every Detail's database full-time for months.

"Come in, come in!" The words floated from inside, and the music stopped.

Only by jiggling the handle could Annette turn it. Even then, the door stuck, and she had to shove it with her shoulder. The door gave all at once. She stumbled into the large old-fashioned kitchen and found herself enfolded in a lavender chiffon embrace.

"Come in, come in. I am so glad you could come by today."

Over Miss Trudi's shoulder, she took in the room.

A large table dominated the right side. Piles of books occupied most of the table, with one end clear. Each chair around the table was covered by a quilt, spread or blanket. Their patterns added a cheerful brightness. So did the lamps around the room, including one with a fringed red gingham shade that was perched in the middle of an expanse of wooden countertop to the right of the stove. Behind the lamp marched a row of teapots of various sizes and colors.

Beyond these overlapping pools of light lurked a cavern of darkness. One rectangle of more intense darkness indicated a hallway to the right.

"My dear, how wonderful to see you. Let me take your coat." It was whisked away before Annette could get her bearings. "Sit down, and I'll bring you some tea."

She selected a chair, watching Miss Trudi at the antiquated stove. "About the front doorbell, I'm sure my brother Max could—oh, no, I was forgetting his wrist—but I'm sure he'll know someone who can fix that bell for you—"

"No need, no need. The tea will be ready in a moment. The kettle was almost on the boil when you arrived—such good timing."

"But the bell—"

"The bell's okay."

Miss Trudi had not said those words. Annette was looking right at her, and the woman's lips hadn't moved. Moreover, the voice was a child's.

Looking around, Annette discovered that the red quilt she'd thought was covering the chair at the head of the table was wrapped around a small figure, leaving only the pale oval of a face exposed.

An odd little shiver took Annette by surprise. Although not yet in the throes of a true Wisconsin freeze, the warm spell was fading and the room *was* chilly, she decided. The quilts and blankets on the chairs were not a fashion statement, but a necessity. She drew a knit blanket around her shoulders.

"The sign says the bell's broken."

"Doesn't say broken. Says it doesn't work."

"The child's right," Miss Trudi said from the stove. "The bell doesn't work."

"But—"

"It makes noise okay. But," said the child, "we don't pay any attention to it, Miss Trudi and me."

"Never have liked rude, buzzing things," Miss Trudi murmured. "Here's the tea. This will warm you both up in no time."

"Thank you, Miss Trudi." Annette's words came out as an unintentional chorus with the child's. She had pushed back the quilt to reach for a blue mug.

Miss Trudi placed a cutting board with a loaf of bread wrapped in a cloth, a knife, a pot of jam with a spoon and two small plates on the table.

"But your back door sticks and…" Annette didn't bother to finish, because Miss Trudi had disappeared into the darkness beyond the kitchen.

She smiled at the child and received a look of unwavering concentration.

Annette considered herself neutral on children. She didn't crave them as many women her age seemed to. Nor was she wary of them. She had made no pronouncements, even in the privacy of her heart, about whether she would ever have children or whether she needed them to live a fulfilled life.

She had the feeling the kid had catalogued every pore on her face, not to mention her long jersey skirt, boots and tunic-length sweater over a long-sleeved knit top. Annette felt justified in looking back.

The quilt revealed only the face. A girl's face. Her cheeks were rosy, with health or cold or reflected color from the quilt or all three. Her features were regular, her nose straight and short, her mouth too wide for perfection, the line of her lips cut in a firm mold. Judging from her brows and lashes, her hair was fair. Her eyes were bright blue. And direct to the point of being disconcerting.

"How is your tea, my dears?" Miss Trudi's voice floated to them from the dimness.

"It's very good, Miss Trudi. I— Oh!" The older woman had stepped into the light, and she wore her red coat. "I am sorry, if I'd known you were going out—"

Annette began to stand, but her action and her words stopped as she wondered if the older woman wore her coat because she couldn't afford to heat her home. Why wasn't anyone doing something?

"Sit, sit. I asked you for this hour." Miss Trudi pressed a surprisingly strong hand to Annette's shoulder. "This works out perfectly. I have an errand to run, so this would be an excellent time for you two to get acquainted."

Annette's heart felt as if it shrank away from her ribs.

She didn't believe in premonitions, but maybe her heart had other opinions. "Acquainted?"

"Yes, this is Nell Corbett, Steve's little girl," Miss Trudi said brightly, as if the child's existence hadn't changed Annette's life. "Nell, I'd like you to meet Annette Trevetti. She's my friend and a friend of your father's."

"Max is your brother," the child declared.

Annette was too preoccupied for more than a nod to Nell. "Miss Trudi, you can't—"

"I must. For a short time." She gave Annette a direct look, all fluttering and twittering gone. "And so must you." And then she whirled out, saying, "Help yourselves to more tea, my dears."

The door slammed closed, but neither Annette nor the girl moved.

Steve's daughter.

Annette sucked in a breath.

Lily standing in the church, smoothing her palm over her abdomen. *This is Steve Corbett's baby.* Images of Steve and Lily. Steve expressionless. *We'll talk about this later, Annette.* This child was theirs. This child was...

Simply a child.

Who had not made the choices. Who had not committed the betrayals.

The breath eased out of Annette, slow and painful.

"Would you like more tea?" She made herself say the child's name. "Nell."

"No." She opened her eyes wide, then frowned. "Thank you."

It was so obviously tacked on that Annette could almost hear Steve saying, *What do you say?* the way parents did, and Nell producing the obligatory thank-you. And then that image of father and child brought stinging heat to her eyes.

"But I'd like some bread and jam."

Annette blinked hard. "Miss Trudi left it for us, so go ahead and have a piece." She tipped her head toward the food, but the girl shook her head.

"I'm not supposed to cut my own bread."

Annette felt like an idiot. Here she'd been trying to force a sharp knife onto the child. She picked up the knife and adjusted the loaf to cut it.

"That's a good idea," she said. "Knives can be dangerous even for—"

"I can use a knife." The girl's haughtiness evaporated with her next words. "But I'm not supposed to use hammers. I used the hammer to open a box and Daddy said I polar iced it."

"Polar iced it? Like the Arctic?"

She shrugged. "That's what he said."

Polar iced...

"Pulverized. Could that be what he said?"

"'Spose. Pullerize?"

"Pulverize. It means smashing to little pieces." Steve used to tease her about using the word, and it became a shared joke. *I'm going to pulverize that final.*

"Pulverize," Nell repeated. "But that's not what Daddy didn't like about the bread. I took too much. Daddy said other people should slice the bread until I know the difference between a slice and half a loaf."

A splutter of laughter took Annette by surprise. It was a good thing she'd completed the cut or she might have sliced herself—and wouldn't that be a fine example.

"He said he wanted two pieces." Nell sounded aggrieved. "So I cut it in half."

Annette controlled her response as she placed a slice on Nell's plate, then pushed the pot of jam forward. "A very reasonable conclusion."

"I know. I like bread."

Nell unwrapped the quilt enough to spoon a listing strawberry mountain on her bread. Apparently she liked jam, too.

"Daddy says liking something's not a good enough reason." She sighed. The kind of exhalation that couldn't quite make sense of the world.

Annette, thoughtfully spreading jam on her bread, could have joined her. *Daddy.* How strange to think of Steve in that connection with this small girl. Even though they had talked about having children. And it wasn't as if she hadn't known he was a father. Still, it squeezed something inside her.

"Can I ask you somethin'?"

"Okay."

"Do you have a dog?"

The question was simple and direct and totally unexpected. "No." Not enough money when she was young, not enough time when she had the money.

"I like dogs."

"I like dogs, too."

"Then why don't you have one?"

"I have to be away from home a lot, so a dog would be lonely."

"I could visit the dog every day after school and all day on the weekends and then he wouldn't be lonely."

Annette caught the insides of her cheeks between her teeth. "I live too far away for you to do that, Nell."

"Oh." Nell immediately jettisoned Annette's dog-owning prospects. "Miss Trudi says her cats catch things that get into the house. Not like burglars—a dog would be good for burglars—but mice and icky stuff. Cats don't like to be squeezed." Which probably explained why Annette hadn't seen so much as the tip of a cat tail. "The ladies at the library say—"

The jangle of the doorknob was the only warning before

the door burst open. Steve came in, propelled by the effort needed to open it.

"Hi, Daddy. Want some bread? She cuts pretty good." Nell looked toward Annette. A frown scrunched her light brows. "Don't be scared, it's my daddy."

"Didn't mean to scare you," he said. "Miss Trudi says to come in without knocking."

The dual references to her being scared made Annette aware she had a hand over her thundering heart. She dropped it to her lap. "You startled me."

His attention had gone from one face to another at first, but now he focused on Nell. A slice of concern showed through as he scanned her face.

But why would he be concerned?

Then it hit her. He was looking for signs that the girl was upset. Because he was worried about how Annette might have treated his daughter. The realization sliced Annette as surely as the knife could have, and much deeper.

How could he think she would be hurtful to a child?

"I should be going. Miss Trudi had to leave, so I stayed to—" To look after his daughter. "But now that you're here…" She stood, looking around for her coat before remembering Miss Trudi had taken it away. "I have a great many things to do. If you would tell me where Miss Trudi might have put my coat…"

He spread his hands. "Don't have a clue."

Steve was relaxed and smiling. Clearly his anxiety had been relieved. Good for him.

"Do you know my daddy?" Nell asked.

"A long, long time ago, your father and I knew each other."

"Are you the one who used to go on dates with him?"

The one? No. That had been the problem. Knowing Tobias, someone would eventually tell her that her father had been about to marry Annette when Lily's pregnancy changed the course of events. Annette would not be that someone.

"Yes, we went on dates." The words sounded fine to her—even and casual. If she had to avoid looking toward Steve as she said them, what did that matter?

"Can I ask you somethin'?" Nell asked again.

"Be careful how you answer this," Steve murmured.

Did he think she would be cold because Nell was his daughter with Lily? Annette bent to be face-to-face with the seated girl. "Of course you can ask me something."

"Is it true you were so poor you had to raise mice in a church, but you drank a lot while you worked, and you made a real big company and now you've sold it for a bazillion dollars and you're going to buy the whole town and tell powers to be dumped in the lake?"

Annette stood up straight.

Steve cleared his throat. "Maybe I can help translate. *Had to raise mice in a church.* Nell, could that have been *poor as church mice?*"

"I guess, but why would a mouse be poor in a church?"

"We'll talk about that later. In fact, I think we should leave Ms. Trevetti alone and apologize for hitting her with all your questions."

"Not at all," Annette said with her best don't-tread-on-me smile. "No sense leaving for later what we can—what we *will*—talk about right now. The answer to your first question, Nell, about whether it's true I grew up poor, is yes. My family was poor. My father went away when I was little."

"Like my mom," Nell said with a wise nod that took Annette aback as much as the words had. Nell was so young to know about such things…as she had been.

With the discipline that had helped so much in business,

Annette focused on what she'd been saying. "My mother worked very hard but she didn't earn much money. After she died, my brother, Max, worked very hard so we could have a house and food and go to school, but yes, we were poor."

"Mr. Max isn't poor now, is he? Because if he is, we could give him the rest of the bread." Nell looked at the remains of the loaf with sorrowful resolve.

Annette and Max had turned aside charity as much as they could during those hard years, but sometimes there had been no choice. That still rubbed raw. But how could she not like this child for her concern for Max? "No, he isn't poor now. Now, what was the next part of your question?"

"You drank a lot while making a big company," Steve supplied. "I'd guess *workaholic.*"

It was rather like doing a crossword puzzle, which he practiced daily. "I did work a lot—you have to when you're creating a company the way my partner and I did. But I didn't drink a lot," she added.

"And now you've sold it for a bazillion dollars," Steve said from behind her while Nell nodded.

"My partner and I are selling our company. Sorry—" She held up a hand as Nell's lips parted. "I can't tell you how much money we'll get, because it's also my partner's business, and that would be telling you someone else's secret. But I'm sure it's nowhere near a bazillion dollars. And…what else?"

"Buying the town. Though if Tobias were for sale, I'd tell you," Steve told his daughter.

"I'm definitely not going to buy this town," Annette said with emphasis. "I'll be leaving as soon as my brother's wrist has healed."

"Sounds like you would be willing to dump Tobias in the lake," Steve said.

She cut him a look. "I could be tempted."

"Not her dumping it in the lake," Nell protested. "Telling powers to be dumped in the lake."

Annette looked to Steve for explanation, but he shook his head. "Sorry, this one isn't computing."

"That's what they said," Nell insisted, growing impatient.

Annette muttered the words again, started to shake her head then stopped. "Tell the powers that be to jump in the lake."

"Yeah," Nell confirmed, as if that's what she'd said all along.

But Steve gave a faint whistle and said, "You're good—very good."

She suppressed a grin—how could she want to grin at him when she'd told him to get lost this morning and he'd thought so little of her that he'd worried how she might treat his child? She faced Nell. "So people said I would tell the powers that be to jump in the lake, and you're asking if that's true, right?"

"Right."

"Do you know what *powers that be* means?" Nell shook her head. "It's people who run something—the ones everybody knows about, like town officials or—"

"Like my daddy?"

"Yes, and others. To tell you the truth, Nell, there are some of them I might be tempted to tell to jump in the lake. But that's not polite, so I'm going to try very hard to not do that."

Nell sucked her lip between her teeth. "It's too cold for my daddy to jump in the lake now. So if you can't keep being good forever can you wait until summer?"

Annette bit the inside of her cheeks. "I can do that. Any more questions?"

"Nah. But I'm not going to build a company, even to make a bazillion dollars. I thought I'd be president of India—prime minister of India," she corrected herself. "And president of the United States. But you gotta be real, real old to do that. So first I'm going to be a great actress. That's better than a star. I'm going to be an actress they talk about forever, like Sarah Bernhardt and Helen Hayes."

Miss Trudi's fingerprints were all over that statement. Then Nell added one that was all her own. "No one will forget Nell Corbett or I'll pulverize them."

"I believe that," Annette said in all sincerity.

"That's if the FBI doesn't get her," Steve added, in an aside.

Nell gave him a quelling look, but relented. "I could be in the FBI, too. I'd make a good spy." Annette wasn't sure if she'd mixed up federal agencies or intended to add the CIA to her resume.

"I meant if the FBI didn't bring you in as a top ten most wanted criminal."

Nell rolled her eyes, then jumped up. "Oh, Squid!"

When Nell dashed across the kitchen, Annette deduced that the exclamation had been in reaction to sighting a mottled-gray cat mincing along the base of the counters and not a menu request—thank heavens.

That left the two of them face-to-face in the pool of light.

"Annette—"

"Acting, politics and law enforcement—that's quite a future she has planned." She cut off whatever he had intended to say with a bright smile aimed toward his daughter, who was discovering the faster she went, the faster her quarry went. Apparently Squid was one of the non-squeezable cats.

Steve's pause was so short it would have been easy to miss. "Oh, this is a big improvement. What worried me was when she wanted to be Amelia Earhart, complete with flying around the world and crash-landing on a Pacific island. Or possibly being abducted by aliens. Now *that* gave me gray hair."

"You don't have any gray hair."

Spoken words should come with a string for reeling them back in. Better yet, a backspace key like on computers, which would wipe them out as if they had never existed. Especially when the words sparked a flame in the depths of his eyes. Blue-gray eyes should be cool and distant. Not smoldering. But maybe the gray was smoke, and the blue the ultra-hot—

"I meant what I said this morning, Steve."

"I know you did."

"About the past. There's no sense talking about it, because it can't be changed. And the future. I'm leaving as soon as Max heals or Juney's back on the job. Whichever comes first."

"I know."

"Okay then."

She was spared from uttering any more inanities by Miss Trudi's arrival.

"Oh, good, you're here." She addressed Steve, though her gaze bounced from him to Annette.

"Miss Trudi, Squid won't let me catch him," announced Nell from a corner.

"Smart cat," Steve murmured. He was enjoying this entirely too much.

"You need the right plan," Miss Trudi called to Nell at the same time she tapped Steve's arm in reproof. "A cat-catching plan. We can work on that next week if Gert is still under the weather."

She looked at Steve in question. Annette didn't give him a chance to answer. "I'm sure you all have things to discuss, and I should be going. Miss Trudi, if you'll just tell me where my coat is—?"

"Oh, my dear! I'm so sorry. Did you think I was holding you prisoner by absconding with your outerwear?" Her trill of laughter didn't hide the glint in her eyes. Miss Trudi knew very well that's what Annette thought, because that's exactly what Miss Trudi had done. "All you had to do was ask Nell. She knows where I keep the coats. Nell, will you please run and get Annette's coat?"

Nell returned with her coat and without the cat, and in another second Annette had said farewell to Miss Trudi and Nell.

Steve reached the door before her, taking a firm grip on the inside handle.

"Sorry about all the questions," he said in a low voice. "I tried to warn you."

She passed him and stepped onto the small porch. Clouds huddled together across the sky, bringing a chilly dark. Compared to the dark and cold outside, Miss Trudi's kitchen glowed more enticingly than ever.

"No problem. It just took—" *My breath away.* Or was it the questions that had done that? "—me by surprise."

After dinner, which Nell picked at, Steve took the trash to the curb for the morning's collection. He supposed strawberry jam and bread had enough vitamin D that she wouldn't become the first reported case of rickets in Tobias. She'd eaten enough of the treat to leave a red crust around her mouth that had stubbornly resisted attempts to wipe it off. Nell had resisted almost as stubbornly. He should have tackled her face before it hardened. He'd had something else on his mind.

His mind…right.

Even as he'd hurried through his meeting, his rational mind had known she wasn't in distress of any kind—not physical, not emotional, not anything. But raising Nell had humbled his rational mind more times than he could count.

The instant he saw she was perfectly at ease, he'd recognized a twin fear had pushed him. Annette's pain. To the world, Nell was the embodiment of his betrayal of Annette. Yet before she'd stepped behind that frosted glass, he hadn't seen pain or hurt in Annette's eyes. He'd seen only enjoyment of his daughter.

And in a turnaround as fast as a snap of the fingers, another reaction far from reason had hit him. Annette and Nell, warmth and amusement on their faces. The two people who had given him the most love and the greatest joy. He'd never thought to see them together. Yet there they sat, eating bread and jam. In that moment, he had known Annette might try to deny the bridge that connected them or dynamite it, but she was way off the mark saying it was gone. And dead wrong in saying it never should have been built.

When they had made love, she would reach to him, ready to take him inside her with a generosity, heat and joy that never failed to amaze him. She gave him the full measure of her response. It had fascinated him, awed him.

When he could hold himself back from his own driving need—or when she had already fulfilled it—he loved to touch her. Sometimes just for the pleasure of her texture. Sometimes to push her toward her pleasure while he watched it magnify her beauty. That he could make her feel that way, feel that joy—

"Frozen in place?"

His head snapped up at a voice from the darkness. He was instantly aware of cold rushing in like someone had opened the freezer door. He'd been standing at the end of his driveway for God knew how long with his thoughts warm enough to insulate him from one of those turn-on-a-dime Wisconsin weather changes.

"Fran?" He spotted his bundled-up neighbor. "What are you doing out here?"

"Rescuing forsythia."

Fran had a penchant for rescues. She'd come to his rescue often as an emergency baby-sitter. And there'd been her good sense in turning down his marriage proposal. She'd also been instrumental in his buying this house.

While Miss Trudi's great-grandfather had kept his land intact, Steve's great-great-grandfather had divided his property into judicious pieces, selling to "the best people." Lots extended from Lakeview Street in front to Kelly Street in back. The Corbett house held the middle, on a significantly wider lot, like a monarch with outriders guarding each flank.

Steve's house was on Kelly Street, kitty-corner behind the house he'd grown up in. He almost hadn't bought it because of that.

After he'd toured the house, Fran asked what he wanted in a house. When he'd ticked off his list, she'd looked from the house for sale to the Corbett house to him. "Seems to me it has only three drawbacks. Location, location, location."

The gentle ribbing stuck. He didn't require physical distance from Lana to raise Nell his way, so down the street or a mile away, what difference did it make? Lana had said he went behind her back, since she expected him and Nell to live with her. He'd wryly acknowledged he was moving in behind her, but that didn't qualify as going behind her back. She hadn't seen the humor. She so seldom did.

"Why does forsythia need rescuing?" He stepped into the street, and Fran advanced into the streetlight's glow.

"A forsythia on the south side was lured into thinking spring was here. If I don't bring it inside, it will freeze. Here, take this—" he took a branch from her "—and put it in water. Nell will love it. How're you? You look a little distracted."

"It's been one of those weeks."

She cut him a look. "So I heard."

He could talk to Fran. She would hold his confidence. But that didn't seem right when there were so many things he hadn't told Annette.

"Next week should be quieter," he said with false confidence.

Chapter Six

Max had to be the worst patient who'd ever fallen off a ladder.

The doctor said to take it easy for the rest of the week. Annette interpreted that as through the weekend. Max declared Friday was the end of the week, and therefore he could work.

In the end, Annette drove him to the work sites and to see a client and heard all about the Hendersons' addition, the Garrisons' basement remodeling and the proposed conversion of a barn into a workshop for Tom Dunwoody, Junior's retired father, who carved duck decoys.

The decoys were beautiful, but by that time Annette was convinced Max was both exhausted and in pain—he'd refused a pain pill because he wanted his head clear. At each stop she'd tried to get him to leave earlier than he wanted. By the time they got home they were both surly.

After lunch, he read aloud from the *Tobias Record* about

Steve's report to the hospital board, and she made a crack about the Corbetts and noblesse oblige.

Max lowered the paper. "I can't say I'm a fan of the Corbetts, but when I look at what Steve's done for this town I've got to respect him."

"Is this the same Max Trevetti who warned me when I got engaged that I was marrying the Corbetts, and I better be sure the man was worth it?"

"I'm not going to pretend he hasn't done good because he's a Corbett." His stern look didn't waver. "I've told you the business has been going good. Why do you think that is?"

"Because people know you're a great builder."

"If there's no money, nobody's going to build—it doesn't matter how great I am. I've got business because this town's coming to life. You saw the new emergency room, but have you looked at the lakefront? There's life downtown. Steve's been pushing that through bit by bit. He found the developer who took over the old resort and re-opened it. He's brought in a lot of jobs."

Using one hand, he tried to fold the paper. The pages resisted, leaving a sloppy lump. "I'm going for a walk."

"You shouldn't—" He was gone before she could finish. Or admit she was wrong.

Max was right, she had no idea what Steve had done for Tobias. Somewhere in the back of her mind she'd wondered if he would follow through on his plans for a legal clinic. Or if, once he had a law degree, he would fall in line with Lana's expectations. Steve's father had been a power in state politics; his mother had expected the next generation to advance to the national scene. Annette had to admit Steve had not followed Lana's script.

It was oddly unsettling that he kept kicking at the sides of the mental mold she'd put him in seven years ago.

The phone rang, and Annette decided Tobias was really getting to her when she looked at a phone as if it were an alien spaceship. Worse, her throat clogged up when she recognized the caller as Suzanna Grant. As if she were some urchin besieged on all sides and Suz were her only friend in the world.

"How is he, Annette?"

"He's being totally impossible. You would think he would be as eager as I am to let this time in Tobias pass with as few ripples as possible. But, no, he pops up all over the place like some six-foot..." She was *not* going to describe him as a guardian angel out loud. "Some six-foot *Waldo.*"

The quality of the silence slid right under Annette's skin.

"Please, don't you tell me, too, that I'm being unfair. I know Tobias is a small town. I know he has reason to be at Town Hall, and I understand the post office. But the grocery store? Cleaners? And Miss Trudi's with his daughter? Always when I'm there? Oh, I know it's not all him. Miss Trudi is in it up to her eyeballs. But let me tell you I am *not* imagining this and I'm *not* paranoid."

"Uh, Annette?"

"I know, I know, you didn't say I'm paranoid, and I'm sorry for snapping."

"Actually, I was wondering about Max."

"Max has been no help. You would think they'd become best buddies." She pushed her hair back with one hand. "Okay, that's not entirely true, but Max has no idea what it's like to keep running into— Not that it's a big deal."

"I want to hear about this, really I do, but first, can you tell me, how's Max? His head, his wrist—is he healing okay?"

Annette felt air flow into her mouth from her jaw dropping. She wanted to drop through the floor. *Max.* Of course

Suz had been asking about Max. While she had blabbed on about Steve.

She dropped the receiver.

Suz's worried voice came clear even before Annette had the receiver to her ear. "Annette, are you okay?"

"I'm fine." Tear-soaked words emerged limp.

"You're fine, but you're crying. Your first thought when I asked how is he wasn't for your injured brother. And you're saying Max—the original and never-improved-upon model for a protective big brother—is no help. All I can say is, I think you're in the Twilight Zone. The rest maybe can be explained, but Max being no help when some guy is stalking you makes the Twilight Zone the only—"

"He's not stalking me. Steve wouldn't—"

"Steve. *Steve?* As in Steve Corbett? And you said you met his daughter?"

Annette was reasonably certain she hadn't mentioned Steve's name to Suz for six years. Maybe five. Or…maybe she hadn't put Steve as completely out of her heart, mind and vocabulary as she had told herself. She nodded as she sank into a kitchen chair then added, "Uh-huh."

"Wow. That must have been tough."

"She's just a little girl. None of it's her fault."

"No, of course not, but she *is* the reason—"

"She's *not* the reason. She did nothing but be born. It's the actions of the adults that—not even so much Lily. Lily wasn't supposed to be getting married…. Oh, God, I can't believe I'm crying about this after all this time."

"You need to deal with all the emotions."

"I *dealt* with these emotion years ago. I dealt with the fact that the man I was going to marry didn't even wait for the wedding to cheat on me. I dealt with the fact that I asked for an answer at the altar and he couldn't be bothered to respond until it was convenient. I dealt with it by making a new future."

"These are different emotions."

Annette opened then closed her mouth. Some people viewed Suzanna Grant as strictly decorative. They were fools.

Yes, the emotions were different, because she and Steve were different people. In different circumstances. In different lives. She stood and walked to the sink, looking beyond blooms of frost on the window to the cloud-spattered sky.

"You're right. Thank you, Suz. They are different emotions, and I will deal with them. But that isn't why you called. Now, about Max…" She gave Suz a no-nonsense rundown of Max's injuries, prognosis and stubbornness. She wrapped up. "I am so sorry, Suz, for not keeping you up to date."

"It sounds like you've had a lot going on. Not that I would pry. I'll just say…so Steve Corbett is following you around, but you are *not* being paranoid?"

"No, you wouldn't pry. Uh-uh, not Suzanna Grant."

"So, when did you first see him? Tell all."

A half hour later Annette had told all…nearly all. And darned if she didn't feel better.

"I can't imagine how hard it must have been to meet that little girl." In Suz's husky voice, Annette heard loyalty and sympathy.

"That was my first reaction, but honestly, Suz, she's such an individual, it's hard to see her as anyone but herself." She gave a dry chuckle. "I hate to admit it, but Miss Trudi might have been right to manipulate me into getting it over with. But I still hate being manipulated."

"No kidding."

Suz slid into discussing the sale of their company. For Annette, it was like the final step onto solid ground. A feeling that didn't evaporate even when Suz shifted gears. "So, what do you think Steve Corbett's up to? Is he playing some game?"

"It doesn't matter because as long as I don't play, it can't be a game."

"You sound like your old certain self. You know, instead of mailing you those papers, why don't I come up tonight and bring them? You need anything else? More clothes?"

"That would be great. Would you bring the TV from my bedroom, too? It's basketball tournament time, and if I want a break, I'll need it. Plan on staying for the weekend. I'll take the couch, and—"

"No problem on the clothes and TV, but it's my turn for the couch, and I'll have to leave tomorrow afternoon. I have a date."

"Anybody I know?"

"No."

"Another first date? Suz—"

"I know, I know. No reason to say it, I'll run the appropriate tape from the Annette lecture series."

She chuckled despite herself. "Yeah? Do I really lecture that much?"

"Only because you love me and want what's best for me. At least that's what you keep saying."

Annette came out of the library and turned in the opposite direction from the parking lot. She needed some air.

She'd stopped at the bank, the bookstore and the video store, then walked to the library on impulse. Three heads had turned in her direction from the checkout desk. She didn't recognize any of the women, but as she passed, three voices said soft hellos, and one added that it was wonderful to see her and asked how Max was recovering.

All three sent best wishes for Max and said to be sure

to call if he or she needed anything. Not likely, she'd thought as she made her way into the stacks, in search of a mystery the bookstore said was out of print, since she had no idea who the women were.

"Hi, Annette." The soft voice came from behind her as she pulled the book off the shelf.

She recognized the speaker—Fran Dalton, who grew up next to the Corbetts. Her brother, Rob, was Steve's long-time friend. Annette had gotten to know Rob when they were all at Madison. A year after the wedding debacle, they'd run into each other in Chicago. She would have kept walking after the initial hello. He wouldn't let her.

Fran, a year behind Annette in school, qualified as only an acquaintance.

Still, Annette's smile and greeting were genuine. Fran still favored bland clothes, but she had a wonderful smile, and Annette had always found the younger woman pleasant.

"It's wonderful to see you, Annette. I'm glad you've come home."

"For a visit."

Fran smiled slightly. "That's what I thought when I came back."

Annette remembered Rob saying Fran had returned home to care for their father during his final illness. "I was so sorry to hear about your father."

"Thank you. Rob and I appreciated your note. It's hard to believe he's been gone this long, that I've been back so long."

"Rob said he thought you might return to Madison after…"

The smile returned. "There's something about Tobias. I hope you rediscover that, Annette. And I know I'm not the only one. It would be wonderful to have you here permanently.''

''Oh, no, I—''

Fran touched Annette's arm. ''I don't mean to pressure you. Just expressing a wish. Let's get together for coffee. I'll call.''

''Yes, that would be wonderful.''

Only when she stepped outside did Annette let the question that had been tumbling around in her head form into something resembling words. *And I know I'm not the only one....* Surely Fran hadn't been intimating she thought Steve had ideas about... Air, yes, she needed air.

The wind was whipping furrows of clouds across the sky, piling white and gray clouds on top of each other to open a strip of blue at the western horizon.

She took the path around the library to the pier. She'd always loved the pier even as a crumbling structure for fishermen filling the tank or buying bait. In the past few years—under Steve's leadership—such mundane matters had been shifted to a nearby inlet that was protected from weather. And the picturesque curve of lakeside in the center of town was no longer viewed through a clutter of fuel pumps and bait shacks.

The pier had been rebuilt to take advantage of the improved views, with park benches built into the wooden rails. Perfect for taking in the sunset.

The strip of sky scrubbed clear of clouds was widening, while the blue retreated before an advancing fire line of red and orange. The underbellies of the clouds that hadn't scurried out of the way fast enough were scorched pink and purple. All the ingredients for a fantastic sunset.

But with her first step onto the wood pier, she stopped dead.

Someone sat atop the farthest bench, facing the sunset.

A blue-jeaned figure wearing a leather jacket with his rear end balanced on the narrow top of the wooden back, feet flat on the seat. Even when he turned, she couldn't read his expression. Except… Was there challenge in that look leveled at her down the length of the empty pier? And something more? Something almost wistful?

Oh, right. Steve Corbett wistful. Sure. The man who never lost his cool, never made a scene, never let the outside world in on what he was thinking. *Even Steven.*

After what she'd told him at the cleaners, she'd thought that if their paths crossed again at all, remote politeness would be the tone. After their encounter at Miss Trudi's, she didn't know anymore.

She took a second step, and a third.

She would find another bench, with a distant nod to acknowledge him. Yes, she had new emotions to deal with, but that didn't require his presence.

Even if he ignored her signal that she preferred solitude, anyone who might see them together would be responsible for any misinterpretations. Looks and whispers had been part of her life for as long as she could remember. As she had grown into awareness of how different her life was from the lives of her schoolmates, she'd understood the looks and whispers and hated them. But she didn't care anymore. She'd proved a lot of things to herself. She didn't need to prove them to Tobias.

So it wasn't about the town—or the man—when she stopped a quarter of the way down the pier and turned around to head back.

She'd just decided the sunset wasn't all that great.

He caught her where the concrete apron of the pier met the path around the library. One hand inside her elbow had her pivoting to face him.

"That is never going to happen again, Annette. This is your home. I don't want you thinking there is anyplace in this town you can't go if you want to."

He'd thought, once she'd met Nell and with the way she'd reacted, that they could go on from there. Then she'd spotted him down the pier and stopped dead.

"It wasn't that—"

"I'll get the hell out of your way if that's what it takes so you feel comfortable." How much of his reaction was that, and how much was seeing her turn away from him and walk away? Again. "Understand?"

"Steve—"

"Good."

"You arrogant—" She shook off his hand. "Is that how you deal with your staff?"

He met her ire with calm. "Yeah. Saves a lot of time."

She stared at him another second then dropped her hands. Not in defeat. She could hide behind frosted glass five feet thick, and he still knew her better than that. He could practically see her thinking she would be here three more weeks and similar circumstances weren't likely to arise, so she might as well let him think he'd won.

He'd take that. Because he also saw that her anger had passed.

"So, let's go watch the sunset," he said. "Unless you're scared."

She snorted.

It wasn't much in the way of a commitment, but it gave him enough hope that he started toward the pier. He'd gone two excruciatingly slow steps before she swung around and followed. He stayed slow until she caught up.

"I just told someone you weren't stalking me. I might reconsider that."

He couldn't decide if it was humor with a bite or a bite

with humor. Either way, it was different. Perhaps part of that new confidence he'd spotted in her the first day. It made her seem less delicate. He liked it.

"My assistant's husband is in charge of the state troopers for this district. I can give you his name and number if you want."

She rolled her eyes. "Great. The town cops are already in awe of the Corbetts, and now you're cozy with the state troopers. They'd all think I was nuts if I said a word against Saint Steven."

That bite was a little close to the bone. He'd hated that nickname, started by his brother. Even more than *Even Steven.* He gestured for her to sit on the bench, and resumed his seat on top of the back.

"This time I'm innocent. I brought Nell and Fran to the library and decided to take a walk. I had no idea you were around. This was purely happenstance."

"Right. Who's going to believe that after the past few days?"

"You." He didn't give her a chance to say she didn't believe that or anything else he said. "Besides, why do you care what people think?"

She followed that turn in the conversation with something like relief, even though he was sure that if she stopped to think about it, she wouldn't want to talk about this, either. But compared to his being obsessed with her, she'd take this topic, hands down. "I don't like people talking about me."

"It's not my favorite thing, either."

She hitched her shoulders. "It's different for you. You never were one of *those poor Trevettis* whose father walked out and left them living in a shack."

She said the words almost lightly, something she hadn't been able to do when they were together. The change didn't hide how deeply the event had lodged in her. She had let him see that from the start. It was a gift he would never get over. It was a gift that had had a profound impact on him. It had widened his view and steadied him when the world shifted under his feet.

Would telling her make any difference? Would it even be fair?

For now he said only, "No child should be without a father."

"No child should have a mother who works herself to death, either. If it hadn't been for Max... It was him and me against the world." Her tone was still light, but from this angle he could see her blink hard.

"Maybe you and Max shouldn't have tried to fight the world so hard."

"You never had to take the charity, see the pity."

"Does pity look different from compassion?"

"Asked like the true golden boy you are." There was no rancor in that. But she clearly didn't think he had a clue. "This was always your town... I was merely Cinderella to your Prince Charming."

"Did you ever notice Cinderella's the one everyone remembers and likes? Prince Charming doesn't have much of a role. No depth, no development, no growth. Doesn't even get any help from cute little rodents who befriend him."

"You? Get help? Even from cute little rodents?" Her chuckle faded. "You were always so self-contained. Never sought or accepted help."

Self-contained, and with no idea how to get out of the container.

"You helped me." He could see she didn't believe it. So he took the easier path. "You helped Tobias, too. I remembered what you said about how hard your mother worked, how few opportunities there were, the lousy pay, no benefits. I had that in mind when we looked at companies to renovate and run the old resort. Nobody working over there is getting rich, but they're not being taken advantage of. Now that the resort's on its feet, we're looking for someone to convert the church camp into something that will bring more jobs here.''

She had turned to face him halfway through. She peppered him with questions and responded to his answers with her experiences, both with workers employed by her company and in negotiating with the conglomerate for their protection after the buyout.

''The long-term result should be improved business for them. It's the short term Suz and I are worried about.''

She put her hands up and started to push her hair back.

He caught the wrist closer to him. ''It would be better if you don't do that.''

The confusion in her eyes burned off under the heat he felt radiating from him. It was replaced by an awareness and a wariness. She didn't know exactly what he meant, but she had the gist. Oh, yeah, she had the gist. She dropped her hands. He held her wrist an extra beat before letting go.

''It's still there, Annette.''

''It's chemistry.'' She didn't try to deny it. Was that her innate openness, or was that progress? ''Chemistry without emotion is…'' She shrugged, signifying nothing.

He had a different view to propose. ''Chemistry *with* emotion is—''

''Impossible.''

''—love, right?''

''Impossible,'' she repeated as she looked at him, letting him see the certainty in her eyes. ''Love without trust is impossible. At least for me.''

"And you don't trust me?"

She gave a mirthless laugh as she faced forward, the sunset bathing her face in ever-changing light. "You don't think I have good reason not to trust you?" As if realizing she'd left him an opening to turn that question from rhetorical to real, she added, "It doesn't matter now. I got over it a long time ago."

Would telling her make her trust him more? Or less?

But telling her, telling anyone… Maybe it was just too far out of that container. He was the one who took care of problems. He was the one who looked out for people. He was the one who accepted responsibility. He didn't burden other people with it. Especially her.

"Some things a man doesn't get over."

She twisted her neck to look at him, humor in her eyes, as he'd hoped. A tacit acceptance of his change of subject. He suspected she would have taken almost any alternative subject he would have offered. "That's a quote from *The Quiet Man*. Did you think I wouldn't recognize it?"

He was sure she would. "Seemed appropriate with Saint Patrick's Day coming up. And I remember your love-hate relationship with that movie."

"Don't get me started. I know it was a different era, and Maureen O'Hara was strong in her own way, but—"

"Daddy!"

Two figures stood at the end of the pier, the taller one holding on to the smaller one, who was straining to come down the pier to them. Bless Fran for the perceptive soul she was in not letting Nell charge in.

"Be right there," he called, waving. "We're going for Chinese. Would you like to come? We could get Max and—"

"No, thank you. I have dinner started. I'm going to sit

here a while longer.'' So she didn't have to walk down the pier with him to join his daughter and Fran.

He stepped off the bench, standing in front of her.

''You know, one thing, Annette…'' She put a hand up to shade her eyes against the sun's final, slanting rays. He realized he'd never looked at the sunset, after all. All his attention had been on her. ''You've covered the past and how you don't want to talk about it, and the future and how you're going to take off as soon as you can, but you skipped one thing.''

''Skipped? I don't—''

''The present, Annette. You've left me the present.''

''Um, Annette? This guy who's not stalking you, he wears a leather bomber jacket, doesn't he?'' Suz asked.

Annette felt a flutter in her chest. It should have been her heart sinking.

Since they were standing in line at the weekend-crowded grocery store, she was grateful for Suz's discretion. Not only for not naming a name, but for keeping her voice low. So maybe that sensation in her chest was gratitude.

Feigning a sudden interest in the alien baby a tabloid proclaimed had come out of a pumpkin, she glanced in the direction Suz had been looking.

She turned her back on aliens born out of pumpkins and on Steve Corbett, who was looking at her from near the exit.

''How did you know that?''

''Are you kidding? The way he's looking at you? The way you're not looking at him? The way everyone else has their necks on swivels to look at both of you?''

Annette tried not to look as their order was rung up. She turned her back. It was just too darned easy to look over her shoulder. Less than a week in this town, and it was a habit.

He leaned against the wall next to the exit. His hands were stuffed in his jeans pockets, and he looked way too sexy to be a town manager. Too casual to be a town manager. That's what she'd meant. Casual.

She had never thought of Steve as contrary, but she was beginning to wonder how much of this seeking her out in public came from the fact that she'd been trying to side-step—not avoid, simply to sidestep—his company.

Steve's smile and hello held definite challenge as he joined them.

"Don't you ever work?" she grumbled. She refused to consider what percentage of Tobias's population was watching them.

"Weren't you complaining about my being at my work-place the other day? Besides, it's Saturday. Even hard-working public servants get an occasional day off. Are you going to introduce me to your friend?"

She stopped on the sidewalk in front of the store. It was marginally better than having him accompany them to her car. This was neutral territory.

"This is my friend and business partner, Suzanna Grant. Suzanna, this is Steve Corbett, the manager of the county and town."

"Please, call me Suz." The traitor extended her hand and added a warm smile. Not the plastic version she usually bestowed on presentable single men, which said, "Ap-proach me at your own risk." Annette had been after her to let her guard drop more with men. Her timing sucked. "You manage a very nice town."

Steve smiled. "Thanks. You have good taste in friends and business partners."

"I do, don't I? I also have the sense not to let a good

friend and business partner get away. Only a fool doesn't hold on to a good thing.''

Annette sucked in a breath, feeling as if she were watching two trucks roar toward each other head-on.

''You're fortunate that you've never been in a situation where you couldn't hold on to a good thing,'' Steve said without hostility.

Suz dipped her head. ''I won't argue that I'm lucky.''

Somehow the head-on collision had been avoided without either truck appearing to swerve out of the way.

''Talking about not holding on to a good thing,'' Steve said, turning to Annette. ''Rob is getting divorced. His wife wants out.''

''Oh, no—he seemed so happy. Fran didn't say anything when I saw her yesterday.''

A glint in his eyes said he remembered seeing her yesterday, too. ''I'm not surprised. Fran's in major protective mode. Rob was set to start a family. Instead his wife asked for a divorce—he's pretty torn up. It's not common knowledge.''

Impulsively, Annette touched the back of his hand. His other hand covered hers, an acknowledgment of her gesture of sympathy. Though whether it was sympathy to Rob by proxy or for Steve himself, she couldn't have said.

''Remember Rob, Suz? And all the advice he gave us about setting up the company, all for the price of a dinner?''

As she turned, she saw an expression on Suz's face she didn't understand. Her friend was looking toward Steve, so Annette followed the direction of Suz's gaze. The skin over Steve's cheekbones stretched tight, and his jaw was clenched, almost as if in pain. But—she checked Suz's face again—yes, her friend looked amused.

"What did I miss?" she asked, turning from one to the other.

Steve said nothing.

"Miss? Nothing." Suz sounded legit, but her mouth twitched like a rabbit's nose. "So, what brought you here, Steve? We picked up ingredients for chocolate chip cookies to help Max's recovery. Forget casts and physical therapy, what the man needs is a good cookie—better yet, a dozen good cookies."

Annette chuckled. "Suz is a great believer in the healing property of baked goods."

"Best thing in the world for broken bones. Besides, there's nothing like chocolate chip cookies after slaving over a hot contract for weeks."

"I didn't get anything as exciting as makings for cookies. Just napkins."

He hefted the bag, and Annette caught a glimpse of blue paper napkins. That was a change. The meals she had eaten under Lana Corbett's roof always included cloth napkins—brunch, lunch or dinner, always cloth napkins.

She tuned in again to hear Steve say, "Quite a coup. Congratulations on the sale of your business."

"Thanks."

He shook his head with a half smile. "I've never heard two people less excited about selling their business for a lot of money."

"It's not that—it's a great offer, an amazing offer. Neither of us would take back the agreement to sell. But now we each have to figure out what to do next." Suz made it sound like a chore.

Annette felt Steve's gaze but didn't return it. "But we can't wait to explore the possibilities," she said brightly.

Suz pinned on a dutiful smile. "Endless possibilities. Which reminds me, now that selling Every Detail is wrapping up, the town house is next.'' She turned to Annette and almost did a double take. ''What? You hadn't thought about selling?''

''Naturally, I've thought about it,'' she lied.

Sell the town house? She would be homeless. No, that was ridiculous. She would have money to buy something—*where?*—and, besides, as long as Max had a roof overhead, she would not be homeless. Of course that roof was in Tobias….

''I thought, without the business,'' Suz said, ''I mean, there's no reason for either of us to be tied to Glen Ellyn or the Chicago area, and with you up here—''

''Temporarily.'' She got the word in fast, because Steve was opening his mouth.

''Doesn't have to be. In fact this could be exactly the sort of great opportunity you're both looking for.'' Annette couldn't pin anything on Steve's tone but would swear she'd picked up a rumble of triumph. ''You should both look around Tobias—lots of opportunities here. We're growing, but not too fast.''

''Yeah?'' Suz's eyes brightened. ''Looks like you've redeveloped along the lakefront. Nice job. You've kept the genuineness of the town while adding appeal.''

''Thanks.'' He gave her the full Steve Corbett smile. ''It's attracting summer folks who come for the lake and resort. But the other seasons are too quiet. And some haven't benefited from the upswing in business, like retired folks on fixed incomes. They're stretching their pensions by selling things like quilts and knitting. We need to include them. We're looking for ideas—the sort of ideas I bet a pair of entrepreneurs like you could provide.''

''We'll keep that in mind.''

Annette glared at Suz for including her, but spoke with

forced cheer. "If we're going to get these cookies made before you leave, we better get going."

"Didn't mean to keep you," Steve said, then added to Suz, "but if you feel the urge to discuss the ins and outs of selective redevelopment, give me a call."

Suz laughed and waved as they said goodbyes. Clearly in danger of bursting, she restrained herself until they were in the car.

"He's very attractive. *Very* attractive."

"Suz, subtlety does not suit you. Come out and say it."

"Remember I said on the phone that you're dealing with different emotions? Well, I want to add to that—you're also dealing with the reality of Steve Corbett. Maybe you'd dealt with some of your emotions about him and what happened, but it's different dealing with a flesh-and-blood man. Very nice flesh, by the way, and don't try to tell me you haven't noticed and felt that."

"How pathetic would that be? Still wanting a guy seven years later who got someone else pregnant while he was engaged to me?"

Suz didn't fall for that nonanswer. "About as pathetic as a guy whose bride walked out during the wedding still wanting her seven years later."

"I had darn good reason to walk out—the best reason. No one could..." Anger had carried her through the first half of her response before the rest of what Suz said sank in. "You think he..."

"Uh-huh, I think he. As if you didn't know."

"I didn't." She backed the car out of the parking spot. Then she admitted, "I wondered. But, really, Suz, how could you... You only saw him for a few minutes."

"Didn't Smokey the Bear say something about it only taking a few minutes to start a forest fire? That grocery story will be smoldering for weeks."

She went right to the crux as she drove through town. "You think I'm falling for him again?"

"I don't know, but that's not what worries me."

"Then what worries you?"

She caught Suz's quizzical look. "Have you *seen* the way he looks at you? And when you touched him, just that little brush on his hand…oh, my."

Heat spread through Annette. It started from the vicinity of her heart. Had she been totally unaware of the tenor of Steve's manner toward her until Suz mentioned it? Or had she been pretending not to be aware so she didn't have to deal with how it made her feel. How *good* it made her feel.

"*That's* what worries me," Suz said.

"You needn't worry. I'm no longer some girl who can't help herself from falling for the guy. I am *not* going to fall for him."

Suz shook her head. "You can guard yourself against falling for him, and I don't doubt that you would keep any such feelings under wraps. But for the first time since I met you, I don't think you can guard yourself against what someone else feels for you. What are you going to do about Steve falling for you again? Or still? That's something I don't think you have any defense against."

"That's presuming you're right he's, um, expressing a preference for me."

Suz rolled her eyes.

"Okay, okay, but it still doesn't mean it's what he really feels. I mean, he could be pretending to show interest to get a response so he could feel vindicated."

"Vindicated?"

Clear of town, they started around the lake. "As you said, I left him at the altar, and even though I had a reason he can't fault me for, his masculine ego might have taken a hit."

"I think it's a fair assumption that his ego and other parts took a hit when you walked out of your wedding."

Annette ignored that. "It would be human nature to try to get me to respond, to show I was still attracted to him. You know? He would feel vindicated—that the woman who left him at the altar still wanted him. That's probably what's going on." She eased her hands on the steering wheel, satisfied.

"Sometimes you think too much," Suz said. "Let me ask you one last question. Do you?"

"Do I what?"

"Still want him?"

"Don't be absurd." She laughed, though her hands tightened on the wheel again. "What I want are chocolate chip cookies...or maybe the dough."

Chapter Seven

If Annette had been asked before she answered the back door Sunday afternoon whether she had any expectations of who might be on the other side, she would have said no. But when she saw Steve and Nell Corbett standing outside the storm door, she knew she must have had *some* expectations, because this pair was way outside of them.

"Are you going to invite us in?"

Steve's question snapped her out of a mini trance. She opened the door, smiling at Nell.

"We come bearing gifts," Steve said, indicating two shopping bags he held as well as a small one Nell carried. "Better put that down while you take your boots off, Nell."

"Not gifts," Nell objected. She sat on the floor and yanked off one rubber boot. "Food. We brought food."

"Food can be a gift, Nell."

Annette bent down, setting the first boot upright. "Do you need help?"

Nell shook her head. ''I can do it.'' But her attention remained on her father, who was wiping his shoes. ''I don't want any of *my* presents to be food. Not Christmas and not my birthday.''

''I'll keep that in mind. But this food is for Max and Annette.''

Nell's shoe came off with the second boot, but she put it on, closed its Velcro fastener and popped up before Annette could help. ''Where's Mr. Max?''

''He's in the other room.'' Nell scooted to the living room. Annette turned toward Steve, who was putting the bags on the kitchen counter. ''It's kind of you, but really, we don't need—''

''Don't get all stiff. It's neighborliness, not charity. Besides, I'm just an emissary. Muriel Henderson and Miriam Jenkins and some of the others sent these things.''

''We brought brownies,'' Nell announced as she bounced into the room with Max following more slowly. While the men said hello, she said to Annette, with the air of someone determined to be straight with the world, ''We bought them. They're not as good as Mrs. Grier's but they're good. And I thought Mr. Max should have brownies.''

''She and your friend Suz apparently belong to the same school of health care,'' Steve murmured.

''What have you got there?'' Max asked.

Steve delved into one bag. ''Looks like Polly Bernard's brats casserole. And I suspect this is Miriam's potato surprise.''

''What's the surprise?'' Nell asked, eyeing the plastic container.

''Four kinds of cheese.'' Until she said it Annette would have sworn she had entirely forgotten this particular culinary staple of any Tobias gathering. She remembered eating it for days after her mother's funeral. She could never see it without remembering the sour taste of charity it had left in her mouth.

To hide her suddenly moist eyes, she reached into the second bag and pulled out a covered rectangular pan. "But… This is the dish." She blinked her eyes dry as Max and Steve looked at her. "The dish that had the lasagna in it that I cooked the first night. I washed it and then I couldn't find it later."

"I gave it to Lenny to give back to Muriel," Max said.

"And she filled it with more lasagna," Steve said, catching her gaze and holding it. "The woman passes out the way some people sneeze, but she can make a mean lasagna. And she was concerned about Max."

Annette turned, busying herself with putting away the food. She'd received his message loud and clear. *Neighborliness, not charity.*

Was that true? Or was it the difference between a man brought up in a home where he never lacked for anything and a woman brought up in a home where the necessities were scarce enough to feel like luxuries?

"Mr. Max knows how to use a hammer, so he could teach me." Nell's voice brought Annette's attention to the discussion. "And then I wouldn't—" Nell looked to Annette. "Pul—uh, pulverize anything."

Annette nodded, then matched the girl's triumphant smile.

"Max doesn't want to do that with his hurt wrist, Nell," Steve said.

"He's got another one that's not hurt." She turned to Max. "Don't you? And you could use that one to show me how."

"Nell—"

But Max had already crumbled. "Sure. I could show you."

"Nell, you can't—"

"It's okay, Steve," Max said, gesturing for Nell to precede him toward his workshop. He stopped in the doorway. "I hope you're grooming this kid for power because I don't think she's cut out for being a foot soldier."

"Please, don't mention the military to her," Steve said. "She already plans to be president of several countries. And the fact that she's talking serial instead of simultaneous power should be a great relief."

"Because she won't try to unite several countries?"

"Because she doesn't plan on being dictator of the world."

"C'mon, Mr. Max!" Nell called, apparently already in the workshop.

"Yes, ma'am." He grinned—the most genuine grin Annette had seen from him all week—then disappeared from view.

Still looking toward the doorway, Steve said, "Now, how about a brownie? That'll teach Nell to railroad Max, she'll miss out on the brownies."

Annette opened the bakery box and gave him a brownie on a salad plate, then took one for herself. They sat across from each other at the kitchen table. They used to sit at right angles—it had made it easier to touch under the table.

"Steve, there's something I want to talk to you about." The way he stilled had her jumping into what she'd intended to say to remove any confusion. "About Miss Trudi. Actually, about Bliss House. Something has to be done. It looks terrible, and it could be dangerous."

He sighed. "Get in line. Half the callers to the office say the same thing."

"Well, then the town could get together and—"

He was shaking his head. "Miss Trudi likes charity about as much as you do. Besides, passing the hat for a Corbett isn't likely to sit well with a lot of people. In case you haven't noticed you're not alone in your opinion of the Corbetts."

"The town likes you."

"I'm doing a good job," he said, making a clear-eyed assessment, not bragging. "That's an even exchange—I work, and they pay me. But even the benefit of cleaning up an eyesore isn't likely to sway many to dig deep to fix Bliss House. Plus Miss Trudi's eccentricities aren't endearing to some people—they just think she's strange. Hey, nobody ever said Tobias was a center of advanced thinking, especially not from the country club set. People like Jason Remtree and his pals."

"Including your mother."

"Including my mother. She has the deepest pockets in town, but she's not going to put money into Bliss House so Miss Trudi can keep living there when she insists Miss Trudi should be in a retirement home if not a nursing home—"

"Oh, no! She'd hate that. That's awful. You can't—"

"Did I say I agreed with my mother? She also believes the property should be converted to more *practical* use."

"In other words, profitable."

"Absolutely. That's another reason Remtree and his ilk won't go for it—they're the ones who would stand to turn a profit if they can get Miss Trudi out."

"That's awful! How can they do that to a wonderful old woman?"

"It's ingrained in them to believe turning that block into high rises or a shopping mall or some other moneymaking venture is the right thing to do. Then they grab on to any evidence that backs their conclusion. Pretty soon they've got themselves thinking they're doing what's right for Miss Trudi.''

She was looking at him, the clean, spare planes of his face. The beginnings of lines not only at the corners of his eyes and mouth, but across his forehead. Lines of concentration…and worry. His job must involve a lot of worry. Trying to anticipate problems in order to prevent them. Trying to fix the ones no one anticipated. Looking out for his town and its people.

''How did you escape thinking that way?'' Where was that darned string she needed to pull her words back in? She could swear she'd spoken the words before she'd thought them, and that left nothing to do but try to explain…or possibly to drown the first words in the ones that followed. ''I mean, people do that, whatever their mindset, they look for evidence to prove what they already think—but mostly what people believe is what they were raised to believe, and that should have put you in the high rises and shopping mall camp. To be raised with that mindset and yet to see a different view…''

He covered her hand. The warm weight of his palm stopped her words.

''It's nice to know you think I escaped. But if it hadn't been for knowing you, I probably would have become a lawyer, and even though I had great plans to help people it would have been a lot easier to slide into politics and all the rest that's expected of Corbetts.''

She slid her hand from under his, acknowledging the sudden coolness as a fact of physics, nothing more. ''I was gone when you switched to getting your graduate degree in public administration.''

''True.'' He curled his hand as if holding a cup. ''So maybe it was heredity.''

''Right. Like Lana isn't more Corbett than if she'd been born to the family.''

He paused so long she thought he wasn't going to respond. She opened her mouth to return to the topic of Bliss House, but he spoke again.

''Try the other side of my family tree.''

''Ambrose?'' She had only vague memories of seeing Ambrose Corbett around town. From what Steve and others said, he was a decent man, though stiff and not at all demonstrative. In that way, a Corbett through and through. ''That doesn't make—''

And then she looked into his eyes and saw exactly the sense it made.

''Ambrose Corbett wasn't my father,'' he said without emotion.

''But... How could you know? Your mother—''

His laughter was so raw her throat hurt in sympathy. ''Did my mother tell me? Hell, no.''

''Then how did you find out? When... Oh, Steve, are you sure?''

''I'm sure. Zach said something before he took off that started me digging.''

''Zach knew?'' That made even less sense. Zach had always seemed to be on the outside of the family, so how could he?

''I suspect Mother let something slip. They had some royal battles the last month or two before he left. I've never heard her lose control except with him. He didn't say anything outright to me. But what he did say...it fit with things I'd wondered about most of my life. So I started digging. Right before our wedding I found proof my parents were married a year later than they'd said they were—after I'd been born.''

''Before our wedding,'' she murmured.

Either he didn't hear or he pretended not to. "Over the next couple years I kept digging. My birth certificate had been altered. The original had *father unknown.* I tracked down an old lawyer Father—Ambrose—had used in Milwaukee. He was in a hospital and glad to have someone to talk to. He told me a lot of things I hadn't known, all the way back to Tobias Corbett. Then he came down to Ambrose and Lana. He clearly thought I knew the whole story, and he let it slip that Ambrose had legally adopted me."

His mouth twisted. "Guess I wasn't Corbett enough to hide my reaction, and when he saw that I hadn't known, he clammed up. I couldn't get anything else out of him then. I went back later, but he'd died."

"You suspected this when we were together, but you never said a word."

He looked faintly surprised. "That wasn't part of the deal you'd signed on for."

"Your worries? Your hurt? That wasn't part of what I'd signed on for? What do you think *for better, for worse* means?"

"But we didn't get to that part, did we?"

His quiet question and steady look should not have made her feel as if she couldn't breathe. Yet her chest and throat ached with the effort of pulling in air.

"Besides, it was more of a relief than a hurt. A lot of things made sense then. There'd been moments…not with Ambrose. He was strict, and the only time he was truly affectionate was when we brought home an achievement. But he was equal in his strictness and when he gave affection. And God knows he raised me to be a Corbett. It was her. The way she would watch me so closely. I'd tried to think it was because I was older, but it didn't feel right. She was always talking about the opportunities I'd been given and how lucky I should consider myself. With Zach she talked about how he owed it to the family name. A small thing, but it stuck with me.

"But Ambrose never once treated me as anything other than his son. His heir. If anything he favored me over Zach. Of course, I was an easier kid to deal with." Steve opened his hand and ran it over the surface of the table. "I respected him. I always respected him, but after I found out... I was lucky. I know that. Every child should have a father, and I was lucky."

Every child should have a father.

That's what he'd said Friday on the pier, too.

She hadn't had a father, and Steve knew how that had affected her. Steve had had a father because Ambrose Corbett had voluntarily fulfilled that responsibility. A fact Steve had been learning at the same time Lily announced so publicly that she was carrying his unborn child. How could that not have affected his decisions?

As she had thought that day at the hospital, out of the mess and pain of his cheating on her with Lily had come one good—Nell had a father who loved her.

She looked at Steve, her movement bringing his gaze to her. "You loved him. Ambrose—you loved him."

"He wasn't an easy man to love."

"You loved him." He didn't argue again—as good as an agreement from him. "It must have hurt you when you found out you weren't his son."

"I was in the important ways. That wasn't what..." He spread the fingers of his right hand in a constrained gesture trapped between dismissal and frustration. Oh, yes, he had surely been raised a Corbett, refusing to acknowledge even the pain of this. But then he added, "All her lies. That's what got me. All her lies, and—God! Her hypocrisy."

He looked over his shoulder. Through her surprise at what he had said and how he'd said it, she became aware of sounds from the workshop, as if its occupants were heading this way.

"I think you should talk to her."

He made a harsh sound that didn't resemble a laugh. "You think I would hear anything resembling the truth from my mother?"

"No." Max and Nell's voices were louder. She had to say this fast. "But maybe it's more important that you tell the truth than that you hear it."

Nell's profession of the moment apparently was prosecuting attorney. She was in the middle of cross-examining the poor guilty slob in the witness chair.

That would be him.

"You said she was your girlfriend," Nell proclaimed, hands on hips.

"You're supposed to be setting the table."

"But you *said* she was your girlfriend."

"She was my girlfriend. Now set our places."

"But you had a wedding—" *Only the first part of a wedding.* "She had a dress and music and everybody was at the church. I heard all about it," she said as she planted silverware atop the peninsula of counter that served as their table.

He kept tossing a salad that was already mixed enough. Damn. If Nell had heard that much about what happened, how long would it be before she heard the rest—that Lily had been pregnant and had broken up the wedding? And how much of it would she understand now...or resent later?

Annette had understood what he'd told her yesterday afternoon. He'd seen her connect his finding out about his birth with the timing of his marriage to Lily so Nell would have a father on her birth certificate.

What he doubted Annette had understood was how his

memory of the things she had said and not said about her upbringing had played into his decisions. How many times had he wished he could somehow take that sadness out of her eyes? Past counting. Even as he'd tried in the ways he could to make up for the losses she had suffered from her father leaving and her mother dying, he had known he couldn't entirely.

Then he was faced with the future of the baby Lily was carrying. There was a child he could give a father. There was a child whose eyes didn't have to be filled with sorrows.

"Yes, Annette and I were at the church, and the wedding was started, but you know getting married is such an important step, and—"

"She was in the dress, but you didn't get married to her. That's *weird.*"

The microwave dinged to announce the packaged noodles were done.

Eventually Lily's choices in life, as well as her death and his relationship with her, were bound to raise questions for Nell. He hoped eventually didn't come until he'd come up with good answers.

Maybe it's more important that you tell the truth than that you hear it.

Could Annette also have been talking about the truths he hadn't yet told Nell? Or had Annette thought there were more truths he hadn't yet told her?

"I suppose it is a little weird." He put salad on the plates and took the chicken breasts he'd browned off the burner.

"Are you ever going to get married again? Or did divorce scar you? Caitlin says divorce scars women. Men run away with the flu and that scars the women. But since my mom left, and you stayed—"

"I'm not scarred, Nell." Part of his mind tried to unravel

men running away with the flu. The rest was divided between being dropped into a pint-size version of the Oprah show and pouring milk. ''Divorce isn't about all women feeling a certain way or all men feeling a certain way, no matter what Caitlin says.''

Who the hell was Caitlin? There was no Caitlin on Nell's class roster. Surely she couldn't be seven, to be telling Nell about scars from divorce and men running away with the flu—

Got it! *Men running away with floozies.* He definitely needed to track down this Caitlin.

''Dinner's ready. Let's sit down, and we can talk about this later.''

She sat, still talking. ''You didn't marry Annette, so you can't get divorced.''

''True.'' He sat back, eyeing her. ''I thought you liked Annette.''

''She's okay. But if you didn't marry Fran—''

''We've been over that. Fran and I aren't in love. We're not going to get—''

''—will you ever get—''

''—married.''

''—married?''

The repeated word reverberated in the kitchen like the echo of a gong.

The gong of his understanding. No doubt someone indulging in Tobias's favorite dish—idle speculation with a side of gossip—had shared with Nell.

''Listen, Nell, if I ever get married again I'll talk to you about it beforehand.''

''You won't get married unless I say okay?'' The kid should be a trade negotiator. The other countries wouldn't stand a chance.

''That's not what I said.''

Her lower lip came out, along with her chin. "I have to take some wife of yours no matter what?"

"That's not what I said, either. For right now, there's no possibility of my getting married anywhere on the horizon. Now eat your salad."

After a perfunctory knock, Annette pushed at Miss Trudi's back door Tuesday afternoon.

She'd spent yesterday paying bills, sending out invoices and doing the accounts with Max. They had started on a bid, with her typing while trying to keep him from using his wrist when he impatiently grabbed pricing files. After a break overnight, they'd resumed this morning. His frustration at the restrictions on him was palpable, and contagious. It had been a long time since she'd done a job she had no clue about, and her frustration level was mounting, too.

Frustration…and confusion.

They had been her constant companions yesterday. It was disconcerting to discover that not seeing Steve for the first time after seven straight days wasn't the respite it should have been. It simply left more time to think.

Why had Steve told her… No. She wasn't going to let questions without answers pound in her head all day.

Max's longtime employee, Lenny, picked him up to check on the Henderson site. Ignoring Max's scowl, she made Lenny promise not to let her brother lift, climb, do any work or otherwise use his wrist, and to return him within two hours. Heaving a sigh as the pickup backed out of the drive, Annette finished the bid in a fraction of the time required under Max's supervision, wrote a list of questions to go over with him, wrote checks and took three phone messages.

As she'd gone to the mailbox, Steve pushed into her thoughts again.

An express delivery from Suz had arrived with teas from their favorite specialty grocery, and she grabbed it like a lifeline. Miss Trudi would enjoy a sampling of these teas. And she could use a break before Max returned.

Annette tried the door again. Definitely locked, not stuck. Miss Trudi never locked her door except at night. It was barely past three. Could she be sick? What if something had happened to her?

"Miss Trudi? Are you here? It's Annette!" she called, her voice and her concern rising with each word.

A scrabbling of locks on the other side of the old door brought a whoosh of air from her lungs. The door opened a crack, and her relief fled. Tearstains tracked over pale cheeks and disappeared into folds created by decades of smiles.

"Miss Trudi, what's wrong? What's happened?"

"Oh, my dear!"

Those shaky syllables were the last coherent words Annette made out as the older woman broke into a torrent of sobs. Only after she wrapped Miss Trudi in a green quilt and plied her with hot tea with sugar did she understand more.

"They want to send me away! Lock me up!"

The middle-aged woman behind the desk in the outer office spotted Annette first. Steve, giving instructions to the woman, had his back to her.

"And after the meeting, I'll give you the rough-out of next week's schedule. But right now I've got to get those figures to—"

The woman nodded toward Annette, and he looked over his shoulder. The corners of his mouth started to lift.

She would not let his charm detour her. "We have to talk."

Her abruptness stopped his smile, but his tone was warm as he said, "Nell and I could pick up Chinese and bring it to Max's for dinner. Maybe a movie, if—"

"No." An edge of panic sharpened the word. The image of Max, Nell, Steve and her, cozy and laughing in Max's living room… No. "This is business."

He studied her long enough that resentment leaped up, so bright and hot that any reasonable man would have backed away. He stayed where he was.

"Since it's business, I'm sure Bonnie can give you an appointment."

"We have to talk now."

"I have a full schedule this afternoon, so—"

"Too full to talk about throwing an old lady out on the street—not only a resident of this town you're so proud of managing, but a former teacher, a friend of your daughter's *and* a Corbett! After everything you said—"

"Annette, we can talk about this later." His reasonableness hadn't changed in seven years, and neither had the words.

Flame singed her throat raw.

"That's your answer to everything, isn't it, Corbett? To an old lady or your daughter's questions or an inconvenient request for the truth when your wedding's interrupted by another woman pregnant with your child."

He went still, retreating into his damned Corbett creed. Don't show emotions—hell, don't *have* emotions. And she'd broken those rules all to bits. Just like before. Tough. She wasn't a Corbett and she wasn't going to live by their stupid rules. She had something to say and she was going to—

"Bonnie, call the judge and tell him I'll get the figures

first thing tomorrow. And tell the department heads I might be late for the meeting. Thank you.''

He pivoted and pushed open a door. With his extended arm acting like an underlining of his name on the door, he held the position as he said, ''Annette.''

It was too even to be a challenge, too cool to be an invitation.

Straight-backed, she passed him, nearly brushing in the limited space of the doorway, and for that instant it seemed as if the rules of the natural world had been suspended. Because instead of coolness, she felt heat radiating off him like an old stove that gave no sign of the fire blazing inside. And instead of adding to her fire of righteous anger, his heat sent a chill of uncertainty through her.

''What is it that couldn't wait?'' he said as soon as he closed the door. His office was utilitarian, but the view took in downtown and across the lake.

''Don't be condescending,'' she snapped, uncertainty wiped out.

''I'm not being condescending, I'm trying to find out what's important enough to cause you to raise a past you've repeatedly said you want to forget.''

''It's a shame if I offended your sensibilities, but Miss Trudi's life is more important.''

''My sensibilities are not so easily offended. And I presume if you meant that literally you would have called nine one one instead of coming to me.''

She narrowed her eyes. ''The quality of her life, not her mortality.''

''Glad to have that cleared up and—''

''How can you joke about this, Steve?''

''Believe me, I'm not joking.''

She barely heard. ''No, wait, what am I thinking? A man who can talk so convincingly about his concern for a woman on Sunday, then plot to drag her from her home and lock her up in a nursing home on Tuesday is certainly capable of joking about it.''

He sat on the front edge of the desk, crossing his arms over his chest, the gesture emphasizing its breadth. The corners of his mouth lifted, but the expression was nowhere near pleasant enough to be called a smile.

''If I didn't already know that in your mind the rule is guilty until proven innocent, I might be offended. But I am still confused. Would you care to explain that off-the-wall accusation?''

''Did you think Miss Trudi would let you do this without telling anyone? Did you think that she has no friends who would come to her aid? Well, let me tell you, you're wrong. You're going to have the fight of your life on your hands, so—''

''What I think is that you're full of bull—''

''Don't you dare say that.'' Through her anger she felt a tickle of recognition—he was angry, too. Impassive face, even voice and all, Steve Corbett was angry.

''You come to my office, taking cheap shots and throwing accusations around like that, and believe me, I dare. I accept that you don't trust me, and while I've always viewed your passionate nature as one of your strengths, Annette—in fact, I've missed it—you've just shown me why some people consider it a flaw.''

At the moment her passionate nature wanted to strangle him.

She'd dealt with tougher cookies than him in running Every Detail. None of them had knocked her off her stride. None of them had gotten the better of her. None of them had made her wonder if that hair would feel as soft as it used to if she reached over and pushed it off his face. None of them had made her palms itch to caress from his neck across the ridge of his shoulders.

She shook her head, trying to track how she had slid from wanting to put her hands around his neck and squeeze to wanting to stroke. This was not good.

"I am not throwing accusations around. I am repeating what Miss Trudi told me."

"She told you that I intend to put her into a nursing home? She said that? *Steve is going to put me in a nursing home?*"

"I don't know that she said those exact words," she admitted, trying to pin down her memory of Miss Trudi's jumbled utterances. "But her meaning was quite clear—she does not want to go to a nursing home."

"You think I don't know that? I'm not the one who's been away seven years."

She took that arrow without retreating, but felt its sting.

"I'll repeat what I said Sunday. I don't want her to go to a nursing home, either," he continued. "Or a retirement home. But you'll find that a group of people styling themselves as concerned citizens went to see Miss Trudi this morning. If the reports I received are accurate, they expressed the opinion that she would be better off in a retirement home if not a nursing home—their words, their opinion, not mine. I wasn't at the meeting. After I heard about it, I went there to try to get her to see that the situation can't go on—not the first time I've tried that."

"And clearly succeeded in only confusing and scaring her more," she said. "You've got to do something about this."

"What would you have me do?"

"Tell the truth. All of the truth. Because it's as bad to tell lies by not saying anything."

Something flickered in his eyes, like a flash of intense

blue. Was it a reaction to what they'd talked about Sunday in Max's kitchen? He had told her a truth then. A major truth. Or had he interpreted her words as a jab at his not telling her that truth or others seven-and-a-half years ago?

An even better question was, how had she meant it?

"Be open," she said, pushing aside other thoughts. "Give Miss Trudi the facts. Don't dole out little shreds. Dump the whole bag, so she knows you're not hiding things."

"Are you sure the listener I would dump this bag onto wants to deal with all those facts, or does she want to be protected, the way she always has been?"

He held her gaze—he was not talking only about Miss Trudi.

"Sometimes," he continued, "people who say they want—even demand—facts don't truly want them. They want someone else to take care of them. They want someone else to fight their battles."

If you're not happy I'll tell Mother to back off. But you have to tell me.

She shouldn't have to tell him. He should just do it, the way Max would.

But that was so long ago. A different century. Different people.

"People grow. Change. Besides, it's not your place to make that decision if they ask for the facts. And Miss Trudi is a grown woman who—"

"Who was looked after by an overprotective and old-fashioned father and then by old-fashioned trustees—until those trustees started dying off, and the new ones opened the purse strings at the same time they made unwise investments. For all her education and intelligence, Miss Trudi doesn't have the slightest regard for or understanding of money. Her whole life she's had whatever she's wanted whenever she's wanted, and she doesn't want to hear any different now.''

Suddenly warm in the small office, Annette pushed her ear-warming band back before yanking it off. The tension in him seemed to shift to a different gear. When he spoke again, his voice had lost that cold edge.

''Do you know she doesn't know how to balance her checkbook? She has this notion that the bank puts money in her account when she needs it, because that's what the trustees did.''

She opened then closed her mouth, the anger draining out of her, the concern remaining. ''No, I didn't know that.''

He levered off the desk, paced around it and stared out the window. ''Her money's nearly gone. What little is left is disappearing fast into that sinkhole of a house, and she won't listen. Won't deal with the realities. Keeps saying she has a pension—like what she gets from teaching would make a dent in making that place livable. Won't let anybody help her. Won't hear of moving out.''

He scrubbed one hand over his face then turned to her.

''And in the meantime, the town's divided into camps— one extreme insisting Miss Trudi should be sent to a retirement home for her own good even if it's against her will, while the other extreme—'' his grimace indicated her ''—wants her left entirely on her own no matter what the consequences.''

''I never said that's what I want. I see what a wreck that place is.'' From Every Detail she knew the first step was to find out the facts. She would go back to calm Miss Trudi, then filter what she said through what Steve had told her. ''I apologize if I formed an erroneous conclusion about your views. I certainly did not intend to take a cheap shot at you. But—'' she squared off to him ''—I stand by what I said about your needing to tell her the whole truth.''

He made no promises, but the steady look he gave her convinced her that he would do his best to get through to Miss Trudi.

There didn't seem anything left to say—maybe Annette had already said too much. ''Goodbye, Steve.''

She had reached the door when he said her name. She turned.

''That crack outside, when you accused me of putting off people—Nell, you—by saying *later,* that was the cheap shot I meant, not about Miss Trudi. I don't try to sidestep people's feelings.''

Conflicting reflexes to spit fire at him and to retreat into icy distance died as she saw that it truly bothered him.

''I'm sorry if you think so, but—''

''It's another part of your saying I'm like Mother. It's no more true than—''

''It's true, Steve.'' She sounded almost gentle to her ears, yet he looked as if she'd struck him below the belt. ''You said *we'll talk about it later* to Nell the other day. And you said it more times than I can remember to me when we…before. The last time was at the wedding, when I asked for the truth about Lily. I swore that no one would ever say it to me again. So I'm sorry you felt it was a cheap shot, but I'm not going to apologize for the truth.''

Tell the truth. The whole truth.

Steve sat at his desk, looking out the window. The old glass waved like a pool not quite at rest. Was that why he'd refused to replace these windows?

In swim workouts, the pool had been his private realm. Water cushioned the world's sounds. Voices barely reached him. The long, steady cadence of his stroke was a form of meditation. As long as he moved, the water cradled him. He'd kept going because of a limb-dragging reluctance to leave the water's refuge.

We'll talk about it later.

Was that another sort of reluctance to leave a refuge? He remembered saying it at the wedding—he remembered every word of that. He didn't remember saying it to Nell when she'd asked Annette questions, but he did Monday at dinner.

There had been pleasures out of the water. Uncomplicated camaraderie expressed in nicknames and backslaps. Straightforward expectations distilled to seconds and their decimals. No lies and few secrets.

Secrets. *It's as bad to tell lies by not saying anything.* He'd considered himself an honest man. But by Annette's definition he was far from it.

Meets had been his least favorite part of swimming. With the cacophony of shouts, buzzers and whistles, the water offered no solace, so he had no reason to linger. That's why his times always fell at meets.

He'd thought Coach Boylan had figured it out, but the coach would simply shake his gray flattop and say, "Whatever works, Corbett. Whatever works."

The hard part was accepting that sometimes nothing worked.

The whole truth.

Not later, but now.

Max had obviously returned, but was gone again—for a walk, according to the P.S. on a note taped to the kitchen cabinet that informed her Suz had called.

A walk along the cold, slick lakeshore. Great, just what a guy with a broken wrist, a cut on his head and bruises needed.

Annette rubbed her forehead. She could go out and see where he was. But Max would take one look at her and demand to know what was wrong. She paced from the kitchen to the living room, looked out the front windows to snowflakes drifting past the porch overhang. Then paced back.

She picked up the phone and dialed Suz's cell phone.

"We're not ordering eight kinds of pizza. Let's get some consensus here."

Steve's turn had arrived to let the sextet practice walking in a straight line for the parade in his living room. Nell bamboozled him into feeding them.

"Common sense? But—"

"Consensus, Nell. It means agreement. In this case—" the phone rang, and he started toward it "—it means I'll order two large pizzas and each half can have a different kind of topping. That's four total. So you girls get your list down to four, and then I'll order." He picked up the phone. "Hello."

"Steve?"

Annette's voice on the phone. Had he dreamed of hearing her voice on the phone? He'd known she wouldn't come back, not of her own accord. But had he allowed himself to dream she might call? Out-of-the-blue unexpected. Maybe on a pretext. And they would start to talk. Talk and heal. Work their way back—

"Is this the Corbett residence?"

"Yes. Sorry. There's a lot of noise here." He held the receiver to absorb the background of Nell and company coaxing one girl to try pepperoni on her pizza.

"Steve, it's Annette…Trevetti."

Like he didn't know. "Yes."

"Steve? I have an offer to make, for Miss Trudi's sake.

If you think it would help, I could come with you to talk to her. Part of my business has been as a go-between for people who need technical work.''

Maybe she'd had it right before. When she'd walked out of the wedding. When she'd turned around instead of coming down the pier. When she'd said they had nothing to talk about that morning outside the dry cleaners. Maybe those were reality. And the other moments, the instances of laughter and connection, floating like perfect bubbles through these past days, were the tease of fantasy.

''Daddy!''

''What?'' It wasn't loud, but it was sharp enough that Nell looked at him with her eyes large. He never shouted at her. Never. But did he sidestep her feelings as he did to Annette at the wedding? *We'll talk about that later.* ''You have to wait a few minutes until I finish this phone call. It's…business.''

Did he hear an indrawn breath? ''If this is a bad time, Steve…''

''It isn't the best time. Come by my office in the morning and we'll talk.''

They set a time, like colleagues. No muss, no fuss, no bother. Only, after she'd hung up, he didn't budge until the phone buzzed in irritation.

''Daddy? Are you okay?'' Nell patted his side in childish consolation.

''I'm fine.'' He hung up the receiver. ''Now, one pizza order coming up.''

Chapter Eight

The meeting had gone as well as it could have, Annette decided as she gathered her coat, gloves and scarf in preparation to leave Steve's office Wednesday. They hadn't come up with solutions, but they had agreed on a sequence of what needed to be done to get some answers.

And Annette hadn't mentally cursed Suz for pushing her into this more than a half dozen times.

He as much as said that I wanted someone to take care of me, Suz. Someone to fight my battles. Can you believe it?

Do you want the truth?

Not really. But of course, she hadn't said that. And Suz had laid out a convincing case. It boiled down to two simple points.

Point one. Annette had always been protected by Max, and that was what she had expected of Steve as a fiancé. Only after she'd left Tobias had she taken care of herself.

Annette had acknowledged that one, remembering Steve's reaction when she'd said he should have shared his discovery—and feelings—about his parentage that last summer. *That wasn't part of the deal you'd signed on for.*

Point two. Annette had jumped to conclusions about Steve's guilt in regards to Miss Trudi because she had wanted a wall to hide her attraction behind.

Suz was way off there.

But, as her friend reminded her when she'd protested, the issue now wasn't Annette or Steve—it was Trudi Bliss. *You could help him tell her the truth, couldn't you?* It had sounded so reasonable when Suz said it. Like it would be irresponsible not to do such a little thing.

Getting Steve to let her help might be another matter.

Steve said he would take it from there; since it was a town problem, it was his responsibility. Instead of arguing, Annette turned to his assistant, Bonnie, who had taken notes, and asked for a printout so she could explore some avenues on her own. Bonnie agreed without even looking at Steve.

"I'm heading for a meeting with the highway maintenance chief—could be a lot of snow later this week," Steve said. "I'll walk you out."

He quirked a challenging brow at her, daring her to argue, while at the same time he held her coat for her to put on. She wasn't going to argue in front of Bonnie. Besides, they had not come back to the issue of whether she was going to accompany him when he talked to Miss Trudi the next time.

Debating with herself how to broach that subject occupied her until he pushed open the massive main door, stepping out ahead of her to hold it.

No time for finesse. She descended the first step and stopped. Another step down, he turned to look at her in question. "Steve, my offer still stands to go with you to talk to Miss Trudi, or I could talk to her first."

"Thank you, but it's my responsibility."

"Weren't you the guy griping that not even cute little rodents helped you? Maybe that's because you—excuse me if I repeat myself here—don't accept help." She came down to the step he was on. "I know you're not used to needing help, but I think this might be one time when Cinderella's got the upper hand."

He'd gone still at her first reference to their conversation on the pier. Still, heck, he looked thunderstruck—at least by his standards. Could he possibly have missed the connection between her offer, his refusal and their conversation?

She brushed a touch to his coat sleeve. Too lightly to press it against his arm. Yet she felt as if a flow of heat had come into her fingertips.

Focus, Annette. Focus.

"I know it's daunting, but I'm sure we'll find a way to help Miss Trudi without hurting the town's best interests."

"We? You know, Annette—" one side of his mouth lifted "—you sound like someone who's thinking about the future of Tobias, like someone who might stick around."

"I can care about an old friend even after I leave Tobias."

She saw the change in him as he looked over her shoulder. She turned. Lana Corbett had emerged from the bank, Jason Remtree holding the door for her. Steve's mother would not be happy seeing him talking to her.

"I have to go—"

He moved in front of her before she could retreat toward the door. "No, you don't."

If a meeting between his mother and Annette had to happen—and her vote was no—surely he wouldn't want it to happen on the steps of Town Hall as if some particularly malicious fate had set them up on a stage for passersby. ''Steve, I…''

He didn't touch her. Just looked at her—he was so close, he had to look down. The vapor of his breath swirled, as if reaching to touch her face. His heat flowed around her. Did he…

No. There was nothing to react to here. Nothing to…feel.

''Steve, let me by.''

''You're not chickening out.''

''Chickening?''

''Steven.'' Lana, climbing the steps at a deliberate pace, gave Annette a long cool look.

Realization hit Annette. To a Corbett, a public street—or even a stage—didn't make a difference. Lesser mortals might make scenes, but Corbetts didn't express emotions in public or private.

She frowned. Yesterday in his office, Steve had definitely shown emotion. And last week in front of the cleaners. And certainly around Nell.

''Good day, Annette,'' Lana said without inflection.

''Hello, Mrs. Corbett.'' Seven-and-a-half years of accomplishments and successes and learning the world. They were all there in her perfectly modulated—neither too warm nor too cool—greeting.

Lana continued studying her with no hint of the result of her assessment showing in her steely eyes. ''Steven, I wish to speak to you about a family matter.''

''I'll just—'' Annette backed up a step.

Steve clamped a hand on her arm. ''Go ahead, Mother.''

Lana's eyes flickered to Annette, then dismissed her.

''Very well. I have told you I disapprove of the company you are allowing Nell to keep. Disregarding your reputation is one thing, but letting Nell go to that hovel Bliss House is a disgrace, and to be in such company—''

"Please don't stop Nell from seeing Miss Trudi because of me—it would break both their hearts." All Annette's resolve to remain uninvolved fled at the prospect of those two being separated because of her. Steve's hand slid to underneath her arm below the elbow, a warm support through her coat. "I'll make sure that I'm not at Miss Trudi's when Nell's there."

Lana Corbett didn't respond.

"It's not you she's disapproving of, Annette," Steve said. "It's Miss Trudi."

"But Miss Trudi's—"

His smile was grim. "A Corbett? Yes, she is."

"Hardly a credit to the family," Lana said.

"I'm not the reason you want to stop Nell from seeing Miss Trudi? Because of...because we didn't..." She couldn't find words that presented what had happened seven years ago in a neutral light.

"Naturally, I fault you for running out of that wedding," Lana said. "After the social capital I expended to create a success. And all for nothing—worse than nothing. If you had stood your ground, we would have emerged from the situation with significantly less damage. It would have looked better if Steve and his wife had united to raise Nell."

It would have looked better.... Not that it might have been easier for Steve or better for Nell. Not even that it might have saved Steve hurt. The woman was entirely heartless. To not even consider what Steve and Nell—

Annette swallowed. Not that *she* had cause to feel protective of Nell, and certainly not of Steve.

"I wasn't concerned with how it would look."

"Yes, you were," Lana said with cool certainty. "You

were concerned that you would look weak and put-upon if you stayed. A woman whose man had strayed before they were even married.''

''Mother—''

Annette overrode Steve, looking straight at the woman who had once so intimidated her. ''Have you ever given anyone the benefit of the doubt?''

Lana Corbett hesitated, and Annette wondered if she had penetrated the shell to reach a softer center.

Then the older woman shook her head slightly and said, ''No, I don't believe I have.''

Stunned, Annette stared at her. Lana looked back with no show of emotion.

To her surprise, a bubble of laughter rose in Annette. ''Well, at least you are honest.''

Lana raised one brow slightly as she looked her up and down. ''And you are considerably more sure of yourself than you were seven years ago.''

Instantly serious, Annette said, ''I should hope so.''

''All this is neither here nor there.'' Lana looked at her son. Annette had to hand it to the woman, she had a gift for dismissing people. ''You have an obligation to the name Corbett in this town, and—''

''Do I, Mother?''

Annette thought Lana saw something in his expression that frightened her. Something like the truth. Then that fleeting impression was gone, and Lana spoke with as much certainty as ever.

''Yes. And you are not living up to it. It's clear that Miss Trudi belongs in a nursing home, and that building must be razed.''

Annette couldn't stop a gasp. Neither Steve nor Lana looked at her, but Steve gave her arm a slow squeeze, as if in reassurance.

"Neither of those items is clear to most people in Tobias, Mother, and certainly they are not clear to Miss Trudi."

"No reasonable person could come to any other conclusion."

"Some reasonable people are convinced that Miss Trudi and her home should be left exactly as they are."

Lana's eyes flicked toward Annette. She willed her face not to inform the other woman that she was not among the people Steve meant. She surely didn't want Miss Trudi sent to a nursing home, but leaving the house as it was? No.

"Furthermore, you have no standing in this matter, Mother. You are not related by blood." Steel flashed in his tone, almost daring his mother to say he wasn't related to Miss Trudi by blood, either, then it was gone. "Nor are you among Miss Trudi's trustees or her immediate neighbors."

"I care about the Corbett name that she is connected to and—"

"No one doubts that. But this is a town matter. Now, if you'll excuse us, Annette and I have a meeting."

He used his grip on her arm to start Annette down the steps. It was a good thing her feet operated on automatic pilot, because her head was elsewhere. Like in shock. She would never have believed someone would dismiss Lana that way. And for it to be Steve…he didn't seem to think it was unusual. She studied his profile. A faint frown, as if in concentration, but nothing more. Certainly nothing that prepared her for his abruptly stopping and catching her staring.

His mouth twitched, but he wisely did not let a grin unfold. Instead, he said, "Where's your car? Where'd you park?"

Boy, she was out of it. They'd gone half a block past the lot. He turned around and headed back with her.

"Sorry about Mother," he said unexpectedly.

"You're not responsible for your mother."

He looked at her, but she kept her attention straight ahead. "You didn't used to think that way."

"I've grown up."

"Yes, you have. We both have." He took her hand and drew it around his arm as if he were escorting her into a ball. It should have been a ridiculous gesture with both of them bundled up for the cold. She wondered if tingling could be considered a normal response to ridiculous. "C'mon, I'm taking you up on that offer. Let's go talk to Miss Trudi."

He was going to accept her help. She wanted to throw her arms around him and hug him. Not a good idea.

"Right now? What about the highway maintenance chief?"

"If he doesn't know how to handle snow after all these years in Wisconsin there's no hope. Besides, setting up an appointment to talk to Miss Trudi would just give her time to fret."

"Okay, but I want to know one thing. Who are the reasonable people convinced that Miss Trudi and her home should be left as they are?"

He grinned. All-out, devil-may-care and totally un-Corbett-like.

"Nell."

"I'll leave you two to it, then."

Annette's smile took them both in, but Steve seriously doubted it had the same effect on Miss Trudi that it did on him.

The door closed, leaving him with Miss Trudi and a stack of bad-news financial reports. The study smelled of damp and old paper. A blowtorch couldn't have ignited the aged photo albums and scrapbooks that lined the walls.

"Such a lovely person, our Annette." Miss Trudi twitched a pink chiffon scarf. Her eyes, though red-rimmed, were sharp and bright on him.

Our Annette. Would she let him claim a share of her?

She'd impressed him during this conversation with Miss Trudi. Impressed him? Hell, she'd saved him.

As soon as he'd tried to make Miss Trudi see her situation realistically, she started weeping and, yes, wailing. Fearing she would stop listening entirely, he'd rushed to get in all the hard facts. It wasn't pretty.

Annette stepped in, soothing Miss Trudi and shushing him.

"Stopping her crying is great, but she's got to hear this," he'd said.

"She can't hear it if she's crying," she'd retorted.

Annette had spent a good thirty minutes listening to Miss Trudi's laments and memories. It took him half that time to recognize how she was bringing the older woman around by acknowledging her feelings, then gradually leading her to accept that she couldn't go back to the past and had to think of the future.

The last five minutes he'd barely heard what Annette and Miss Trudi said.

How many never-acknowledged feelings had piled up in him in seven-and-a-half years? Had he truly accepted that they couldn't go back to the past? Or deep down, had he thought he could rewrite it, now that Annette was in Tobias?

When Max heals, I'll be leaving.

She'd said it enough that it should have sunk in. Apparently he still needed the reminder—he'd be a damned fool to let himself fall again for a woman who wasn't going to stick around. And then there was the matter of the things he hadn't said to her in the past and the things she had said to him.

I'm tired of having my feelings scheduled so they're more convenient for the Corbetts to ignore. This isn't going to work.

"Steve?"

Annette's hand on his arm jolted him upright. Both women looked at him, Annette quizzically and Miss Trudi with growing speculation.

After that he'd followed Annette's lead by giving Miss Trudi smaller doses of reality than he'd first tried and letting her digest them before serving up the next batch. By the end, they had agreed Steve and Miss Trudi would go over the details of her finances right now. Annette would watch Nell when she arrived from school.

They had also agreed that Max would give Miss Trudi a realistic appraisal of needed repairs and costs as soon as possible.

"Such a pity it didn't work out for you and Annette," Miss Trudi said.

Steve gave her a warning look. Some people thought she was harmless. Some people also thought poison ivy was an attractive plant. Having known her all his life, he'd felt the itch too often to fall for the mild-looking leaves.

"But past mistakes can often be remedied," she added.

"Don't even think about it, Miss Trudi."

She fluttered her eyelashes. "Why, whatever do you mean? I'm simply referring to my lamentable lack of attention to Bliss House. Shall we start?"

He answered by arranging the financial reports in front of her.

Nell arrived as Annette lit the balky burner on her third try and put the kettle on to make tea. Nell immediately set out on a Squid hunt.

Where had Steve gone to in those moments she'd been helping Miss Trudi come to terms with the reality that faced her? It had been nearly impossible to concentrate on Miss Trudi when he sat there with the color of his eyes changing like a sky with wind-driven gray clouds coming and going.

The gray won out. Not like thunderclouds. But like a raw, chilled rain. A day that clamped down on your spirits, making them as listless as the sky.

"Can I ask you somethin'?"

Annette started, more from the realization she'd been staring into space contemplating the intricacies of Steve's eyes than from his daughter's return.

"Okay."

"Why didn't you marry my daddy? You had the dress and everything!"

Annette sucked in air super chilled by surprise and choked on it, coughing and gasping.

The girl considered her gravely, then whacked Annette on the back with the heel of her hand—Annette's lower back, because that was as high as Nell reached.

"Okay!" Annette managed to speak between gasps. "I'm—okay." *Whack!* "No more!"

"Because I'm pulverizing you?"

"Yes!"

Nell peered at her, nodded in satisfaction and went to her favorite chair. The instant Annette drew one steady breath, Nell pounced. "You *were* gonna marry my daddy, weren't you? So, why didn'tcha, when you had the dress and everything?"

"I, uh, I'm not sure what the dress has to do with it."

Nell frowned. "Laura Ellen's big sister said the reason to get married is for the dress and presents and party. Caitlin said you can do the other stuff without getting married. And Caitlin's *sixteen*. They said you were dressed up and at the church with flowers and all the people, but you left him right in the middle because you changed your mind. Why'd you change your mind?''

You left him. Underneath the little girl's directness, Annette heard a vulnerability that reverberated in her memories. *Daddy's not coming back, Annette. He's left. But why? Why did he leave?*

''Sometimes you make a decision you think is right. But then you realize you made a mistake. So I...we decided we wouldn't get married. Because two people who get married should truly love each other.''

''But you musta thought you loved each other, right?''

''Well, yes, when we decided to get married, we thought...but it wasn't...'' She was not going to get tongue-tied by a seven-year-old. ''Not getting married was right. Your daddy married your mommy and had you. And I've been very, very happy building my company. So you see? Everything turned out fine.''

The kettle whistled, and Annette tended it gladly. She even welcomed a minor crisis over not enough lemon in Nell's tea.

Then Nell said, ''Can I ask you somethin'?''

Annette remembered Steve's advice—*Be careful how you answer this.* ''You decide if it's a good question to ask, I'll decide if it's a good question to answer.''

Nell's blue eyes bored into her. Sitting still under that gaze was a greater challenge than sitting across a table from the toughest negotiators.

Finally, the girl nodded. ''Daddy doesn't want me to believe everything I hear. I asked Miss Trudi, but it's her song and she thinks it makes sense.''

''Song?''

"The one about the butterfly woman."

"Butterfly wom— Oh. *Madame Butterfly*. I thought I heard Miss Trudi playing that. It's actually many songs put together in a story called an opera."

"All that singing makes it hard to hear the words. They should just say the words, like on TV. Miss Trudi had to tell me the whole story."

"Is that your question? About opera? Because—"

"No, Miss Trudi told me *all* about that. She says I'll like it better when I'm older." Her face screwed up in disbelief. "This butterfly woman kills herself because some guy picks another girl. Does that make sense?"

Oh, fine, Miss Trudi got opera. What did she get? Cultural differences. Historical inequities. Issues of a woman's self-worth and, oh, yes, suicide.

"Um, well…killing yourself is never a solution. But it was a different time."

Nell nodded "They wear strange clothes on the front of that big CD Miss Trudi plays. But Caitlin says lots of girls have babies when they're not married."

Annette closed her eyes, wishing she could get her hands on Laura Ellen's older sister. Now she was supposed to discuss children who may or may not be legitimate depending on which opera expert you listened to? "That's something you need to talk to your daddy about, Nell. But even if that were entirely true, it can be very difficult for a grown woman to have a baby alone, much less a girl."

"But this butterfly woman's all gooey about the baby. It's the guy who went away that she gets upset about."

Annette dived into the sliver of daylight that statement offered. "That's another part of what the story's about— losing someone you love. Losing him by discovering he doesn't love you the way you love him. By counting on him and then having him let you down completely."

She had no awareness of movement or sound, but she looked over Nell's head and saw Steve leaning one shoulder against the door frame. His eyes contradicted the ease of his pose.

"And then he comes back, but she's already dead," Nell said. "If she'd waited, he wouldn't be yelling *Butterfly! Butterfly!*"

"That's true. That's part of the lesson, to think hard before you do big things. Because you might regret them for a long, long time."

Only when Annette met Steve's gaze did she consider that he might read a subtext from their history into the words—but what subtext? That she lived with regret for leaving or that he should live with regret for betraying her with Lily?

Nell said, "Well, I like the one about the fig guy better."

"Fig? Oh, *The Marriage of Figaro.*"

Nell made a gagging sound. "That one's about marriage, too? Does everybody in the whole world want a dress?"

Steve cleared his throat from the doorway. "Came to get Miss Trudi some tea. She—" his gaze flashed to Nell "—needs time to absorb what's been said."

"The water should still be hot. Let me help you." Standing beside him at the stove to keep her voice low, she added, "How is she?"

"Rocked. It's a lot of reality to swallow when she hasn't had to face it before."

She was aware of him watching her profile as she put tea into another pot then poured the hot water in. He wasn't talking only about Miss Trudi.

That wasn't part of the deal you'd signed on for. Sometimes people who say they want—even demand—facts don't truly want them. They want someone else to take care of them. They want someone else to fight their battles for them.

"Hasn't had to face it, or hasn't been allowed to face it? Hasn't been allowed to grow up." She put a cup and saucer on a tray. Pink roses twined around the translucent cup, and blue geometric designs ringed the saucer. "Do you want to take the pot?"

He looked at her a moment before saying, "Yeah, that'll be good. What was that all about—*Madame Butterfly* and *The Marriage of Figaro?*"

"Apparently Miss Trudi has been teaching her about opera, and Nell isn't enamored with the subject matter of love and marriage."

"Who can blame her?" He took the tray and walked out.

Was that what had been bothering him? Had something triggered memories of his marriage to Lily? It ended in divorce, but Annette had no idea why. Could Rob's situation have opened old wounds? If Lily had left Steve and Nell...

A surge of something like anger hit her. Absurd. The woman had to have been six kinds of fool to abandon her child and husband, but that was no business of Annette's. It could, however, cause a man to think poorly of love and marriage as the topics for operas, she supposed.

"Can I tell you somethin'?"

Having Nell tell her something had to be easier than answering Nell's questions—or trying to figure out her father. "Sure."

"Sometimes my daddy's not happy. He doesn't have a special grown-up like Laura Ellen's mom and dad do."

Oh. She swallowed twice. "Sometimes when grown-ups get a divorce like your mom and dad—"

The girl shook her head. "He said divorce didn't scar him. I asked."

Annette blinked at the image of *that* conversation—no doubt it had started with *Can I ask you somethin'*—but Nell was already continuing. "I thought he could marry Fran, but he says he's not going to marry her."

So much there to consider—*Steve and Fran?*—but no time to think about it because Nell had placed her hand on Annette's arm and leaned forward in the posture of all children telling secrets.

"Sometimes he opens a box in his dresser, and he's sad. Once he saw me looking and pretended nothing was wrong. But he was sad. So I looked in the box."

"Nell, you shouldn't—"

"Daddy says sometimes you have to do things that aren't fun to protect somebody you love—like making me stay in my room after I crossed the street when I wasn't supposed to. So I looked in the box." Her defiantly raised chin dropped abruptly. "But the only stuff in there was some rings and torn gloves."

"Rings?" Annette felt as if she couldn't breathe. As if the air in her chest had heated to meltdown temperatures. Yet that single word came out clear and urgent. Rings and torn gloves. The silk had flowed against her skin as she yanked them off, but the sound of ripping had been harsh.

"One's a diamond and two are just plain gold. I like rubies."

"Rubies are nice." But her engagement ring and their wedding bands had been beautiful. Why would Steve keep them? Or maybe he'd given them to Lily and— No. He wouldn't do that.

The man had conceived a child with another woman while engaged to her. Yet *that* betrayal—recycling of the

most callous kind by giving her rings to another woman—
was not in him. She knew it with every atom in her.

"Shh! Here comes Daddy. Don't tell him—please?
Promise!"

Nell had an obvious case of confider's remorse, but she
didn't need to worry that Annette would bring this up to
Steve.

"Promise."

Warned by the rattle, Steve opened the back door to let
Max and Lenny enter, stamping snow off their work boots.
A wad of note-loaded pages stretched the jaws of Lenny's
clipboard. He looked shell-shocked.

Miss Trudi smiled. "Don't see buildings made like this
anymore, do you?"

Max's injured arm was inside his coat. He was trying to
remove the glove from his left hand by rubbing it against
his leg when Annette reached him.

"No, ma'am," he said dutifully, then added in a mutter
Steve barely caught, "not standing, you don't."

Annette sighed as she pulled off Max's glove. He backed
away before she could reach his jacket zipper. Steve
watched her and wondered at his own surprise. He'd understood intellectually that Annette was taking care of Max,
yet mild surprise bubbled up at the sight of her looking out
for her brother. Maybe he hadn't given her as much credit
for being grown-up as he had thought.

Then she propped her hands on her hips, and intellect
took a vacation. She'd slipped her hands under the hem of
the bulky cardigan she wore over a white shirt that probably
looked plain as sin hanging on a hanger. On Annette it
looked like plain sin, sliding over her breasts like a silken
sheet after a night in bed. Her gesture pulled up the sweater
to reveal her rounded butt in jeans tight enough to—

"Steve, you want to close the door before we all freeze?"

Max's words and accompanying glare jolted him back to the moment.

They had all arrived an hour and a half ago. They'd agreed Max and Lenny would check the house, ranking what needed to be done based on urgency. Then Max and Annette would work up figures for what the various levels—from necessary to keep the place standing, down to decorative touches—would cost.

The first stage—the outside inspection—had taken depressingly long. Nell used the time to make inroads into Miss Trudi's jam pot, while Miss Trudi filled the silence between Steve and Annette by telling stories of growing up in the house when it had been at its elegant best.

From the look on Max's face, Bliss House was further from that standard than they had feared.

"So, what needs to be done?" Miss Trudi asked brightly.

"I need to check inside before I can tell you." One-handed, Max maneuvered a powerful flashlight out of his pocket. "Annette, if you come and hold the flashlight, that'll help. Miss Trudi, how do I get to the furnace and the attic?"

"I'll show you. There are a few little places where it can be ever so slightly tricky for someone not familiar with the house."

Nell popped out of her seat. "I know the hole in the stairs, and where water runs down the wall. And I can hold the flashlight. I wanna go."

That started a rapid-fire discussion of who should go. Max and Lenny, of course. Miss Trudi insisted. Steve volunteered to wait in the kitchen. Annette thought she should go, leaving Nell with her father. But Max said Nell not only knew the house, but took up less room in exploring close quarters.

That left Steve and Annette on opposite sides of the big table...for about four seconds. Until she jumped up and started clearing the table.

He picked up a cup and saucer and followed. "Spill it, Annette."

"What?" She stopped in the act of testing the water filling the sink.

Based on experience, he turned the burner on under the kettle to add hot water to the tepid stuff from the tap.

"You've gotten better at hiding your feelings, but I can still tell when you're working up to saying something you're not sure you want to say."

Her eyes widened. He caught that in the second before she dropped her head, her hair swinging forward to obscure her expression. Then she reached up with both hands and pushed her hair back. *Damn.*

"And you better say it fast," he muttered.

"All right." Her tone and the tuck between her brows indicated she interpreted his reaction as impatience. Just as well, or she'd be running.

"Look, if we're going to work together helping Miss Trudi, I think...I wanted you to know...I don't want you to think—"

He had no idea where she was going with this.

She took a deep breath and started again. "This doesn't change what I've said before, but something your mother said—that I took the easy way out—I just... I know you hate public scenes, and the one at our—at the church was a doozy. If there'd been another way... But there wasn't, not for me. Still, I want you to know that leaving that church was the hardest thing I've ever done."

He felt an odd lightening. It didn't make sense. He'd

never thought she'd acted on a whim. Hell, his rational mind could see that, from her standpoint, she'd had good reason. It was just that his heart hadn't been rational. Maybe the lightening came because she was talking about it without anger.

"The only thing harder I can imagine," she continued, "would have been staying there after... I couldn't do that."

"No, I don't suppose you could have. Not any more than I could have done differently than I did." The weight of each word felt like putting down a stone he'd been carrying. "But I am sorry, Annette. Sorry I didn't do better. Sorry I wasn't someone you could believe in. And especially sorry you were hurt. Letting you get hurt was the last thing I wanted."

Her eyes came to his, and for the first time they held an openness. She was giving him what he had so wanted before and what had come in snatches against her will from that first day at the hospital. Letting him see inside her. What he saw was that she had interpreted his words as an apology for a sin he'd committed. He'd been thinking of all she didn't yet know.

He gave one short nod, an acknowledgment of the corner they had turned. A blind corner, with no way to see what was ahead on the road.

While she started to wash dishes, he returned to the table to gather the rest. And maybe to put some distance between them.

"The jam knife's so sticky, it's going to have to soak."

She offered a return to the mundane, and he accepted it.

"Wish I could do that to Nell's face." He started drying what she'd washed.

Her chuckle faded into a sigh, and she glanced toward the doorway Miss Trudi and the others had gone through. "I'm not looking forward to this."

"None of us are. It almost doesn't matter what total Max comes up with. It's going to be more than she can afford."

"Then why are we putting her through this?" She knew why. It was frustration and pain for her friend talking.

"To shock her into facing the reality that she can't stay here like this."

"She'll be heartbroken." Annette put a handful of silverware in the drainer and wiped her hands on a towel.

"I know."

She scooped her hair off her forehead with both hands again. "What are we going to do?"

It had no planning. No will. No intent. Solely need.

He leaned across the corner of counter that separated them and kissed her.

Heat blasted through him, along with something that would have made him laugh and shout out loud if his mouth hadn't been better occupied in renewing its acquaintance with hers.

Ah, yes. That rounded curve that led to the dip below her lower lip. This sweet tuck at the corner. The full press of her lips against his. The seam where they met, and where his tongue demanded entrance. Her taste. Ah, her taste.

He wanted to grasp the instant, suspend it, extend it. And he wanted to drive past it, go deeper, harder, faster. Now, right now.

He held her shoulders, held them tight, like that might give him a grip on his desires. No way.

He negotiated the corner of the counter without releasing her mouth.

In a gasp of loss so sharp he wanted to curse it, he released her mouth to gulp in air. They were separate, yet so close they couldn't look at each other. He could only feel the accelerated pace of her breathing.

She'd suspended motion in mid-gesture the instant his

mouth touched hers. Now he was aware her hands were moving. She could push him away. She would push him away if her brain was working. He had to do something.

He shifted, bringing their bodies in contact and nudging her off balance. At the same time he took her mouth again, pushing insistently at the renewed seam of her lips. She backed up half a step in pursuit of balance, but stopped abruptly—it must have been the counter—and gave a soft *oof*. That tiny breath was all he needed. He stroked his tongue inside her mouth and surged against her. She pressed against him as her mouth opened to him.

She touched his jaw, fleeting and soft, then grazed a caress of her palm on his cheek before her fingers slid into his hair and around to the base of his neck.

Her hands on him were a benediction flowing over him and into him, reaching to where the need for her resided. Never gone, never forgotten.

A change in the pressure of her hands registered first. She was pushing against him, not holding on. Then noise penetrated. Noise from the hall. Of people approaching. He released her, pulling in air. She didn't look at him as she stepped back, then turned.

He retreated behind the corner of the counter. It provided cover without requiring much moving, and both were essential at the moment.

Her brother paused in the doorway as he looked from Steve to Annette. Max's gaze landed on Annette, and his grimness deepened. Miss Trudi advanced while her gaze flitted from Steve to Annette, ending on him, and her grimness lifted.

"What's—" Annette's voice came out half an octave higher than usual. She cleared her throat. "What's the upshot of your inspection, Max?"

Max's frown deepened, and Steve could almost hear her

brother's voice demanding to know what the hell was going on.

Instead, he said, "I couldn't write as I went so I have to make notes." Having Miss Trudi and Nell along made dictating to Lenny, as he had outside, awkward.

"Of course, of course." Miss Trudi bustled around to make the two men comfortable at the table. Nell peered over Max's arm until Steve shooed her away. Annette stayed at the sink, as if that lone jam knife required constant supervision.

Miss Trudi took the chair at the head of the table. Steve sat beside Nell, pretending he was watching Max laboriously write with his left hand and pretending he wasn't watching Annette.

After all his lectures to himself to remember what she said about leaving, his hormones sure as hell had pushed them around another blind corner. But was it heading toward or heading away from something—and *what?*

Max raised his head and cleared his throat. Annette walked over, wiping her hands on a towel. Steve couldn't take his eyes off those slender hands. Those fingers had touched his cheek, threaded into his hair, caressed his neck....

A dual gasp from Annette and Miss Trudi snapped him to now.

Max had given a figure, and he'd missed it.

"Oh, but if we don't do everything," Annette was protesting, "if we do the absolute necessities for safety and to prevent more damage..."

"That's what I just gave you."

"Oh, my." Miss Trudi's chin wobbled. "We'll just have to do a bit at a time."

"That won't work. Most of these jobs fit together," Max said.

"Is there anything that makes the house dangerous to live in?" Steve asked. He didn't want to force Miss Trudi to leave, but if staying here endangered her…

"Immediately?" Max rubbed his chin. "The wiring's sh—crud. But as long as she doesn't use more than one plug in an outlet and no extension cords, she should be okay. But as far as comfort's concerned—"

"Oh, I don't mind about that!"

"There's also the matter of code, Miss Trudi." Max shot a look toward Steve. "This place isn't up to code—not close. It's been grandfathered in, but once you start renovating and modernizing, the new codes kick in. The furnace isn't too bad, but there's no insulation to speak of, and there are so many gaps and splits and holes that it's like you're trying to heat all of Tobias. And the plumbing…"

The news only got worse.

Chapter Nine

Following Max out of Bliss House forty-five minutes later, Annette pulled the collar of her coat around her throat and shivered in the wind that was piling up snow clouds like a miser's bank account.

Or maybe the lingering effect from Max's litany had chilled her.

She hadn't been chilled after that kiss—

No. She wasn't going to think about that. It was a hormone flashback. There was no sense rehashing or reliving... Steve's mouth, hot and firm, familiar and strange, insistent and compelling...

"So now what?"

I don't know.

A second after that mental wail, she realized Max's question was about Bliss House. He and the others had stopped in front of Steve's SUV.

"Like Annette told Miss Trudi, we'll all think about solutions and get together Tuesday night," Steve said. "That gives her time to come to terms with the reality."

"It doesn't have to cost that much. I can work on it for the expenses—"

"Max, how could you?" Annette said. "Your business is growing so much you won't even take time to heal properly."

"I could do it in my spare time."

"What spare time? You work constantly."

Lenny nodded agreement until he caught the sharp look Max sent him.

"It might take a while, but I could do it," Max said stubbornly. "Enough that she can live in it and it won't fall down around her. At least not all of it."

"That's very generous of you, Max. But I doubt Miss Trudi would agree to have you working for free, and it doesn't solve the problem for the neighbors," Steve said. "And if we stand here discussing this, Miss Trudi will know we're talking about her."

Annette pivoted toward Max's truck. Steve's hand on her arm stopped her, and heat surged through her. She should invest in armor. "If you come with me, Annette, we can start brainstorming for solutions."

"No, I—"

"We're going to need all the time we can get to find a workable solution. Max and Lenny are welcome, too, but I got the idea they've got other work this afternoon."

"That's why I can't. I have to drive Max to—"

"Lenny, you walked over, didn't you?" Steve's eyes turned almost silver with challenge. "You could drive Max home when you're done and keep the truck a while."

Max frowned, but said, "Lenny and I could go right out to the site, and I was thinking he should take the company truck in for a tune-up first thing Monday, but if you want to go home, Annette…''

Nell was the only one not staring at her. Lenny looked curious, while Max's concern was almost as blatant as Steve's challenge.

''If you don't need me to drive, I'm happy to get started brainstorming.'' In case it wasn't clear, she added, ''Miss Trudi needs our help.''

Steve had eased his SUV away from the curb when he lobbed his next hand grenade. ''Before we go to my house, I have to drop off Nell at her friend Laura Ellen's. Laura Ellen's mother is a saint. She's taking four of them to a late matinee then feeding them.''

''Your house?'' And without Nell as a de facto chaperone. Sure, he waited to mention that little fact until she was buckled into a moving vehicle.

''Not scared, are you?''

''There's nothing scary at our house,'' Nell said from the back seat.

''Except for the mess under your bed,'' her father said. Paper napkins and messes under the bed? Lana Corbett must be loosening up.

Nell giggled. ''It won't hurt you, Annette. Honest.''

''Thank you, Nell, and I'm not scared. However,'' she said to Steve, ''your office would be better. If we need background material or—''

He shook his head. ''We shut up tight and turn down the heat on the weekends to save the taxpayers money. My house will have to do.'' He flipped on the turn indicator and pulled into a driveway. ''Here we go.''

A woman in a Green Bay Packers sweatshirt and jeans waved from the front door. Steve waved back then turned in his seat to instruct Nell. ''You be good and do whatever Mrs. Volz says.''

"I'm good all the time," she said. Nell leaned across the back of the front seat to kiss Steve on the cheek. "You know what would make our house even more not scary? A dog. Bye, Daddy. Bye, Annette. I sure hope Caitlin's here."

With that she scampered up the walk. Not until she disappeared from view did Steve shift to Reverse. Instead of backing out, however, he sat staring at the house.

"Darn. I meant to… Sorry." He set the emergency brake. "This won't take long, but I've got to find out who this Caitlin is that Nell keeps quoting."

He put the car in Park. Although Annette suspected Steve's peace of mind was in more immediate danger from Nell's campaign for a dog than from Caitlin's pronouncements, she leaned forward and covered his hand on the gearshift lever.

"Caitlin is Laura Ellen's older sister. Sixteen and apparently eager to impart the wisdom of her years to the younger set."

He had turned at her touch, and she was near enough to feel the full impact of his eyes. The girls at school used to gush about Zach's startlingly blue eyes, but she'd always preferred Steve's. They were subtle and changeable and fascinating…and Steve's.

This close, she could distinguish each emotion in his eyes. Surprise, probably at her knowing about Caitlin. Amusement, no doubt at a sixteen-year-old sage. Heat, at—

She lifted her hand, but before she could withdraw it, he'd turned his over and caught it.

Two pairs of Wisconsin-hardy gloves—his and hers—separated their palms. Tell that to the nerve endings in her hand, or the ones running a conga line up her arm to her shoulder, where it made a U-turn and brought heat and tightening to the point of her breast.

One touch couldn't do this. One simple touch. Not even skin to skin, the way he'd touched her when they'd kissed.

She pulled her hand away, leaving the glove in his grasp. His gaze dropped to the empty glove he held, masking his expression.

Four times she drew in a breath and slowly released it—hoping it wasn't audible—before he wordlessly held out the glove, then backed out of the driveway after she took it from him, equally wordlessly.

She scoured her mind for an excuse to cancel the brainstorming session that would make him think this *awareness* wasn't the reason. Not an easy task, since that was the reason.

They had crossed to his side of town and were climbing toward the hilltop where Corbett House sat when he finally spoke.

"Thank you for clearing up the mystery of Caitlin."

"You're welcome."

"I owe you another thank-you, too. For being so nice to Nell."

She frosted his profile. "Did you truly think I would take it out on her?"

"Even for someone who's closed the door on the past, the history can't be completely ignored. But, no, I didn't think you would." He glanced toward her, leaving no doubt that he meant it, before returning his attention to the road. "But sometimes what I feel when it comes to Nell isn't totally rational." His brief half grin faded. "So, I'm not surprised, but I am grateful."

She made no effort to break the silence as he turned onto the street that ran behind Corbett House. A half-circle drive marked the front, but the multi-car garage was at the back, off this secondary road.

"What you said in my office," Steve finally said, "about me putting off people's feelings, about saying *later*..."

She waited.

"I know at the wedding, after Lily..." He slowed the car. "I don't know how much I say it, to Nell or... But you were right to call me on it."

She swallowed, buying time to search for the right words, which apparently were spending the winter somewhere on a beach. Because there had sure been a shortage of the right words in her life these past two weeks.

As she opened her mouth to let out whatever subpar comment had formed, he passed the back entry to Corbett House and turned right into a driveway on the opposite side of the street.

"What's this?" She stared at the compact brick Cape Cod.

"My house."

"Your house? *Your* house? But—"

She glanced over her shoulder toward the big house where he'd grown up. His gaze followed.

"You thought I was living there? Under my mother's roof?" His mouth twitched. "And under her thumb, presumably."

"It's not that. I..." Assumed. Yup, she'd assumed, and now she felt like an ass. "With Nell to raise... It can't be easy to be a single father. And it would make sense to have your mother help with child care."

"No, it wouldn't." He gave her no opportunity to respond. "Or is it that you thought that in my mother's house you wouldn't have to worry about your virtue? That I would behave like a perfect gentleman?"

"Of course not—I mean... I don't mean you wouldn't be a gentleman anywhere. Everywhere. And I'm *not* worried."

She was protesting to air.

He was out of the car, and the door closed behind him with a *thunk* that made her jump. He opened the passenger door and held out a hand to her.

"Steve, maybe it would be better if we did this another time."

His hand, outstretched at her eye level, didn't waver. It was a dare. Just like coming to his house was.

She didn't run from dares. Besides, if he thought that kiss had changed things, better set him straight now.

"There's nothing scary here. If you won't take my word for it, take Nell's."

"I'm not scared." Defiantly, she placed her hand in his, but then got out on her own steam so it was more like they were holding hands than anything else.

Rather than make a big deal of it—that had been her mistake at Laura Ellen's house—she stepped away, extending their arms almost straight out. He grinned but released her hand before leading her in the back door.

The kitchen was extraordinary in its ordinariness. White painted cabinets, pine stools pulled up to the outside of the counter that separated the working area, French doors that would open to a deck in good weather. Practical flooring and easy-to-clean counters. No restaurant-grade appliances or gourmet touches here.

Her attention snagged on wipeable boards marching across one wall. Three were marked with calendar grids under headings that read This Month, Next Month and The Month After. Notations written in red, blue or green, like the one under Tuesday saying Town Hall Field Trip, clogged the boxes.

"That's quite a calendar system."

It was also an insight into his life as a single father. She hadn't realized the full impact of that status before—*single father.* A man raising his daughter alone, since Lily left when Nell was a baby.

Had he been scared? Spent nights up with a crying baby? Wondered if a fever warranted calling the doctor? Worried that he wouldn't do enough, or might do too much, for Nell?

"That calendar is all that keeps Nell and Gert and me from sinking into chaos. And sometimes not even that works. Let me take your coat, then go on into the living room where it's more comfortable while I make coffee. I'll light a fire, and that should take the chill off. Unless... You're not scared, are you?"

"Not scared at all." But her moments of empathy for his years of single parenthood sank under a renewed tide of being on guard.

In the living room she staked out a dark blue wing chair set at right angles to the couch.

"Sorry about the mess," Steve said, grabbing two open books from the ottoman that matched her chair. "Obviously, I didn't plan on having anyone over. That should relieve you about this being a plot."

"I didn't think—"

"Sure you did." He bent to scoop newspapers from the couch. The motion stretched his shirt across his back and shoulders, and his jeans across his narrow hips. "And if I'd been smart I *would* have thought of it. I'll be right back."

The print couch was cushy and comfortable. More books, a stuffed dinosaur and one green mitten were on the end table between the chair and couch. An open cabinet held a TV. Bookshelves flanked a fireplace. The mantel held three photos of Nell and a framed child's drawing of a house that a generous viewer might think resembled this one.

"Okay, here we go," Steve said. He dropped a legal pad

and pen in her lap, then took a seat on the couch with another pad. "Any ideas how to tackle this?"

She picked up the pad and pen. No more noticing how fabric stretched when he moved. No paying attention to the way his fingers wrapped around a pen, the way his hand moved over paper with a faint sound of friction. She was going to concentrate on the task ahead of them. Only that.

Steve dropped his pen to the legal pad and stretched.

Annette abruptly twisted away and searched for something in her purse on the far side of the chair.

He got up to add a log to the fire. It was an act of defiance. The previous time he'd added a log, she'd acted as if it were a commitment to staying the night.

"So you're going to look into grants and tax breaks if we could get historical status for Bliss House," he said, "and I'll check on reverse mortgages."

"With Remtree?" Her voice sounded strained. "He'll never agree. Nobody from that side of Tobias will help her."

He turned from the fireplace. "I'll check with Rob first, but don't count out Tobias. I'm part of that side of town, and here I am. Besides, I believe in this town."

"Of course you do. Kids who get dollars under their pillow after a tooth falls out believe in the tooth fairy. Kids who find the tooth still there in the morning without a dime doubt the first time and stop believing the second."

"If you gave the tooth fairy a second chance, why not a town?" But he knew it wasn't the town he was talking about.

"I gave Tobias a thousand chances, because I had no choice. I was stuck here."

"Those weren't chances, those were expectations, always expecting the worst—and self-fulfilling prophesies being what they are, that's what you got."

"You've got the order wrong. That's what I got, so that's what I expected. And now look at what this town wants to do to Miss Trudi."

"You're not doing Miss Trudi any good by blaming the town, Annette. It's not Tobias trying to bully some poor old lady for the hell of it. There are serious issues. Bliss House is an eyesore that's costing the business owners and homeowners nearby. You think it's fair to them to have their business go under and their property values drop because she's failed at keeping that place in any kind of shape? And that's the hell of it—knowing how much she hates knowing she's failed at this. It sucks, but that's the truth."

God, when was the last time he'd spoken such unvarnished truth? When was the last time he'd simply come out and told someone what worried him?

Feeling oddly heady, he added, "And it's not going to get easier. It's just going to get harder."

Then he looked at Annette.

He swore under his breath. "Annette, don't... I didn't mean to be harsh—"

He reached to her, but she stood, moving away from him.

"No, it's not you. It wasn't what you said—well, it was, but not how you said it. That was...human and real and...refreshing."

"Nice to be refreshing." He chuckled and earned a watery smile in return, though it edged toward wariness when he came closer.

"It's what you said about Miss Trudi and what a mess she's in." She crossed her arms at her waist, not looking at him. Her breasts rose and fell as her breathing quickened.

The motion visibly pushed her nipples against the fabric of her top. "It's so impossible."

He stepped closer, demanding that she look at him. She did. Their eyes locked. He held the connection as he shook his head.

"Nothing's impossible."

Her gaze dropped from his eyes to his mouth. Her mouth softened. Then she slowly raised her lashes, revealing the rich brown by maddening increments. But what he saw there was worth any amount of excruciating wait.

He leaned into her, the force of that movement and of his mouth on hers opening her arms so nothing separated them but a few layers of clothes as he wrapped his arms around her waist. That was still too much between them—but so damned much better than the thousands of hours without touching her at all.

She spread her fingers across his cheeks, slid them into his hair, then stroked one hand across his shoulder before looping it around his neck—as if there were any chance he might pull away.

At Miss Trudi's the kiss had caught her by surprise—hell, it had caught him by surprise—but this one, this one they'd both seen coming. And neither of them had backed away.

The joy of that pounded in his head. He changed the angle of the kiss and stroked his tongue into her mouth, tasting her quick moan with fierce satisfaction. And then her tongue met his, matching its renewed exploration.

His hands at her waist brought her hips flush against him, then slid to her derriere to hold her even tighter. He wanted to fall into her, drive into her.

Slow, slow. His mind issued the order, intent on not letting his fierce need frighten or overwhelm her.

He wanted to hold her so he could rock against her in a

rhythm only they knew. Instead, he forced his hands to the small of her back, still holding her tight but the urging not quite so blatant. She made a sound deep in her throat as he slowly slid his open hands up the center of her back, feeling the rasp of her bra strap against his palm but imagining only the flow of her flesh. He cupped her head and kissed her long and deep. Then soft and slow.

There were infinite kisses between him and Annette. He wanted them all.

Eyes closed as he explored her taste, he traced with his thumb the remembered curve around the back of her ear, down to the turn of her jaw, along the decisive line of her chin. It seemed to him that if he could capture the true perfection of these curves, turns and lines he might hold the mysteries of the universe. At least his universe.

He released her mouth only long enough to slide his hands between them, pushing back the fabric that kept his touch from her.

Like a blanket of fire, a fierceness smothered all but his need of her. She was his. She had to know that.

Buttons fell before that need. He stroked his hands across her shoulders, carrying the straps of her bra down. His palm was cradled against her breastbone, sliding down to caress the full sweetness of her breasts. To take her into his mouth, to—

She jolted against him with a wordless cry. An ice shower would have been easier to ignore.

Holding her shoulders, he forced himself to straighten his arms to gain distance. Backed up against the side of the chair, she had her hands crossed over her breasts, her head down.

He swore in a stream under his breath.

"I can't, Steve."

"I'm pissed at me, not you." He touched her hair, a

silken brush against his fingertips, then dropped his hands to his sides and stepped back. "I'll get your coat and take you home—"

"You don't have to do that. I can call or—"

"I'm taking you to Max's, Annette."

He turned in the doorway. She'd already restored order to most of her clothes, though the third button down was still undone. The puffiness of her lips and the flush across her cheeks she could do nothing about. Thank God she didn't try to hide them behind that frosted glass.

"Do you want to know why I gave up swimming competitively in college?" he asked on impulse. "Because you'd come into my life."

Her brows dropped in puzzlement. "I never objected to you swimming or—"

"I'm not blaming you, Annette. I'm thanking you. Can't you hear the difference? In high school, when I was living at home, I needed the pool for the solitude. In the water for those long hours of practice I was totally alone. Totally myself. That's how I coped. Shutting out the world. But you showed me I didn't have to do that. Maybe I didn't learn as much as I could have, but I started."

He walked out of the room to retrieve their coats, and with any luck to retrieve his control, too. He wanted her. Bad. He felt the aching proof of that. But was he prepared for what was at risk if this had gone any further?

He handed her the coat instead of holding it for her to put on. Not trusting himself to come that close, or to set her mind at ease? Hell if he knew.

With his jacket on, he turned to find her fiddling with the end of her scarf.

"I'm glad if anything we…if our being together helped you in any way. Very glad." Her head came up on those last two fierce words. "But it doesn't change— I wasn't fair just now, and I'm sorry. But I want to be clear about—'' The end of the scarf made a tight circle in the air as she gestured. "I didn't say anything before—I mean, when you kissed me at—''

"We kissed each other.''

''—Miss Trudi's, that was sort of, um, sealing what we'd said.'' She pulled her coat on with quick, jerky motions. "That we'd made peace. But this—''

"That kiss had nothing to do with sealing a statement or making peace. And neither did this. I'm an ass for pushing too hard and too fast, but I'm not going to pretend I didn't want this and more. And I think you do, too. I hope you do.''

She was shaking her head. "If I'd thought you were misinterpreting—''

"I didn't misinterpret.'' He gestured for her to precede him toward the door. "I had the complete and full translation from the way you felt and the way you touched me. And you didn't say anything because you didn't know what to say.''

She looked at him, then immediately away. "Yes, well... Now I do. This can't—won't—happen again.''

"You can say *can't*. I won't say *won't*.''

Even if he should.

Driving all his life in Wisconsin had benefits. Like even though the snow was coming down with determination and the plows were just starting their rounds, he knew how to drive in the stuff well enough that he had plenty of concentration left over to ask himself what the hell had gotten into him.

Maybe it wasn't such a benefit.

He knew what got into one part of his anatomy. But what about his head? Even if they somehow got over what happened—a damned big if—the fact remained that she'd be leaving in a month. No. Half of that. Two weeks and two days before Juney was back on the job.

So what kind of hell was he letting himself into by getting all tied up about her again? Those first months after...

Her voice coming abruptly in the silence of the car brought a stirring not only in his groin, but in the nerves up the back of his neck and along his arms. And that was a kind of answer to his question. Not one he liked.

"Was it a surprise to you that Lily was pregnant?"

The meaning took longer than the sound to register, and then she had his complete attention. He cut her a look. She wanted the answer to be yes. Would that make a difference? Win him a pardon?

"Where does that question come from?"

She looked out her window. "You'd been seen together. You and Lily. A few weeks before the wedding."

"Ah." The gossips had run to her. Damn. *Damn.* If he'd known that... But even if he'd known, could he have reassured her with a partial truth? Giving her the whole truth then had been so far outside his view of their roles that wondering about it now was a hypothesis without any basis in reality—useless to consider.

"*Ah?* Is that all you're going to say?" She was ticked, but with a sort of ironic amusement, too.

"No. I'm going to say that the timing was interesting, don't you think?"

"What does that mean? The timing was interesting?"

"The timing—Lily and I were seen together a few weeks before the wedding. You told me before that you knew who and what and when. But did you?"

She didn't see the significance, that was clear. He could tell her. Tell her all of it. But... *Two weeks and two days.*

"But that isn't what you asked, is it?" For *this* answer,

he wouldn't tell her *later*. That was the best he could do. ''Was I surprised when Lily came in to the church and announced she was pregnant? I was damned surprised she burst into the church. But, no, I wasn't surprised she was pregnant. I already knew that.''

Stupid. Entirely stupid to feel such disappointment. Just because he'd kept the rings… Just because her hormones…

Oh, God, she'd wanted him. Right there, right then.

But chemistry had led her astray before. From the earliest days of their dating, she'd had doubts—Steve Corbett and poor little Annette Trevetti? Come on. But never when he touched her. As simple as holding her hand, as tender as kissing her, as powerful as making love with her—she had never doubted the sincerity of his feelings when he had touched her.

And she'd been wrong.

Maybe he had loved her in his own way, but not in the way she had needed. Not so completely that he didn't want another woman.

And that memory had materialized just in time. A few minutes longer, another stroke of his tongue in her mouth, another slide of his hand over her skin, another— But there hadn't been. Because she had remembered. Remembered more than her desire for him.

Of course he'd known Lily was pregnant. How could he have been so calm in the church if he hadn't known?

Yet, she had seen him calm in other moments of great distress. When Zach left, Steve had clamped down. Even though she knew he was concerned about Zach, he hadn't talked about it.

She frowned. That wasn't entirely true.

It'll be okay, Annette. It's another of Zach's rebellions, but everything will smooth over by the wedding. Don't worry.

Why can't you rebel? Annette had thought. Then squelched it as disloyal. Now she recognized that she'd been wrong. Steve didn't make a show of rebelliousness, he simply lived his life. Not an easy task for a son of Lana Corbett. As Zach's taking off showed.

Another thought hit her. She had never again asked Steve about Zach.

Why not? She'd known he was worried about his brother. If it came to that, why hadn't she asked him about all the things that had bothered her—the wedding, the sense they were drifting apart, her uncertainty that she could live in the world of the Corbetts. That he truly loved her.

Snapshots of the weeks leading up to the wedding pin-wheeled through her—not visual snapshots, but emotional ones.

She hadn't asked him because she hadn't wanted to acknowledge those questions and feelings, much less deal with the answers.

He was right. Suz was right. She had wanted to be protected. She had had hard knocks early, and Max had tried to cushion her from them. She loved him for that, but it also had taught her to expect other people to protect her.

She picked up those emotional snapshots one by one. She had known Lana did not approve of their marriage, but as with Zach's departure, she had not asked Steve about it, instead letting him—no, expecting him to—deal with his mother. In fact, she'd been disappointed in him for not insisting Lana leave their wedding alone when she hadn't stood up for herself. Even after her outburst about Max not being in the wedding, *poor little Annette* backed down. She had been a champion ostrich.

Had been. Past tense.

That was one unforgettable lesson from the disaster at their wedding—to face facts, because turning her back let them sneak up and grab her around the throat. She'd put that lesson to use in forming, running and selling Every Detail. In a way, she had Steve and their aborted wedding to thank for making her business a success. Although she had not been doing such a great job of facing facts since she'd come to Tobias. Especially when it came to Steve.

All in all, she had been wrong about Steve just about every step of the way.

First she'd thought he was perfect. The person she had looked to to protect her, to reassure her, to lead her…maybe even to define her. Then, in a handful of moments, he had turned out not to be the person she had built him up to be. For seven-and-a-half years she had defined him by how he had failed her. For failing her she had stripped him of all his strengths. She'd been wrong. And unfair.

He was a decent man with many good qualities. She could cooperate with him for Miss Trudi's benefit. Respect his good qualities. Even acknowledge an attraction as a result of those flashback hormones.

But she knew better now than to let it go any further. He'd taught her to face the facts. She'd grown past the stage where she could be devastated by a man—*this* man—disappointing her. Again.

"Sorry I can't give you better news." Rob Dalton's voice came over the speakerphone. "Hope it's not too unpleasant a surprise."

Steve had called and asked if she wanted to join his discussion with Rob. One part of her—cautious, *not* scared—wanted to say no. Another part noted that, considering the lectures she'd given him on accepting help, she should encourage this overture. So here she was at his office on this snowy Monday afternoon.

"Surprise, no," Steve said.

"I'm not saying we couldn't do it," Rob added, "but I don't see how it will get enough money to restore that house. What about other avenues?"

Steve had Annette fill Rob in on their conclusion that tax breaks from historical status wouldn't do much good without having money in the first place. Historic property loans had too many strings, or weren't big enough, or both.

"What about a local bank? Could we get a better reverse mortgage here?" Annette asked.

"No way Remtree will match the figures I gave you, Annette, much less do better. If you're interested, we better do it soon. I'm thinking about taking a page out of your book and returning home for good."

She didn't look toward Steve as she said, "I'm not back here for good, Rob. As soon as Max doesn't need me any more, I'll be considering all my options."

"Oh, I thought… I, uh… With selling your company, I thought you might be in the same boat as me, with nothing to keep me here. If I didn't have a buddy going through hell right now…" Rob changed the subject.

As soon as he'd disconnected, Steve said, "You're not considering all your options if you rule out Tobias."

"We're here to talk about Miss Trudi's options. Not mine."

He held her gaze for an extra count. "You hate it when I'm right. Okay, okay. What else is on our list?"

Max had said she didn't need to come inside Town Hall while he submitted materials for the Dunwoody building permit and checked Bliss House's files. But Annette had finished at the bank and had sat in the parked car long enough to be chilled, so she decided to check on him. Maybe he'd found something useful.

Inside the main door a high-pitched sound hit her ears. Another few seconds and she'd reached the door to the permits section. She encountered a moving, squirming, chattering groundcover of children. Trent Lipinsky cowered behind the counter. Max and two women stood amid the fray.

Annette retreated two steps before Nell squirted out of the mass, calling her name. Nell took her hand and led her to the bench at the base of the main stairway, talking all the while.

They were on a field trip, Nell said, but she already knew all this stuff, since her daddy was in charge of the whole town hall.

Apparently Nell's thoughts shifted to a topic she didn't know everything about, because her next words were, "Can I ask you somethin'?"

Annette eyed Nell with resignation. "Sure."

"You knew my mom, right? Did she love my daddy?"

Who knew a child's question could land such a blow to the gut? Had Lily acted out of love? Or spite? Or something else entirely?

"When they were in high school," Annette said carefully, "they were the most popular couple. They were king and queen of homecoming. They drove in a red convertible in the parade, and your mother wore a blue sweater just the color of her eyes. She was dazzling." Steve had looked uncomfortable but determined.

Nell was interested in the stories, though not as enthralled as Annette might have expected.

"Do you know my uncle Zach? He went away, and I never met him."

He went away. Such a simple phrase for something so

complicated. She and Steve had been sitting on the front porch drinking iced tea after playing tennis. Zach had come storming out, followed by Lana, with red blotching her neck and cheeks and her movements fast and jerky. Zach had thrown out accusations that Annette only half heard. But she remembered Lana's words.

"You have an obligation to the name Corbett in this town, and if you can't live up to it, then you shouldn't carry it."

"No problem, Mother," Zach had shouted as he pounded down the steps to his motorcycle. "No problem at all."

Her expression impassive, Lana had watched Zach leave, then went inside with the roar still echoing. She never acknowledged Steve by so much as a glance.

But none of that had disturbed Annette as much as the pale stillness of Steve's face when she'd turned to him. "Steve…"

"We'll talk about it later."

But they hadn't. Like so many things then. And she hadn't asked.

"So is he?" Nell demanded. Her eyes glittered. "Is he really a pirate?"

"I don't know what Zach's doing now, but I very much doubt he's a pirate."

"That's what Caitlin said her best friend's mother said." She clearly preferred that explanation. "My Uncle Zach was a pirate and a real wash bucket."

A *wash bucket?* A pirate and a *real wash bucket?* Aha! "Swashbuckler? Is that what Caitlin said?"

"I guess." But Nell was on to other matters. "Did you know he brought a dog into Grandmother's house? A muddy dog." Her eyes grew wide, but an impish smile overtook the expression. "With big muddy paws. The whole downstairs—even the music room—and all the way upstairs. That's what Fran said."

Annette had the oddest certainty that Nell was plotting how she could reprise this feat. Nell was fortunate that the flair for the dramatic she'd inherited from Lily was tempered by Steve's good sense.

The child heaved a sigh. "I want to meet Uncle Zach. He sounds *so* fun."

"I'm sure you would like your uncle Zach very much. But you know your dad is pretty spectacular, too. Did you know he was a state swimming champion? And when he raced, it was so exciting."

Annette didn't have time to wonder at her defense of Steve's excitement quotient to his daughter because Nell peppered her with questions.

As she finally ran out of steam, her classmates were emerging from the permits office. She scooched close to Annette and said, "My daddy's neat, isn't he?"

Impulsively, Annette put her arm around the girl. "Yes, he is."

She couldn't have said what surprised her more, her own words, Nell's response of flinging her arms around Annette's neck or how good it felt.

Steve stepped back so the corner at the top of the stairs provided cover.

Annette and Nell sat together on the bench at the bottom. He'd been about to wave to attract their attention over the growing noise of the second grade field trippers. He'd come to collect the class and lead them upstairs. How Annette came to be there he didn't know but took it as a pure bonus.

Then Nell had cuddled close and Annette had put her arm around her, and they had hugged.

He felt as if his body were trying to go in two directions

at once. His throat constricted, and his heart gave an outsize *ka-thump* in his chest. But at the same time his stomach clenched and his head pounded.

Maybe it's more important that you tell the truth than that you hear it.

Twelve days until she left.

What would she take with her? His heart? Nell's?

The truth?

Having hit a wall in trying to come up with the total figure Max had set for making Bliss House livable, Annette had suggested they try a different approach.

So that Tuesday night, while Max was at a brick mason's birthday party, she and Steve sat at Max's kitchen table trying to schedule a five-year plan of work based on the funds Miss Trudi had. So far, the house was going to fall down before the rewiring could be finished.

"God, this is impossible." She pushed her hair back as she raised her head from the column of uncooperative figures.

"Then go ahead and give up. Why not leave? It's what you plan to do in the end anyway. And you've proven you're good at it."

Annette had been getting up to get them both more decaf when he started that little speech. One sentence into it and she stopped, staring at him.

Steve had been edgy since he'd walked in. If he rearranged the three pens on the table one more time she might scream. Triangles, Fs, lines, Is, Us and a V and a half. At first she thought his mood had something to do with the other night at his house when they'd kissed and she'd stopped them from... But he hadn't been this way at his office talking to Rob.

Whatever it was, she'd been careful to keep this meeting

strictly on topic. Well, not any more. No more kid gloves. In fact, the gloves were off.

"Odd how finding out at her wedding that her groom got another woman pregnant will send a girl running in the opposite direction. And if there'd been any doubt, any sliver of daylight left, well, you slammed the door good and hard when you married Lily."

"I married Lily because it solved a lot of problems. Besides, I had no reason not to marry her. You'd left me."

He seemed oddly at ease now, as if a decision had been made, and that made her angrier.

"You're blaming *me?* You're saying my absence was the reason you married Lily? When my presence hadn't stopped you from getting her pregnant? And you knew she was pregnant. So what were you doing, weighing up until the end which of us to marry? Was I supposed to feel special because you were going through with our wedding and all you did was sleep with Lily and get her pregnant?"

"I didn't sleep with Lily that spring or any time you and I were together."

She crossed her arms. "Right. And how do you explain Lily giving birth to your daughter without—"

"She's not my daughter."

"—your sleeping with her."

The two phrases echoed in the suddenly silent kitchen.

She's not my daughter. How could Steve say that? If she'd ever seen a man who adored his daughter…

He slowly raised his head, revealing his face inch by inch.

All shadow had cleared his eyes, and she could see into them. The blue and the gray together, steady, balanced. His gaze met hers, open and direct. The look that had always had her believing. Whatever he said now would be the truth.

Chapter Ten

"Nell is not my biological daughter. I didn't sleep with Lily that spring. I didn't get her pregnant. I didn't cheat on you."

Annette sat down. Hard.

She didn't remember reaching for the chair or even considering if one was there.

"But...but how? She looks like you."

That wasn't what she wanted to ask, wasn't what she wanted to know. But she couldn't channel all her questions into anything except a big, jumbled, howling *why,* a word too small and a question too large.

"Zach is Nell's biological father."

"Zach." She wasn't questioning what Steve said because she hadn't taken it in. She repeated the word to make sure her mouth was working.

"He and Lily had a thing going that spring before he left town."

"He told you?"

"Not directly. But I knew. Even before Lily came to me. That—"

"Wait—Lily came to you? Before the wedding?" Those weeks when people had seen them together and had been oh, so eager to tell her that Steve was seeing his high-school girlfriend again. "So you knew before the wedding what she planned—"

"No!" he roared.

She couldn't ever remember Steve raising his voice, and certainly not to her. But what surprised her the most was how unsurprised *he* seemed. He resumed, his voice strained but at its usual volume.

"I had no idea she would do that. I thought it was all taken care of. A couple weeks before the wedding—that was, what, three months after Zach took off—she came and asked me if it was true that we didn't know where Zach was or how to get hold of him. Of course, none of us knew then that Zach was gone for good. When I said it was true, she became...upset."

"What did she say, Steve?"

"Among other things," he said slowly, "that she was damned if she was going to be left taking care of a kid on her own. She would sue the family, she would drag Zach's name through the mud. She would bring the Corbetts down—that was a favorite phrase.

"I told her the baby was a Corbett, and the family would stand by her. I gave her money to make sure she got the right prenatal care, things like that. And I promised we'd keep helping her—financially and otherwise. She wanted a legal document. Right away. I told her we could get something drawn up, but not until after—" he closed his eyes for an instant "—you and I were married."

"That's when you were seen with Lily. When she made her demands."

"Yes. That's what I meant the other night about the timing—I was seen with her so close to the wedding, but her baby had to have been conceived months before. Nobody saw me with her then, because I was always with you."

Annette was trying to take it in. Trying to keep her thoughts from speeding after one implication, only to dash off in pursuit of another. Trying to break it into basic facts. She stood, needing to move. From the refrigerator to the door to the sink and back.

Nell was Zach's daughter.

Lily had lied when she burst into their wedding.

Steve hadn't been two-timing her, cheating on her, running around on her—all the phrases Annette had tormented herself with.

"...still trying to find Zach. I hired several detectives," Steve said. "We were under the gun because Lily's due date was getting close. She'd made it clear she had to be married to a Corbett or she would keep the baby away from us and make any legal fight public and ugly. Not only for Zach, but for the baby."

"Did your mother know?"

"No. I thought it would be best for the baby. I kept thinking about you. Kept seeing your face...."

She stopped pacing to look at him.

"When you talked about growing up without a father. And I kept thinking about this baby Lily was carrying. Lily couldn't deal with life, much less motherhood. This baby wouldn't have the kind of mother you had, sure wouldn't have a big brother like Max."

But the baby did have Steve Corbett.

I married Lily because it solved a lot of problems. Besides, I had no reason not to marry her. You'd left me.

If she'd stayed… If he'd told her—

"But…but then you knew. At the wedding, when I asked you—you knew Lily was pregnant with Zach's child. All you had to say was it wasn't your baby, and we would have been married."

Even as she said the words, a discordant jangle scraped along her nerves.

"Was that all I had to say? No, I'm not the father of Lily's baby? Would we have been married? Would you have stayed? I sure didn't get that impression standing at that altar with you."

"What was I supposed to think when Lily said she was carrying your baby and you said nothing—nothing!"

His mouth formed a faint, rueful smile, though his eyes remained stormy gray. "I hoped you wouldn't think. I hoped that you loved me enough to trust me. To believe in me."

"Love doesn't mean you stop thinking, Steve. And I remember that day so clearly. I didn't move when Lily came in, or when she said the baby was yours, or even when you didn't immediately say it wasn't. It was when you wouldn't answer me. When you said we'd talk about it later."

"You think I didn't know that you'd already convicted me? You weren't asking a question, you were demanding a guilty plea."

"How could you possibly know what I—"

"Your face, Annette. Your beautiful, emotional face. You hid nothing. It was part of what I loved about you. I knew where I stood. I knew you were doubting me, *us,* in the weeks leading up to the wedding. Until, at the end, you closed off from me, and I had no idea how to reach you."

She stopped pacing, staring at the kitchen window for a

full minute before she realized the pale woman with the lost look reflected there was herself.

"I...I want you to leave now, Steve."

The pause was long enough to make her wonder, then she heard the scrape of his chair being pushed back slowly.

"Okay. There's one thing, though. You said sometimes it's more important to tell the truth than to hear it. And maybe that's so. But sometimes it's just as important to hear it."

She listened to him taking his jacket from the back of the chair and putting it on while her thoughts whirled and clashed. But she grabbed onto that word *truth* and held on. The discord she'd felt earlier suddenly made sense.

"Steve." He stopped at the doorway, not turning. "You were right before—if you'd answered me at the wedding, everything wouldn't have been okay. By the time Lily walked into that church, the foundation between us had revealed its flaws. You wanted my unthinking faith, and I wanted your unthinking protection. We were propping each other up. That's not a real partnership. And it surely wouldn't have been much of a start to a marriage. Everything turned out for the best."

He said nothing for a moment. Then he faced her. The bedrock structure of his bones stood out as if the skin had suddenly been stretched tighter. His voice came low and tight. "There's nothing better in my life than Nell, so I'll take Nell coming to me any way fate wanted to do it. But I'll be damned if I'll agree that your walking out of our wedding means everything turned out for the best."

Annette pulled the collar of her coat up to add a layer of warmth to the scarf around her throat and dug her gloved hands deeper into her pockets.

It was darned cold for a parade. So why was she smiling

and cheering for the third flotilla of green crepe-paper-festooned bicycles to go by? And so disappointed by a gap in the parade that she was on her tiptoes looking down the empty street, eager for the next group.

Especially since she'd been manipulated into attending by Max.

He'd walked into where she was on the computer, already wearing his jacket and carrying her coat. "C'mon, let's go. The parade's going to start soon."

"Parade? It's two forty-five on a Wednesday afternoon."

"Yeah, and it's St. Patrick's Day."

"Since when does Tobias have a St. Patrick's Day parade, and since when does someone named Trevetti care?"

"Since Steve started one a few years back, and since my kid sister needs to get out of the house and quit moping."

She wasn't moping. She just had a lot to think through. Alone.

It wasn't until closer to dawn than midnight that it had hit her that she had never once questioned whether what Steve had told her was true. She knew it was. She sat up in bed, wrapping the comforter around her as she stared at the fragmented moonlight on the wall.

How was that for irony? Steve had needed her belief seven-and-a-half years ago. He had it now.

She needed no proof. No DNA test. Nothing more than Steve telling her he was not Nell's father. But if he had said those same words at the wedding would she have believed? *Could* she have believed, as the person she was then?

"I am not mo—"

"Okay, brooding. Are you going to drive or am I?"

"I'm coming, I'm coming. And I'm driving. You know what the doctor said."

So here she was. Hearing how Steve had instigated several kids-only after-school parades, with the kids voting to choose which ones to do each year.

She heard that not only from Max, but from numerous people who stopped to chat as they waited for the parade to restart. The route circled two big blocks downtown, keeping the spectators in a compact area. She considered that coziness a benefit with the temperature dropping as the late-afternoon sun lost power.

She rethought her position on coziness when Steve showed up and the crowd pressed him in close to her. He said hello and met her eyes for one instant that left her chest burning and her stomach rocking. Then he focused on Max.

At one point last night she had thought it might be easiest to cut all contact with him for her remaining time in Tobias. Juney would return, and she could go back to her life and forget all this. That was where the thought had broken down. She hadn't forgotten before; she had frozen events in her heart. Better to deal with it now than to carry another lump of ice around. Besides—

"There's still the matter of Miss Trudi," Steve said abruptly from beside her, as if picking up the thread of a conversation or as if he'd read her dark-of-night thoughts. "We haven't made much progress. If you're still willing…"

"When?" she said as if they were business associates and she might pull out a PDA any second to check her calendar.

"I've got meetings all day tomorrow and a full schedule Friday, but Friday evening at my place would work." He glanced at her then at the parade. "Nell is going to be at a sleepover."

It sounded more like a warning than an invitation. She could issue warnings, too. "With so little time before I leave, if Friday is all you have, then Friday will have to do."

He grunted—warning received and understood.

A snowflake dive-bombed her nose. She looked up to find more zipping around like they didn't know whether to go up, down or sideways.

"It's snowing."

"It always does for the St. Patrick's Day parade," Steve said. Would anyone else recognize the strain beneath his seemingly casual comments? He didn't look as if he'd slept, either.

"Always? You've only had the parade for a few years."

"A few years is always for these kids."

Someone called Steve's name. He gave her another searching look and a would-be offhand nod before working his way through the crowd.

But he left behind that sentence. *A few years is always for these kids.* She doubted he'd considered it profound, yet it kept running through her head as the parade restarted.

She found herself calculating. Easily half of the kids trooping, skipping, biking and marching past her hadn't been born or had been far too young to have cared about the circumstances of her departure from Tobias. Subtract the ones who had been toddlers or younger when she left for college, and there were maybe a smattering of upper-classmen from the high school band who might have heard of poor little Annette Trevetti. And how many of them would remember or care?

In their *always,* Annette Trevetti hadn't even lived in Tobias. It was a startling thought, and freeing. An entire parade through the heart of Tobias, and she was a stranger to virtually all of them.

Of course the adults were a different matter. She scanned

the spectators' faces across the street then craned her neck to look around where she and Max stood.

"Something wrong?" he asked.

"No…except maybe me. Never mind," she added at his puzzled frown. "Everything's fine." She recognized a third of the adults.

Maybe a town was like a snake, shedding its skin every so often. Or maybe it was more like that saying about how a human being replaced all its cells in seven years. So each cell had its own short "always" that wasn't recognized by the larger organism.

"Here comes Nell."

She jumped and turned to find Steve at her shoulder again, his face so close she could see distinct flecks of blue and gray like snowflakes swirling in his eyes. Her lips parted. His gaze dropped to her mouth, and instead of getting any sound out, she sucked in a breath.

"Uh-oh."

Max's grunt had her spinning around, away from Steve and temptation. Max wasn't looking at them, he was watching the parade. She became aware that the crowd, while clapping and cheering, was also drawing back from the street, opening a wider path for the marchers.

She saw Nell and five of her friends, dressed in green from head to toe, tossing sparkling sticks into the air, which mostly landed on the ground nowhere near their throwers, who darted after the sticks and tried to scramble into a line that continually dissolved as the other marchers pursued errant throws.

"What on earth?"

"Baton twirling," Steve said, removing his gloves to clap louder. "First time any of them has held a baton."

The two girls at the back of the line, apparently tired of chasing their batons, started gently tossing them to each other. They still missed now and then, but they didn't have as far to chase them.

"But…but they had all those practices."

"They practiced forming straight lines—mostly standing still since there wasn't room to march in anyone's house. And then they ate and giggled."

Laughing, she asked, "Why didn't you let them practice with batons?"

But the laughter hid a surge of emotion that had rocked her. Respect, admiration, affection…that was all. Affection. How could anyone not feel that for a man who would raise his brother's daughter as his own to protect her? In the long dark hours of thinking, she had separated that thread from the tangle and set it aside. Whatever Steve—and she—had done wrong more than seven years ago, she knew his every action regarding Nell had been guided by wanting to do what was best for the child. She could not second-guess him there.

"Are you kidding? Would you want them throwing those things around your house? That a girl, Nell! Way to go!"

Nell beamed at the wild applause she received for catching the baton neatly on the first bounce. Annette joined the cheering, trying not to laugh.

There were only two more groups before a band brought up the rear, playing "When Irish Eyes Are Smiling."

Steve remained at her shoulder as she and Max headed toward her car. A trio of women around her age passed them, saying hello to Max and Steve. In quick introductions, Steve said they were all teachers at the high school.

"Hey, Max, will we see you at the Toby tonight for the St. Patrick's Day party?" asked one. "We've missed you these past few weeks. And now that you have a broken wrist I might finally beat you at darts."

Max's brows knit as he looked toward Annette, "I don't know if I'll—"

"He'll be there," she interrupted, careful not to catch Steve's eyes. "Can't have him moping around the house."

Hell, if Steve had known that the way to get Annette to mix into what passed for Tobias nightlife was to make her think she was doing Max a favor, he would have bribed Trevetti weeks ago to come to the Toby.

The Toby served simple meals and provided standard bar entertainment in addition to drinks. Max didn't come often enough to have a set pattern, but his being there didn't surprise anyone, either. Steve stopped in mostly to pick up the conversation, which told him more about how the town and county were running than a dozen formal reports.

Tonight, the crowd was bigger and more boisterous than usual in honor of the holiday. He had no opportunity to talk to Annette alone even after she moved from the dart board and found a relatively quiet corner to listen to the local band playing Irish songs. Four downtown merchants surrounded Steve to talk about the need to build their out-of-town customer base for the non-summer months. Since they weren't telling him anything new, he felt no compunction about breaking away after a few minutes and heading toward Annette.

"Nice to see you giving Tobias a chance."

"I couldn't let Max disappoint the folks wanting to beat him at darts, could I?"

"Not just here. The parade. You seemed to have a good time."

With so little time before I leave... That's what she'd said. Had she realized she'd said it that way? Almost as if she would regret leaving? That had to mean something, didn't it?

"I did. Nell has true star power." The corners of her mouth started to lift in a grin that went flat when she met his gaze. "Stop it. Stop worrying I'm going to treat her any differently. She's herself, and that's all that matters."

How had she known? Having his emotions read when he wasn't consciously telegraphing them was rare. Hell, he'd flat-out told her he was nuts about her back when they were first dating, and look how long it had taken her to believe that. And when push came to shove, she hadn't believed it enough.

"I didn't really worry. Well, maybe some. I told you, I'm not entirely rational about her."

"I know." Her voice softened. "She couldn't have a better father."

He swallowed against the sudden bite in his throat. Not just her words, but the warmth in her eyes. A man could live the rest of his life in that look.

"Do you think he knew?"

He tried to make sense of her words—hard to do when watching her lips form the words was so fascinating. "Who knew what?"

"Zach. That Lily was pregnant."

"Lily said he didn't. I hope to God she told the truth about that."

"Where do you think he is?"

"I don't know. If he's okay, he doesn't want to be found. All the detectives came up empty. No answer to the ads that run every few months in papers across the country."

Her eyes changed, reflecting what he feared she'd heard in his voice—his worry that Zach might not be contacting his family because he couldn't.

He touched the green scarf looped around her throat, wishing it was her skin. Sliding his fingertips through the folds of silk, he stepped closer, needing to taste the warmth and concern he saw in her face.

She stepped back, covering his hand with hers, using gentle but firm pressure to end his caress.

"I can't…I'm not sure I can…"

At arm's length, he cupped the back of her arm and stroked down it.

"What? Forgive? I'm not asking for forgiveness, Annette. And I'm not offering it. We did what we did based on who we were then. We're different people now. I see it in you so clearly, and I know I'm different. I just hope you can see it in me. And that we can go on from there."

Aware of a knot of people approaching, he dropped his arm and stepped back from her.

Greetings and chatter surrounded them. Max looked from one to the other of them with a frown, but said nothing. Ten minutes later Annette and Max left.

Steve waited fifteen minutes more to leave. In the parking lot, standing beside his SUV, he hunched his shoulders against the biting cold and looked up at the hazy moon. A howling moon, Zach used to say.

He'd once asked his brother to define what kind of moon was a howling moon. "All of them," Zach had said.

He'd never understood Zach's taste for the wild side. But for all their differences, Zach was his little brother. That's why he'd felt he had to say something after he'd seen Zach and Lily coming out of a motel over spring break. Months earlier he'd spotted them together on campus, but he'd been so lost in Annette he hadn't thought much of it.

But this was different. Not only because it was a less-than-reputable motel, but Zach had had his arm slung around Lily's shoulders, and she'd had her hand on his chest, looking at him. Wheedling him for something, if he knew Lily.

When he heard Zach in the hall that night, he'd opened his door.

His brother gave a fair performance of an amused sigh, but even in the dim light Steve had seen him tense. "I thought I recognized your car passing the motel. So what are you going to do? Tell me the facts of life?"

Torn between wanting to steer Zach clear of danger and knowing the more he said the less Zach would listen, he'd settled on the all-encompassing, "Be careful."

Zach grinned without easing. "Too late. Don't worry, big brother. I didn't go into this blind. I knew she really wanted you. She thought going after me would get to you. I also knew it wouldn't get to you. I even tried to tell her that—can you believe it? Zach Corbett being gallant? But she didn't believe me. Even swore it was me she'd always been crazy about." He shook his head. "Oh, I know, Saint Steven would have resisted temptation. But nobody's ever accused me of being a saint. There are benefits to being the fallen Corbett. Definite benefits."

They had never talked about Lily again before Zach's blowup with their mother. There'd been scenes leading up to that final one. Some Steve had simply sensed. But one he'd come in on the tail end of. They had been in the small office near the kitchen where Lana wrote notes and read the paper.

He'd heard snatches. About how she was making the best of this inferior marriage Steve insisted on. About how it remained up to Zach to carry the Corbett family banner.

"This is more fitting, anyway. I had hopes for Steven, but he always had disadvantages that you did not."

"I won't be your—"

"You have no choice, Zachary." She had cut across Zach's protest. "You are a Corbett, your father's son, and that is all there is to it."

That final morning, as Steve left to pick up Annette for tennis, he'd walked out and found Zach on the back porch, his head in his hands, his wrinkled clothes and beard stubble attesting to yet another night spent away from the house.

"She's already up," he'd warned his brother.

Steve had reached the bottom of the steps when Zach's voice came. Not loud. Almost as if he were talking to himself. But when Steve turned, Zach was looking at him.

"I always resented your being the frontline Corbett while I was second string. Be careful what you wish for, huh?" Zach had met his eyes for an instant, then looked down. "You can get out. You can take your Annette and get the hell out of here. All you have to do is give the door one hard shove, and it'll swing free."

Steve had thought about those words a lot after Zach left. *All you have to do is give the door one hard shove, and it'll swing free.* Except by the time Steve had proven to himself the existence of that door, Annette was gone.

With Lily about to give birth to Zach's child, marrying her had seemed the simplest way to protect the child and clear up the mess. At that point who he married hadn't mattered. Nothing had mattered much.

And then there'd been Nell. And everything mattered again.

Steve shuddered. What was he doing staring at the moon outside the Toby when he had a daughter to get home to? Whether he would ever have more than that, like a woman who loved him…well, he wouldn't mind a little Irish luck to help with that, no matter what his ancestry might really be.

Steve wadded up another sheet of yellow paper and sent it toward the fireplace. It went in like all but one of the others.

"I should have played basketball," he mumbled. "I sure as hell haven't done much in the way of problem solving tonight."

Neither of them had.

Annette cleared her throat. "There's one thing we haven't talked about yet."

His head came up, and those eyes pinned her. "There's a lot we haven't talked about."

"On my list." She swallowed and shifted in the wing chair in his living room. "One thing on my list. Whether Miss Trudi should stay in Bliss House. She doesn't belong in a nursing home and she doesn't want a retirement home. But say we do come up with a way to get the house restored to functioning status. What then? How long could she keep it that way? Could she afford it? Could she handle it physically? Does she want to devote the time and attention to keep up a house of that size and age—not to mention the grounds?"

"Good questions."

"Now all we need are answers to them, along with all the other questions."

She pushed her hair back, pulled in a deep breath, then glanced at him. She dropped her hands, and her inhalation hitched in the middle before coming out in a rush.

Steve wanted her.

She hadn't doubted his desire for her when they'd dated. But she had never seen such intensity in his face. Did he hide less than he used to? Was that part of the change in him he'd talked about? Did she read him better now that she had cleared some of the static of insecurity?

And she wanted him.

She wouldn't deny that. She just knew it wasn't that simple.

Twice yesterday the wheel spinning in her head had stopped at Talk About It, so she'd driven here. And twice, by the time she'd arrived, the wheel had moved on to Don't. The first time, he'd been outside with Nell, creating a snowman under the maple tree out front. He'd stilled, watching her car, watching her. The second time, no one was outside, yet she sensed he knew about that pass, too.

He hadn't said a word about it since she'd arrived nearly two hours ago.

"I told myself I wouldn't ask. I told myself it can't change the past so it doesn't matter," she said. "And it *can't* change the past, but it *does* matter. I can see your reasons for not telling me before the wedding, feeling you needed to protect me. Maybe even at the altar—the shock and your upbringing explain that. But you didn't come after me. I keep hitting that fact these past three days, and I'd like to know if I'm right about why—you were angry at me."

She had been so certain of her wounds for so long, she had not considered he might be angry at her, not until she'd come back to Tobias. And even then she hadn't stopped to consider if he had any cause.

"Every time I thought about going after you, I saw the ring on that desk. You took off my ring and just…left it there."

She opened her mouth then closed it. He knew what she had thought, and perhaps had some sense of what she'd felt. What had he been feeling? Shocked. Stressed by the wedding and Lily's demands and suspicions about his parentage. He shared it with no one because Steve Corbett was the golden boy. The handler of all problems. *Saint Steven. Even Steven.* And his family's approval—and what love he was given—was based on how well he adhered to the Corbett code.

No wonder he had craved unconditional love.

I hoped you wouldn't think. I hoped that you loved me enough to trust me. To believe in me. Instead, she had left his ring on the desk.

She didn't blame herself, and now she didn't blame him, either.

"Why did you want to talk to me that Thanksgiving after Lily died?"

"To set things straight. There's something about burying someone your own age that makes you want to settle accounts." He spread his hands on his thighs. "Hell, maybe I hoped it would make a difference."

"You could have told me as soon as I came to take care of Max."

"No, I couldn't. Not until I knew the person you are now. Because of Nell. I had a lot of time over the years to think about ways you might react. They weren't all pretty."

"Like?"

"Like you didn't believe me. At least not without proof, like DNA tests. Or you accused me of protecting the Corbett name at the expense of your feelings. You refused to have anything to do with the baby. You insisted that the truth be broadcast so everyone would know you hadn't been cheated on."

"The first few years…" She flipped her hand, dismissing it. "Now it's old news. How about you? You carry the label of getting another woman pregnant just before your wedding."

"Prince Charming as a cad, you mean?" He shrugged. "I didn't give a damn, especially after Nell was born. It was amazing. Astounding. The most… I held her in my hands." He opened his hands, looking at them. "Literally, in my hands. One under her head and one under her bottom. That's all it took to hold this life.''

Pressure in her throat and behind her eyes nearly caught her. ''Why tell me at all, then?''

''What you said about needing to speak the truth. And something else. What you said to Nell when you were talking about opera. *Losing him by discovering he doesn't love you the way you love him. By counting on him and then having him let you down completely.* You needed to know I never loved you less than completely. There wasn't anyone else. And I suppose I wanted to ask a question myself. Why you believed it without waiting to hear what I said— even if it did come later.''

''Because it was what I feared the most.'' That understanding had come in last night's deep, sleepless dark.

He turned toward her. ''That I would be unfaithful to you? Had I ever given you any reason—''

''Not just unfaithful. Lily. She was everything I wasn't. She was willowy and blond, knew the right fork and how to shop without looking at a price tag. She was part of your world—Wilbanks to your Corbett. While I was Cinderella, the girl who lived among the cinders but was all dressed up for a dance with the prince because of magic.''

''You were everything I wanted.''

''I was terrified, Steve. Of being a wife. Of being a Corbett.''

''You are everything I want.''

She gasped. Heat and longing were like a fireball that passed through her.

He stood, holding his hand out, steady and open. Not a dare this time, but a declaration.

She was shaking her head, but she put her hand into his, palm to palm, and let him draw her up. ''Steve...''

''I screwed up, and you screwed up, and we screwed up.

We can see it and we can let ourselves and each other off the hook, even though we can't take back what happened. That will always be there. But this isn't the past. And it's not the future. It's now. It's the present, and that's what you left me, remember?''

He swooped in to kiss her, touching only mouth to mouth. Then not even that, as he ended the kiss.

He backed up a step, and another. There should have been pressure on her arm, but there wasn't. Because she was following him, and then she was beside him.

Upstairs they walked down a hallway into a simply furnished bedroom with a dark green bedspread across an acre of bed.

They sat side by side on the edge. For long moments they held each other. Then he stroked her hair and dropped kiss after kiss along her hairline. By some alchemy the sweetness of those kisses turned to fire in her bloodstream.

If he had laid her back then, taking her fast and hard, she would have met him gladly.

He didn't.

Still sitting beside her, he unbuttoned his shirt with deliberate, almost solemn motions. Pulled it from his waistband and dropped it to the floor. With the same deliberateness, he removed his shoes and socks, then started on his jeans.

A tear slid down her right cheek. Then another. A thread of moisture traced her right cheek, while the tears in her left eye welled and welled, yet did not fall.

He was offering himself to her. Physically, yes, but more. Exposing his nakedness without asking her to keep pace. Acknowledging beyond words how the events seven-and-a-half years ago had left her exposed.

Stripped, full evidence of his desire apparent, he stood beside her and bent to kiss her lightly on the lips. He took a packet from the bedside table and prepared to protect her in the way she needed protection.

No one had known how she had failed him because he held it all inside—which had been her failure.

No more.

She took his face in her hands and kissed his bottom lip. Then touched her tongue there. He groaned, igniting sizzling all along her nerve endings. She kissed him, open, hard, full, long.

She twisted, and he picked up the motion and amplified it, dropping to the bed just beyond her. Leaving her room to reach between them and touch him, rediscovering that broad line of muscle and sinew across his shoulders, the flat of his belly, the slope to his hips, the thrust below.

Her clothes were a nuisance she was satisfied to let him dispose of while she otherwise occupied herself. He muttered a protest when she bent to lick first one then the other brown disk on his hair-dusted chest. But she judged he didn't really mean it, because his body told another story.

Besides, he was turning about the fair play for all he was worth, touching everywhere. Some of it was to rid her— *finally*—of all her clothes, but not the slow, thorough strokes that had her panting and shivering. Then his mouth on her breast, flicking his tongue over her nipple, then sucking, so her back came off the bed. He slid his palm up her thigh.

"Yes," she said to the question his body asked.

He found his place between her legs, and she opened to him.

He looked into her eyes and slowed, pushing deeper inside her with maddening patience while the colors sparked and flamed in his eyes. At last he stilled. With reverential hands, he cupped her head, dropping one soft kiss after another on her mouth, her chin, her eyes, her brow, while the effort not to stroke sheened his face. She knew the strain of his effort to rein back by the tension of his muscles, by the rasp of his breathing.

Having him inside her was so *right*…and not yet right enough.

She lifted her hips to him, feeling the power and heat as a rolling explosion through her bloodstream, then experiencing it again when a groan rumbled through him.

He raised up on his arms, bracketing her head, trying to hold on to his control, to be contained. She balled up a fist and tapped the inside of his right elbow, knocking out his brace so he collapsed onto her. She wrapped her arms around his neck and for good measure wrapped her legs around his thighs, bringing him deeper.

"Annette—"

"Show me, Steve. Show me I'm everything you want."

He wasn't contained at all. He was around her and inside her and with her. Praising her, urging her, kissing her arched throat, rubbing the sweet friction of his chest against the taut tips of her breasts.

She was pushing against something. Trying to break through. And he was her only way out. Harder and faster. Straining and stroking. Pounding to be released. To… yes…yes.

"You are," he said. "Everything."

And a universe shattered into joy-sharp shards sparkling like crystals of ice raining around her.

Steve piled pillows behind his back as he sat in his bed looking forward to…ah, this moment. The moment Annette walked out of the bathroom wearing his shirt and only his shirt. It joined all the moments of the previous hours.

"Come here."

"That sounded like a Corbett, giving orders." But she smiled and sat on the edge of the bed beside him.

"Hey, watch it. I'm not a Corbett, but Nell is."

"Oh, you're a Corbett all right." He slid his hand up her thigh under the shirt, but she stopped his foray with a hand on his wrist, her eyes turning serious. "How are you going to tell her? That you're her biological uncle, not her father."

When he didn't answer, she searched his face. "Oh, Steve... You can't not tell her. I know she's young, but before she's much older, you have to tell her."

"What good will it do?"

"Steve, which hurt you more—knowing that Ambrose wasn't your biological father or knowing that your mother kept that a secret from you? Nell loves you so much, she'll know you love her."

"There's already so much she's had to deal with—the divorce and her mother's death." He stroked her hair and kissed her temple. "If she starts digging when she's older, she'll find out Lily had drugs in her system when she ran her car off the road. And her passenger was a known dealer. Why add any more that I don't have to? As long as everybody in town thinks I'm her father, why—"

"Because you know it's a lie. Keeping secrets is like poison, Steve. No matter how well you think you have it bottled up, there's always the danger of it spilling out. I'm sure your mother believes she has her secret locked up tight. But you found it. You don't think Nell will be as much of a digger as you are?"

"She's just a little girl."

"I know." She touched his cheek. "When would you have wanted to be told?"

Early. When he was too young to take it in too deep. So

he already accepted the fact of it before he dealt with the pain.

She was good. She was really, really good. She left him no place to hide from the truth.

"I don't mean to give you a hard time about this," she said as she stood.

He circled her wrist. She cooperated as he guided her onto the bed, bridging his lap as she knelt. "You're giving me a hard time, all right."

"Is that a fact?' The shirt covered her from her collarbone right down to his lap.

"A hard fact." He bent his knees, pulling away the sheet and bringing his thighs against her derriere.

She rested back against him. Without taking her eyes from his, she started unbuttoning the shirt. "Guess we'll have to do something about that."

He reached under the tail of the shirt, cupping her hips, drawing her down the descending slope of his thighs to the part of him straining to meet her.

"Steve—"

"I made good use of my time while I was waiting for you." He nodded toward the freshly emptied condom packet on the nightstand. "I had a feeling…"

He adjusted. She leaned forward.

And then the feeling was ecstasy.

She lightly kissed his jaw, then edged carefully away.

"What are you doing?" he asked, drawing her back with one easy movement.

"It's getting light, and I should go. Max might be wondering—"

"Max isn't wondering. He might come after me with a shotgun because he's not wondering. But I guarantee he's not wondering."

"Nell—"

"Is taken care of until after lunch. And—" he reached his other arm behind him to the nightstand, easily finding the large box "—look what I have here."

"Do you always keep the giant economy size?"

"Bought it special. You had to know I was hoping."

She kissed him. "You believe in the tooth fairy. And want cute little rodents to help you. Your hopes aren't grounded in reality. They're…"

He kissed her. And both their hopes were soon being realized to their fullest.

He started awake to the phone ringing. Annette was still curled in his arms. The first surge of joy at that shifted as his mind kicked in.

It was after ten. He wasn't supposed to pick up Nell until one, but if something had happened—

He snatched up the phone.

Something had happened, but it wasn't with Nell. Negotiations with the company that collected garbage had fallen apart overnight. Both sides were asking for him. He hung up with a promise to be there as soon as possible.

"Let me tell you about my glamorous life," he said, as he rolled over and took Annette's warm, soft body into his arms for one final second.

Even in Tobias, parents worried, so when the knock came at the back door Sunday afternoon, Steve said, "Nell, don't open the—"

But Nell, encased in her snow clothes in preparation for a rescue mission on her sinking snowman, opened the back door a split second after the knock and long before he could hoist himself off the couch. The negotiations had gone all

Saturday night and into the mid-morning hours, but they were done.

Now maybe he could catch up on his sleep…if he could figure out what to do about Miss Trudi and Bliss House. Not to mention how to keep Annette here.

"Hi, Annette! Wanna help me make my man hard?"

He relaxed into the couch and let the laughter come. He could imagine most people's reaction to that comment, but Annette took it like an old pro.

A minute later, the back door closed behind Nell, and Annette came in still wearing her coat but having left her boots by the door. She put down two bulging shopping bags with a thud that attested to their weight.

"Before you turn me in to child protective service, I can explain that comment of Nell's," he said.

Nell had been distraught when she came home after an extra night at her friend Laura Ellen's house to discover her snowman had shrunk. He'd suggested she put a thin coat of slush over him just before dark, so the colder night air would freeze it and he would be somewhat protected…and hardened.

"I'd love to hear that explanation, but not just yet. I have an idea." Her eyes were sparkling. "Do you want the supporting evidence or the broad outline first?"

"Broad outline."

She sat on the couch, not as close as he would have liked, but slewed around with her bent knee between them. That knee brushed his hip, and all he had to do to see her face was roll his head against the back of the sofa.

"Okay. Miss Trudi signs over the main house and three-quarters of the grounds to Tobias on a lifetime lease, with the property deeded to Tobias in her will. In return, Tobias renovates the carriage house as a new home for her, along with a stipend for her to live on."

He could see the advantages. Miss Trudi would be in a smaller, modernized home she could handle, yet on part of her beloved property, and wouldn't feel like a charity case. But Tobias would hold a white elephant.

"Don't get that look, Steve. Just listen. Tobias also renovates the grounds and main house, turning it into a crafts center. A showpiece that will be a draw and an outlet for those people you told Suz about that day at the grocery store. Tom Dunwoody's carvings and Muriel Henderson's knitting and Miriam Jenkins's quilting could be displayed—and sold. Maybe a tearoom in the kitchen, and the ballroom for talks or crafts demonstrations.

"Make Tobias a Mecca for people who love handmade items but don't make them. The whole town can play up the historic look—you've preserved the old buildings, so make use of them. Have festivals—Christmas and spring for sure. Make Tobias a destination for crafts, and make Bliss House the hub."

He was clicking over the possibilities, but there was one thing... "Would people buy things like quilts and baby blankets?"

She cupped her hand to his cheek. She was laughing at him, but who cared with the feel of her palm, soft and warm, against his face?

"Oh, my dear Steve, you have a lot to learn."

"Are you going to teach me?"

She touched her mouth gently to his. He felt the tip of her tongue line his bottom lip, and he opened to her immediately. "Yes," she breathed into his mouth. "I'm going to teach you."

As he was reaching to fold her in his arms, she jumped up and grabbed one of the shopping bags, tumbling stacks into his lap.

"Here's the start of your education. The magazines show

what our competition's doing, and the catalogues show exactly how much people are willing to pay for things like quilts and baby blankets.''

He was all for education, but there were limits. He pushed aside the reading material and pulled something much better into his lap—her. With Nell just outside, this could not reach the most satisfying conclusion. But with kisses and caresses, they rediscovered the tantalizing joys of an old-fashioned make-out session.

When Nell came in, she and Annette made hot chocolate while he lit a fire, then ordered pizza. In between, they looked through the material Annette had brought and talked about the potential of Bliss House. She included Nell, letting her thumb through the magazines and flag what she liked. Tired out by her snowman rescue efforts, Nell snuggled between the two of them on the couch. He put his arm around Annette, drawing both her and Nell closer.

Like a family.

Annette couldn't believe how fast this was all happening.

Monday morning she had dropped Max off at his work site then met Steve to sound out Miss Trudi. At first, she had inclined toward weepiness. But within a half hour of Annette hitting on the idea of pulling out the old photo albums, Miss Trudi was relishing restoring Bliss House to its glory. She'd also started a wish list for her new living space, headed by a dishwasher and modern bathroom.

They had shanghaied Max and spent the rest of the day at Steve's office, researching grant programs and figuring out an approach. Steve had worked his connections all day Tuesday, while she and Max roughed out a presentation.

And now, three days after she had taken her idea to Steve, she was waiting for him to arrive to go over everything a final time. He and Max, who was making rounds of his work sites with Lenny, were supposed to leave mid-afternoon for a full schedule of meetings with movers and shakers in the capital.

It had been exhilarating to see Steve's eyes light up with the flame of her idea Sunday. It also made her nervous. A lot was on the line. Steve had staked his prestige and accumulated goodwill in Madison on this project. What if it fell apart? What if her idea turned out to be lousy? What if—

Steve's SUV pulled into the drive. When she greeted him at the door, he was grinning and holding a packet of papers aloft in one hand. "Here they are."

"Steve, maybe we should reconsider this."

"No." He grabbed her with his free arm, curling her in close and kissing her hard. "It's a great idea. We've done a great job pulling it together in an amazingly short time, and I'm supposed to pick up your brother in three hours at the Hendersons' to head for Madison. You know what that means?"

"That we're crazy?"

He took her mouth again, stroking his tongue against hers with an unmistakable rhythm that had her holding on to his shoulders for balance.

"It means you and I have three hours." He tossed the papers on the counter and, still holding her, started unfastening his jacket. "Together. Alone." He kissed the side of her neck under her hair. They had carved out only enough time and privacy for a few kisses since Saturday. "We can spend it listening to you worrying. We can spend it eating lunch. Or we can put it to better use."

He dropped his jacket to the floor and started on his shirt, still exploring her neck and ear.

"Steve..." It came out breathless.

He yanked the tail of his shirt out of his pants. "Okay, okay, if you insist we can have something to eat…later."

He quirked a grin at that last word. His shirt fell at the threshold into the living room as he backed her up through the house. She was laughing in addition to being breathless. "You're making a habit of these stripteases."

He stopped dead, a ferocious frown crashing down. "Hey, you're right."

"Oh, no, what have I done? I didn't mean to make you stop."

"Stop, hell. I'm going to make sure we're even this time." He grabbed the bottom of her fleece pullover and bundled it up her body—with a few interesting sidetrips—and over her head.

She reciprocated with his undershirt. They helped each other out of shoes and socks on the far side of the living room. His pants and her jeans entwined on the floor of her once and present bedroom. He handed her the foil packet he'd snagged from his pocket so he could unhook her bra, then follow the departing fabric with tormenting hands that cupped and stroked her breasts.

He bent his head to take one peak he'd won into his mouth as she stroked his shoulders.

She tried to reach his briefs, but couldn't quite snag the fabric. He straightened, pressing their bodies together from knees to shoulder. She shuddered with delight…and resumed pushing down his briefs with more success, even though she still held the foil packet.

"Hey, we're supposed to be keeping this even," he protested, but stepped out of the fallen briefs.

"Then hurry up. I want you inside me."

She'd hardly finished the sentence when he cupped the back of her neck as he spun her and lowered her to the bed, covering her with his weight and warmth.

"There is no place I would rather be."

Together they pushed down her panties. She thought they might have torn. Too bad.

Together they fit the condom to him. At one point he stilled her hands, dropping his head back and muttering. She kissed, then licked his arched neck and he groaned. So good.

Then they shifted, wrapping their arms around each other. She opened, he stroked, and they were joined.

"If this doesn't work—"

"Don't worry, if we don't get what we want on this trip to Madison, we'll go back until we do. Or maybe we'll look elsewhere, but it will work."

She propped herself on one elbow to look at him. "You are a very misleading man, Steven Worthington Corbett. For all that *Even Steven* and *Saint Steven* stuff, you don't give up. You're quiet about it, so people miss how pig-headed you are."

"I prefer persistent."

"Persistent *and* pigheaded. I wonder… Is that what some of this is about?"

"This?"

She waved a hand, indicating their entwined bodies. "This. Us."

"You didn't seem to mind my, uh, persistence a little while ago."

Heat flowed as visible color up her body. He grinned and raised his head to kiss her shoulder. But she resisted the temptation. "I don't just mean this part of this. I mean, us revisited. The return of Annette and Steve."

"You think this is all based on me trying to prove a point?"

"I don't know." She pleated the sheet. "Wasn't some

of coming back to Tobias after college about proving a point for you? Proving that you can be your own man no matter what your family and this town's expectations are?''

Steve pushed himself up to sit against the pillows. Holding the covers over her, she twisted to meet his look as he said, ''Wasn't leaving Tobias about proving a point for you? Proving that you can be your own woman on your own terms no matter what this town's expectations of you might be?''

''Touché,'' she acknowledged with a lightness she didn't entirely feel.

''Listen, I want you to think about something while I'm gone.'' She opened her mouth, but he kissed it before she could say anything. ''Listen, not talk. Okay?''

''Okay.'' Because if he stopped her from talking that way a second time he might never leave for Madison. On second thought, maybe she *should* talk.

''I want you to think about staying in Tobias—''

''When Juney—''

''No, don't answer. Just think about it. I know you're not ready to hear all the things I want to say. Including pointing out how we've been building a new trust based on truth and experience instead of a starry-eyed demand for blind faith. And since trust's the other element that needs to be added to chemistry to create love—''

''Steve—''

''No, don't answer, remember? Besides, that's not what I'm telling you now. What I am saying is there's no magic rule that you have to leave when Juney comes back. You've made it a habit to think you can't or won't stay here, and all I want you to do is challenge that habit.''

''Just like you make it a habit to assume you'll stay in Tobias. With your skills you could find a rewarding job anywhere.''

"This is Nell's home. This is where she has family and history."

"That can be as much of a burden as a blessing. If you moved away from Tobias, you would never have to worry about people telling her all that history."

"What's the alternative? Never show our faces in town again? Or slip in for a day at Christmas while everyone's preoccupied?" She flinched. "Sorry."

"Sure. You didn't mean it, I know."

He met her gaze and held it. "Actually, I did mean it. I hated that you didn't want to—or thought you couldn't— show your face here. It made me feel like…"

"Even if that was true then, you have no reason to feel that way now. I won't stay away from Tobias like I used to. I just… Staying permanently isn't…" She pushed out the words. "I couldn't bear going back to being *poor little Annette*."

"So don't. Show them who you are now. It might take some in the town longer, but they'll get the idea."

And then he kissed her again.

Chapter Eleven

Annette picked up the ringing phone thinking Steve had forgotten something. He'd been running late by the time he got dressed to leave.

A young woman's voice said, "Annette? Is that you? It's Juney. How are you? How's Max? How's the business? How's the weather? The islands have been so gorgeous. I kept telling Max that I might not come back, so I wanted to reassure you—" she laughed "—that I'll be at work first thing Monday. Oh, but I can't bear the thought of wearing winter coats and gloves and everything!"

Annette made all the appropriate noises, answering Juney's questions and saying how glad they would all be to see her. But beneath that functioning surface, everything had frozen into a single phrase. *Her time was up.*

Steve had said there was no magic rule that she had to leave when Juney returned, but there was. Because she wouldn't be staying for Max anymore. She would be staying for Steve. It was a commitment, a promise.

And a danger.

But why should living here scare her this way? She didn't have anything to hide from the people of Tobias—they already knew everything about her. That should be freeing, in a way. And she'd come up against plenty of people in business who had treated her like a nincompoop—at the beginning. Most had seen the light quickly. Those who hadn't she'd worked around or left behind.

What was so different now?

She didn't have to earn everything on her own here. She could lean on Steve—not financially, the way she had once expected to, but emotionally. She could turn to him when things got tough, as she had in the situation with Miss Trudi?

Why hadn't she handled it herself?

God, she came back to Tobias and she reverted to...

That was it. It wasn't fear of Tobias making her *poor little Annette*—she could fight that. It was fear that she would make herself *poor little Annette*. Riding along behind Steve, hoping he steered her away from choppy water.

Because, let's face it, there were some perks to being *poor little Annette*. No great expectations that she might disappoint. Built-in excuses if she wimped out. Sure made life easier.

Like reverting to childhood when you came home.

She had stood in this room that first night and she had revisited the bedroom of her memory. Was that an unconscious desire to revert to the girl she had been, too? What if the room hadn't been changed into an office? Would she have sunk into the bed and wallowed in her childhood?

Look at the way she fell apart on the phone with Suz. Only at the end of that first conversation did Suz say she sounded like herself—because she *hadn't* been herself, at least not the herself Suz knew. She'd been *poor little Annette*.

And the proposal for Bliss House—since when did she second-guess what she *knew* was a great idea? Yes, there was a lot at stake, but there'd been a lot at stake with decisions she and Suz had made, too.

She'd realized at the parade how few people in Tobias would cast her as *poor little Annette*. But what about herself? How did she fight that?

If she reverted to that wimpy Annette of old, how could she even consider staying?

Halfway to Madison, Max reached over and turned off the radio sports talk show about the college basketball championship game coming up.

"You know if you hurt her, I'll come after you again," he said.

"You didn't come after me last time, I came to you."

"You just saved me the trip."

"Two years later."

Max grunted, but Steve caught the flicker at the corner of his mouth. It was gone when he said, "I mean it, Steve."

"I know you do. But what are you going to do if she hurts me?" She'd given him the present these past few days. But time was running out on the present. He wanted a future with her. He was going to have to push for an answer…with the potential for the answer he dreaded.

Max looked out his window so long Steve thought he wasn't going to answer.

"Get you drunk. And get drunk with you."

Resenting the intrusion, Annette answered the door Friday with a stack of papers in one hand and the pen in her mouth so she could pull the door open.

She had spent the rest of Wednesday going over files and paperwork and bank statements. She'd worked well past midnight, until her eyes couldn't focus any more. Unfortunately that didn't keep her mind from working.

Thursday she drafted the bank draw Max had said to leave for Juney. She'd roughed in quarterly taxes. But what else was there? That's when she realized she'd never examined the Every Detail contract as closely as she should have.

She'd had Suz e-mail it to her and she'd buckled down. It required research and calls to the lawyers, with faxes of their answers coming back. Several of their answers raised more questions. When Suz called last night asking what was up, she apologized for letting her personal life interfere with her obligations to the company. Suz was sweet to try to reassure her that she hadn't slacked off, but she knew better. She'd ended the call and returned to work.

The corporation's negotiators had called first thing this morning screaming bloody murder. She was not going to be railroaded because they wanted things easy. She'd left the phone off the hook so she could concentrate.

And now people were showing up at the door. She'd tried to ignore the knocking, but it wasn't going away.

She yanked open the door, and there were Nell and Fran. With her head still wrestling with client list confidentiality, she blinked at them uncomprehendingly. Nell didn't wait for an invitation, but marched right in.

"We tried to call for a long time but kept getting a busy signal," Fran said. She gave a faintly apologetic shrug, but looked serious. "Nell insisted I bring her over here. She wouldn't tell me what it's about, just kept saying she had to talk to you. She's very upset."

Annette knew she was tired, but she wasn't totally out of it, and a glance at the clock confirmed it. Ten-thirty. "You should be in school," she said to Nell.

The child ignored that. "You've gotta stop her, Annette. Pulverize her before she does something to Miss Trudi."

Annette scooched down to be eye-to-eye. "Nell, it's okay. Your daddy's working to take care of all of that. That's why he's away in Madison and why you're staying with Fran."

She shook her head. "Grandmother's doing something now, while Daddy's gone. I heard her." She hiccupped a sob. "I heard her."

"Okay, Nell. Okay." She stroked the girl's hair. "Start at the beginning. How did you hear your grandmother?"

"I told Fran I had to walk to school early, but that was a fib. I wanted to go to Grandmother's house because Fridays are waffle days. Mrs. Grier makes the best waffles ever. Lots better than Fran's oatmeal."

She looked over Annette's shoulder toward Fran, who said, "I understand. I'd take Mrs. Grier's waffles over my oatmeal, too."

Nell looked at Annette again. "Mrs. Grier's okay. She doesn't tell Grandmother I come for waffles. Mrs. Grier was in the basement, getting more jam, and I heard Grandmother in this room by the kitchen, talking on the phone about Miss Trudi. About being at Bliss House at one o'clock, and she said it would be all settled before my daddy gets back."

Nell's distress must have been contagious, because Annette felt a swell of concern. "What would all be settled?"

"Dunno." Nell gulped back tears. "You gotta help Miss Trudi!"

"We will," Annette promised. "We all will. And the

way you can help is to think hard if you remember anything else that your grandmother said."

Nell's face scrunched into lines of concentration. She repeated much of what she'd already said before adding, "She talked about an attorney with power."

"Power of attorney? Is that what she said, Nell?"

"Maybe." Nell couldn't be any more positive.

Power of attorney. If Lana could get Miss Trudi's power of attorney…

Annette looked at the clock again. One o'clock was not that far away.

"Okay, this is what we're going to do."

Miss Trudi was so primed that when the doorbell rang— they'd removed the sign for this occasion—she yanked the front door open practically before it sounded.

From a triangle of space Annette shared with Fran behind the partially open door to the back hallway, she sent up two quick prayers—that the others waiting in the kitchen would not give themselves away before the cue and that Miss Trudi would play her part.

Lana Corbett swept into the house followed by a quartet of men in designer suits and topcoats. Miss Trudi flattened herself against the wall and fluttered a hand to point them toward the parlor, as if that were all she could muster.

Annette amended her prayer. *Please don't let Miss Trudi overplay her part.*

After a few minutes to let Lana and company settle in, she and Fran exchanged a nod, then eased forward, hoping the creaks of their footsteps would blend in with the old house's noises.

"But I don't understand," Miss Trudi said as Annette caught her first glimpse into the room.

Miss Trudi was a trouper. She had maneuvered Lana and

the four men—all still wearing their coats against the house's chill—so they sat with their backs to the door. She occupied the center of a horsehair sofa with a shawl wrapped over her layers of chiffon, looking small, alone and confused.

"It's simple, Trudi. This house and this estate have become too much for you. No one blames you." Lana's crisply impersonal style robbed that statement of reassurance. "Now something must be done. As trustees of your father's estate, these gentlemen—" she gestured to her left to two of the suits perched on spindly-legged chairs "—agree. My lawyer has drawn up the papers, and his associate is here to represent you."

Lana deftly shuffled legal-looking papers, moving one to the top and setting them on the table between her and Miss Trudi, along with a pen, which she opened. "All you have to do is sign."

"But what is it?"

"It's a power of attorney, so someone responsible can oversee your finances."

"But Steve is working on something. I'm sure he said that…almost sure…"

"Trudi, we both know Steven is reluctant to make difficult decisions. Whatever he might have said to you, this is what Steven wants."

"That's a lie."

Lana's head jerked around. Annette had stepped into the doorway. She supposed her entrance caught the interest of the men, too, but she didn't care. As Annette went to Miss Trudi's side all her attention was focused on Lana.

"You are dead wrong about Steve, Lana. He does not flinch from difficult decisions. And as for Miss Trudi's situation—"

"This is family business—Corbett business—and you are not a Corbett."

"This is the business of Miss Trudi's friends, and I am her friend. She has a lot of friends. And Steve is—"

"You think you know my son so well, but you don't know anything. I have had to spend his entire life doing what is best for him, even when he is too foolish to know it. I should have stopped his idiotic notion of marrying you in the first place. If I hadn't given in to him, he would be building a political career instead of letting himself be dragged down by this—"

Annette never knew what Lana might have added, because apparently the group in the kitchen interpreted her comment about Miss Trudi having a lot of friends as their cue, and they were fast filing into the room—Fran, Nell, Gert, Lenny, Muriel Henderson, Kim Jayne and two fellow checkers, Miriam Jenkins, Tom Dunwoody Senior, a trio from the library and many more. Some Annette knew and some she didn't, but each had answered the call when she and Fran started a telephone campaign saying Miss Trudi needed help.

The men flanking Lana looked nervously around the room as it grew crowded, but Lana's face remained impassive.

"Miss Trudi, do you mind if I—" Annette nodded toward the papers.

"Not at all, my dear," Miss Trudi said in her usual voice.

"These are private papers," said the older of the two lawyers.

Annette gave him her best don't-tread-on-me stare. "Papers that have Trudi Bliss's name on them, and you heard her give me permission." Without waiting for his reply, she scanned the sheets then looked at Lana, who returned her gaze without any reaction. ''Papers that give Lana Corbett power of attorney for finances and property for Trudi Bliss.'' Speaking over a growing grumble from Miss Trudi's supporters, she added, ''Among other things, as Miss Trudi's agent, Lana Corbett could *sell, convey and mortgage realty for prices and on terms as considered advisable.*''

''Sell!'' squawked Miss Trudi. ''You were planning to sell Bliss House? How dare you, Lana—''

''No one would buy this rubbish, Trudi. It's only the land that has value. It could be doing this town some good—and you. You could go away, travel the world. But no one has had the nerve to do what needs to be done.''

''I think we should, um—'' Fran tipped her head toward the kitchen, and Annette nodded.

''Yes, I think Mrs. Corbett and Miss Trudi have more to say to each other in private.''

Miss Trudi grabbed Annette's hand. ''I want you to stay, Annette. And the rest of you, please, wait in the kitchen. It's good that you all know what she was up to, but don't go away yet. I don't trust her.''

Lana stood, and Annette thought she might walk out. Instead, she went to the window that looked out on the wreck of a front garden. ''This is absurd.''

But no one else objected. Lana's attorney joined the other suits being herded out by Lenny and Tom Dunwoody. Fran escorted a reluctant Nell out, leaving Annette, Miss Trudi and Lana.

''You've gone around the bend, Lana,'' Miss Trudi said.

Annette supposed Miss Trudi was entitled to be irked, but as a conversation opener it ranked with a battering ram.

Without turning, Lana said, ''I am not going to tolerate this any longer. To let my granddaughter acquire habits that are totally inappropriate for a Corbett. To see Steven brought down by his unreasoning devotion to a crazy old woman. I will not tolerate it.''

Lana Corbett was jealous. My God, why had Annette never seen that before? The green practically oozed from the woman's beautifully maintained pores. She was jealous of Nell and Steve's genuine affection for Miss Trudi.

Her motivation was not to make money out of selling the Bliss House property, but to give Miss Trudi no home in Tobias along with the means to travel far, far away from Steve and Nell.

For an instant, sympathy pulsed through Annette. Sympathy and something close to pity because Lana thought the way to win a closer relationship with her son and granddaughter was to send Miss Trudi away.

That was a short instant, however, as Lana turned from the window.

''Steven has ruined every single thing I have done for him. I gave him the Corbett name. I gave him position and family he never would have had otherwise.''

Lana's voice was even and emotionless. But the words somehow twisted her mouth, spotlighting the lines around it that were otherwise so cleverly masked. Did she realize how clearly she revealed her deepest secret—that Steve was not a Corbett by birth? Annette started to look toward Miss Trudi to see if she caught that implication, but Lana's next words recaptured Annette's intention entirely.

''And after I saved Zachary from marrying that harpy Lily, Steven stepped right into her trap—ever noble. The fool. If I'd known he intended to marry her after the way she'd acted—''

''You saved Zach?'' Annette demanded.

''Are you really naive enough to think Lily didn't try something before that disgusting scene at your wedding? She came to me when she realized Zachary wasn't coming back and threatened to make public her situation—threatened! *Me!*" Lana's expert makeup couldn't hide the veins throbbing at her temples. "She talked some nonsense about Steven but said she wanted more. I told her the Corbetts would never submit to blackmail—"

"When? When did she come to you, Lana?"

Lana flicked her hand in the air as if the question were a pesky bug, easier to dispose of by answering than ignoring. "Before that debacle of a wedding, I told you. The cleaners were there. She would have made a scene in front of them, so even though I had no time to spare... Thursday. Two days before the wedding."

"Oh, God."

Annette was vaguely aware of Miss Trudi blasting Lana's interfering ways, but her mind was too occupied to pay close attention.

Lily must have panicked before the wedding. Whether she had been trying for more money than Steve had promised or had simply wanted reassurance, they would never know. Lana had not only turned her away but had refuted Steve's pledges of support. So Lily had taken a desperate gamble at the wedding, probably hoping to startle a public acknowledgment out of Steve or Lana or both that Zach was the father of her baby, paving the way for her claims on the family.

She couldn't have guessed how well her gamble would pay off when Annette walked out and Steve took on the responsibility for her and her child.

All because Lana, in her hypocrisy, had—

No, not all because of Lana.

Lana, in her wrongheaded way, had been trying to protect her sons. But she hadn't accounted for Steve's reactions, or Annette's. None of them had accounted for the others' reactions.

Noises from the kitchen yanked Annette's attention to the moment. Or perhaps it was the growing stridency between the two other women in the parlor.

"Steve wants to—"

Miss Trudi's protest of something Lana had said died under a spurt of ugly laughter from Lana. "He doesn't want to be saddled with worry over you and this monstrosity. You are just another problem to him. Deep down he would be thrilled to have me take care of this. I'm doing what Steven really wants and doesn't have the strength to acknowledge."

"Steve has more strength than any man I know. A hundred more times than you have." Annette was on her feet. Her throat was raw from not letting herself shout. "He has the strength to care about people and to let them care about him. He has the strength to worry about how people feel and not what they think of him or the damned Corbett name. Steve is a far better man and a far better son than you have any earthly right to expect and far, far better than you deserve. He's the best man I know, and I love him."

Annette felt the silence drop on the room like a curtain. It took another second to realize the silence was too big to have come from three women.

She looked past Lana's tense form and saw Steve standing in the doorway, the complete cast from the earlier confrontation, with the addition of Max, ranged behind him.

In that moment Annette discovered a new law of physics—wanting both to run to and to run away from a man looking at her like he'd been hit by a bolt of lightning could hold a person utterly motionless.

Steve felt the sizzle run through his body as he watched her eyes widen. The dark chocolate depths of them encompassed joy and fear, the past and the present…and so much uncertainty about the future.

Uncertainty was a hell of a lot better than what he'd been seeing. But he wanted more. He needed more.

Without releasing her gaze, he advanced into the room. What he wanted to do and what he was going to do were two different things. She might say it was because of his Corbettness. But it was really because of her and that uncertainty.

"Miss Trudi, this is the paperwork for the program we talked about. We will go over it in detail before you sign—'' he cut a look toward his mother without making eye contact "—and we have a good start on the funds.''

He and Max had tried to call Annette with the good news as they left Madison, but Max's phone and her cell had been busy. Attempts on the road had gotten more busy signals, then no answer. So they'd decided to stop at Miss Trudi's.

The clutter of cars behind Bliss House had been a surprise. The crowd in her kitchen had been a shock. The casseroles on the table proclaimed it a true Tobias crisis. Five voices had come at him at once with scraps of information that had no pattern until Fran stepped up and gave a succinct recap of what had happened and what was happening in the front parlor.

Nothing could have prepared him for walking in on Annette telling off his mother in his defense, with that kicker of saying she loved him.

Once his heart restarted, all he wanted to do was grab her and kiss her and escape. But there was that uncertainty.

He lifted the papers to the view of the people behind him.

"This is the outline for a plan to give Miss Trudi an updated, convenient home on the grounds, and to convert

Bliss House to a major center to sell and promote local crafts, making Tobias a regional draw. It's going to be a big project, an important project, not just for Miss Trudi, but for all of us." Still looking at Annette, he said, "And no one could do a better job of overseeing it than Annette Trevetti—getting it started and then running it."

"Marvelous!" Miss Trudi said.

The confusion in Annette's eyes quadrupled. She started to shake her head.

"I know it's not what you had in mind. I know you have reservations." About Tobias. About him. "But I hope you'll give it a chance. Stay and give it a chance."

"I can't." Annette turned to Miss Trudi. "I'm sorry. I just can't. No. It's not—"

A chorus of voices urged her to accept. Miss Trudi clasped Annette's hand. With her free hand Annette pushed her hair back, the confusion in her eyes deeper.

"Steve, let's talk about this—"

"Later? No need." He was going to say this now, in public. He should have said at least this much seven-and-a-half years ago. "I thought that might be your answer, so I have a couple of things to say. First, I love you. I've never stopped loving you." Her mouth rounded into an O, but no sound escaped. "Second, when my current contract runs out at the end of June, I will be leaving Tobias. I—"

"No!" She pulled away from Miss Trudi and took two steps toward him. "You won't. You can't."

"I can." He cut the gap to arm's length. "You were right—there are some choices you might not want to have to make, but when it comes down to it, it's so damned obvious."

"Nell—"

"Will be happy wherever she's loved, and she'll be

loved wherever she is with us. If you'll let there be an *us*. We'll go wherever you want for that chance.''

''You can't, Steve. You're not done here. There are so many things you want to do, and the town needs you, and you and Nell belong here.''

''We belong with you.''

''I couldn't be the one who takes you away.'' Twin trails of tears silvered her cheeks. ''I couldn't—''

She bolted past him, past Fran, into the hallway, then out the front door, since the spectators blocked the other exit.

He followed. She was already down the front steps and disappearing around the side of the house. ''Annette!''

''Give her a little time, Steve,'' Miss Trudi said from behind him. ''My, my, you do pick the most surprising times for drama.''

''It's disgraceful. Making a spectacle that way again,'' his mother said. ''She's not worthy of a Corbett. It's bad enough that she left you at the altar once and that she can't control her emotions, but now she has you acting like—''

He turned toward his mother, and her words stopped. Only his mother and Miss Trudi had followed him onto the porch, but the entire state of Wisconsin could have been listening. It wouldn't stop him.

''Annette has me acting like I have emotions because I do. And the most important emotion is that I love her. And you will never criticize her again if you want any contact with me or Nell.''

''You have a position to maintain in this—''

''Damn right. A position as the man who loves Annette Trevetti. That's what—''

''As a Corbett!'' Lana's voice rose over his.

''As a Corbett, Mother? Exactly how did I come to hold that position and that name?''

This time the lacquer, instead of preventing any expression, set in place the lines of strain. She said nothing.

"I will carry Ambrose Corbett's name for the rest of my life, and I'll respect that name. But that's not the position you've been pushing me into all these years, is it? It's being *your* son. Being like you—hiding the truth and living lies— that's the position you've tried to make sure I maintained. Well, the hell with it, Mother. It's time for the truth between us. I'm not counting on you to tell the truth, but someone very wise said to me that it was more important that I tell the truth than that I hear it. So sit down and start listening."

The open trunk of Annette's car, parked in Max's driveway, showed suitcases and a hanging bag. She closed the trunk lid, and through the rear window, Steve saw a large box and two shopping bags.

He was out of the SUV practically before the engine stopped.

"Annette."

She turned, her eyes widening.

"You're not leaving like this. If you go, I'll follow you and I'll keep following you. You thought it was bad when you first came back? You have no idea—"

"Steve—"

"No. Not this time. No Even Steven. No Corbett code. No Trevetti running away from Tobias. And no damned being apart. This town isn't worth losing you again. This time we're going to talk it out. Right now. I love you. You love me. And we both love Nell. There's a way to make a family out of that, and we're going to figure it out if it kills me."

"All right."

"All right?"

"Well, I don't like the if it kills you part, but the rest of it, yeah. All right."

He stared at her. Wanting to touch her but afraid to. If he touched her, he knew what would happen, and the words would go unspoken. Sometimes words really did need to be spoken. And spoken in the moment. He'd learned that.

"I told my mother I know I'm not Ambrose's biological son." He saw her searching his face for signs, and to his surprise he gave a half grin. He would never have thought he could come close to a grin in connection with that confrontation, and certainly not so soon. "It's okay, Annette. She didn't leave any wounds—visible or invisible."

He wasn't sure he could say the same about leaving his mother unwounded. But the only way to do that would have been to live life according to Lana Corbett's twisted rules, and he'd decided a long time ago not to do that. He just hadn't taken the final step by bringing her secrets and lies into the daylight between them. Until today. Until Annette came back into his life.

A soft breath slipped from between her lips. "I'm glad."

He jerked his gaze from her lips. Had to finish this now. Say the words now. If he let himself get sidetracked…

"I also told her I'm going to tell Nell the truth about Lily and about Zach. She's going to have all the facts to go on."

"Oh, Steve—"

"Gradually, and as gently as I can, I'm going to give her the whole truth. Then it will be up to her if she wants anyone else to know the truth."

"I know you'll do it the best way possible."

"I'll do it even better if you're there to help me."

"Steve—"

"I know—I know it's no bargain to have this town thinking you've signed up to raise a daughter I had with another woman, but unless Nell—''

''I don't give a damn if anyone in this town or anywhere else thinks that, but I don't think you're giving most of Tobias enough credit.''

He grinned. ''No?''

''No. Look how many came through in such a short time for Miss Trudi. I realized something when your mother went on the warpath and Nell came to me. It wouldn't have been that hard to track you down in Madison, but I didn't even think about trying to get hold of you or Max. I didn't slip back into poor little Annette mode. I stayed who I've become.''

He didn't see the big surprise in that, but if she was happy, he was happy.

''And then I had this interesting conversation with Miss Trudi while we were waiting for your mother to show up.'' She extended her closed fist, turned it over, then slowly opened her fingers.

Resting in her open palm was a familiar big old-fashioned key. Miss Trudi's back door.

''I figured we needed some time to…sort things out. But I couldn't very well stay in Max's office anymore with Juney coming back.''

''Stay.'' He cleared his throat. His hopes of a future with her had been soaring, but he'd figured it would be elsewhere. ''You've decided to stay? But you said no to the job.''

''I'm not staying for the job. I wasn't absolutely sure until you made that idiotic announcement that you would be leaving, and that was so clearly wrong I couldn't let that happen. I was going to wait to move my stuff to Miss Trudi's on Sunday, but then I thought why not do it now, since Miss Trudi was offering me a room, which happens to have a private door outside and to be in the opposite wing from the rest of the livable rooms. Lots of privacy.'' Her dark eyes caught fire. ''Starting tonight.''

''I have a house with a nice, big bed.''

''A very nice bed.'' But she shook her head even as her eyes heated. ''And an impressionable seven-year-old down the hall. This is better. I can help Miss Trudi out and plan her new home.''

He pressed his palm over hers, holding the key between them, then curled his hand around hers and tugged her to him.

''That sorting out you mentioned, I think we've done most of it, don't you?'' With his free hand he brushed wind-whipped strands of dark hair from her face.

''Yes.'' Her voice had gone whispery, and he liked that.

''So, this time you think we need…we could use it for something else.''

''I suppose. If we had something else we needed to use that time for.''

''We do.''

''Do we?''

''Yeah. To arrange a wedding where we can say we do.''

She tipped her head. ''Aren't you supposed to ask, not tell?''

''I asked once, and we never got to the we do part. I thought I'd try something different this time. One thing I should warn you about in the interests of full disclosure. It's not just me and Nell you're signing on for. Looks like we're getting a puppy come spring.''

As desperate as he'd been to go after Annette, he'd taken a few minutes to tell Nell he hoped Annette would marry him. Somehow he'd heard himself promising she could have a puppy, and then she threw her arms around his neck and said she loved him and loved Annette.

"I know."

"You know? But how? I just told her—"

"Shut up and kiss me."

So he did. And that led to another thought, when he could think again.

"How soon can we arrange a wedding?"

"A simple wedding?"

He nodded, rubbing his cheek against her hair. "Simple, and fast—that's my idea of the perfect wedding."

Epilogue

"If anyone knows just cause why these two people—"

Annette heard the side door of the Chapel of the Woods outside Tobias, Wisconsin, emit a squawk at being opened, but she didn't turn.

It was the day of her wedding to Steve Corbett, the man she loved. The man who had pledged to love and stand beside her.

The man who'd planned every detail of this simple ceremony with her—a new wedding for a new century.

She also heard the ripple of uneasiness from some people in the church behind her and the faint questioning in the minister's voice as she repeated, "Why these two people—"

Next to Annette, her seven-year-old maid of honor craned her neck to see what was going on. Beyond Steve, she was aware of Max, from his position as best man, turning toward the side door.

But all that was peripheral. Because what was at the center of her attention was the man standing beside her.

Steve's eyes met hers, and the glint was already there.

That's all it took. She pressed her lips together, but the laughter burbled out anyhow, and his chuckles were right there with her as he grasped her hand.

The quiet of the church behind them and the startled expression of the minister in front of them said no one knew what to make of this bride and groom.

Then Nell giggled, and soon the sound spread across the church.

Only then did Annette look over her shoulder and see that the latecomer was Suz, sinking into a pew as if she wished it would open up and swallow her. Annette sent her friend a reassuring smile even as she wiped a trickle of moisture from the corner of one eye.

Steve leaned over and dabbed at her other eye, his smiling mouth providing a sore temptation so close.

"I know," he murmured, and she saw the same heat and impatience in his eyes. "Go ahead, Jean," he told the minister. "Hurry up and get to the we do."

The minister continued the ceremony, they each said I do, strong and clear and unmistakable, and at the end the minister declared what Annette and Steve had known for some time—that they were joined as husband and wife.

* * * * *

If you enjoyed WEDDING OF THE CENTURY,
*you will love Patricia McLinn's next romance
from Silhouette Special Edition:*

THE UNEXPECTED WEDDING GUEST

*Available May 2003
Don't miss it!*

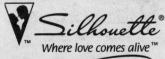

Don't miss the latest miniseries from award-winning author Marie Ferrarella:

The MOM SQUAD

Meet...

Sherry Campbell—ambitious newswoman who makes headlines when a handsome billionaire arrives to sweep her off her feet...and shepherd her new son into the world!
A BILLIONAIRE AND A BABY, SE#1528, available March 2003

Joanna Prescott—Nine months after her visit to the sperm bank, her old love rescues her from a burning house—then delivers her baby....
A BACHELOR AND A BABY, SD#1503, available April 2003

Chris "C.J." Jones—FBI agent, expectant mother and always on the case. When the baby comes, will her irresistible partner be by her side?
THE BABY MISSION, IM#1220, available May 2003

Lori O'Neill—A forbidden attraction blows down this pregnant Lamaze teacher's tough-woman facade and makes her consider the love of a lifetime!
BEAUTY AND THE BABY, SR#1668, available June 2003

The Mom Squad—these single mothers-to-be are ready for labor...and true love!